LONER

PINE RIDGE

BOOK TWO

ASHLEY A QUINN

TCA PUBLISHING LLC

ISBN is 9798985344127
Library of Congress Control Number: 2022903302

ONE

"Olive! Stop chasing the chickens and come help me." Sofie McAllister leaned out the back door of their little two-bedroom bungalow on the Stone Creek Ranch and hollered for her four-year-old daughter. The little girl ran around the yard in her bright purple boots and coat, the pom-pom on her purple stocking cap bobbing as she chased one of the hens. Olive loved the chickens, but right now, Sofie needed her to help carry a few things to the car.

"What do you need, Mommy?" The girl came running up to stop in front of her mother.

Sofie held the door and motioned her inside. "We're supposed to meet Daisy, Sara, Marci, and Grandma to make centerpieces for the wedding." She picked up two sacks of silk flowers from the counter and held them out to her daughter. "I need you to carry these, so I can get the box."

"Okay." Olive took the bags.

Already wearing her coat, Sofie picked up her purse and slung it over her shoulder and across her chest. Gripping her keys in one hand, she lifted the box. "Let's go." She gestured toward the door with her head.

Olive ran to the door and held it open.

"Make sure it's locked."

The girl turned the button on the knob, then jiggled it once the door closed. "It's locked."

"Good." Sofie pushed the button on her key fob to raise the lift gate on her SUV, then set the box inside. Olive deposited her bags next to the box, then ran around to get in the car. Sofie helped her buckle in, then got in the driver's seat.

The trip down the lane to the main house was quick. She pulled into the yard and parked next to her stepdad's truck and got out.

She still couldn't believe after ten years of being single and hardly ever dating, her mother married Silas Mitchell within months of meeting him. Sofie wasn't upset about it, though. He was a good man. And he made her mom smile.

After retrieving the items from the rear of her vehicle, she followed Olive up the steps into the mudroom.

"Take off your boots," she told her daughter before she could scamper into the kitchen for hugs from her grandma and cousin. Not to mention the cookies surely waiting in the cookie jar. Sofie hadn't bothered to bake in the two months they'd been living on the Stone Creek. Daisy always had more than enough to keep their sweet cravings satisfied.

Olive sat down on the floor and tugged off her boots, then stood, tossing her hat and coat onto the pile. She flew inside.

"Grandma!"

"There's my button."

Sofie smiled as her mom, Nori, greeted Olive. She stepped out of her shoes, doing her best not to crash into the wall as she held onto the box.

"Do you want help?" Sara Katsaros asked, as Sofie stepped into the kitchen.

"I've got it." She walked to the island and set the box down. "Olive, you left your bags in the mudroom."

"Oh!" The girl let go of her grandma and ran through the door, reemerging a moment later with the flowers. She held the bags up to Sofie. "Here you go."

"Thank you." She took the sacks and set them next to the box, then shrugged out of her coat.

Sofie's cousin, Daisy O'Malley, pulled a bag toward her and peered inside. "Oh, I like these." She looked up at Sofie. "Thanks for getting them while you were in Billings. I thought we had enough, but Marci said we were short."

"Of course. No sense in you making a trip when I was already there."

"No doubt."

"So, are we ready to get started?" Marci asked.

"I think so." Sofie sat on a barstool and picked up a jar. "So, what exactly are we doing?"

Daisy picked up a jar of her own as well as a ball of jute. "We're wrapping the tops of the jars in this stuff, then filling them with glass beads, lights, and flowers."

"Why did you decide against real ones?" Sara asked. "I'm sure Asa wouldn't have minded spending the extra money."

"No, but some people are sensitive to flowers. I didn't want that on the tables where we were eating. Plus, we can fill the jar with fairy lights since we don't need to add water."

"Kind of like mood lighting," Nori said.

"Exactly."

Sofie picked up a glue gun and plugged it in.

"Mommy, can I have a cookie?"

She looked over to see Olive standing at the counter, pointing at the cookie jar.

"Just one. Once you're done, why don't you go find your coloring books? You can sit at the table while we work."

"Okay." The girl spun around and opened the jar, sticking her hand inside and coming out with a chocolate chip cookie.

Sofie smiled as she took a big bite. It hadn't taken her

daughter long to adjust to her new surroundings. Having her grandma and her favorite cousin close by helped, she was sure. It had helped Sofie adjust, that much she knew. She never would have had the courage to leave Chicago if her mom hadn't come with her. Though it was really the other way around. Nori moved, and Sofie tagged along. There was no reason not to. She and Olive needed a fresh start after what happened with her ex-husband. And it meant she could stay close to her family.

"Bring me one of those, too," she told her daughter.

Olive took another cookie from the jar and brought it to Sofie.

"Thank you."

"Welcome!" The girl spun on her heel and ran from the room to get the coloring supplies Nori kept on hand.

"Can you bottle her energy and give me some?" Marci asked.

Sofie grinned. "Trust me, if I could, I would. I need it just to keep up with her."

"I need it to stay awake."

"Sloan keeping you up?" Daisy asked, mentioning Marci's almost one-year-old son.

"Yes. I thought he'd get better as he got older, but he hasn't. Oh, he'll sleep longer stretches at a time now, but he's still up every three to four hours instead of every one to two. And he's always up and ready for the day at five a.m. I've tried pushing his bedtime back to eight or nine, but he's still up before the sun. He'll just take a longer nap in the afternoon." She sighed. "I'm exhausted."

"Is he teething?" Nori asked.

Marci nodded. "So bad. I have to keep a bib on him all the time to sop up all the drool. It's insane. I didn't know such a small creature could produce so much saliva."

Sofie laughed. "Olive was like that. Once all their front teeth come in, it slows down. How many does he have now?"

"Four. The two in the middle, on the top and bottom. He's working on the ones beside those now. I'm glad to know there's light at the end of the tunnel, however dim it may be at the moment."

They all laughed.

"There is," Sofie said. "And if you ever need a break, I'm happy to babysit."

"I might take you up on that. I could do for a few hours of me time. A hot bath and a long nap sound wonderful."

"You just let me know when. I'd love to have him."

Sofie's ringing cellphone cut off any reply Marci might have made.

"Sorry." She stood to get her phone from her purse at the other end of the island. "It's probably a client wanting to place an order." She found the device, answering it. "Hello?" Turning, she picked up the pad of sticky notes and a pen from the basket by the wall and walked out of the kitchen for some privacy.

"Sofie, it's Jim Blackwell."

Her heart stuttered in her chest as her attorney identified himself. She cleared her throat. "Jim, hi. Um, I don't mean to be rude, but why are you calling? I didn't think we had any more business left to discuss."

"We didn't, but I'm afraid I have some bad news, Sofie. Lance has been released from jail."

Sofie's breath left her in a whoosh. Her lungs froze along with her mind as she struggled to process what he said. "What —how?"

"Overcrowding. He's been a model prisoner and served half his sentence, so they let him out two weeks ago. But not without conditions."

"Two weeks? And I'm just now finding out? I thought we were supposed to be notified right away?"

"We were, but his paperwork got stuck in the system somewhere. It just landed on my desk half an hour ago. I verified everything, then called you."

She ran a hand over her face and blew out a breath. "Okay. Um, you said there were conditions to his release?" Sofie walked to the window and looked out. She ran a shaky hand through her hair and drew in a deep breath to steady herself. This wasn't a big deal. She knew he'd get out at some point, and they weren't in Chicago anymore, where he could just show up and threaten her. But it was still a shock. She'd been mentally preparing herself for his release in February, not now, almost four months early. She let her breath out on a slow exhale.

"He can't contact you, even through the guise of checking on Olive. Any inquiries he makes about her have to go through an intermediary. The judge appointed one when he granted Lance's release. You should get a letter soon explaining how it works. I can tell you that if he contacts you at all—and you can prove it—he'll go back to jail. This is for the duration of his parole, not just the remainder of his sentence."

"How long is his parole?"

"He has to meet with a parole officer weekly until his sentence is technically up, then biweekly for six months, then monthly for eighteen months."

Two years. That was good. Hopefully, by the time his parole was up, he would have moved on and their only contact would be about Olive. Though she wouldn't be upset if he decided to just walk away completely. Lance was poison. Sofie wished she'd never met him, but also didn't. She wouldn't have her beautiful daughter if she hadn't. Olive was the best thing in her life, and she couldn't regret her relationship with Lance because of her. She just wished she'd walked away sooner and spared herself and Olive some heartache.

"I'm sorry, Sofie. If I'd known, I would have lobbied to keep him imprisoned for his full sentence, but he's been a model prisoner, so they let him out."

"It's okay, Jim. I appreciate you trying. Thank you for calling to give me a head's up."

"Of course. If you need anything, please don't hesitate to call."

"I won't. Thank you." She bade him farewell and hung up. Clutching her phone, she rested it against her chin for a moment as her thoughts whirled. She prayed Lance would leave them be and abide by the conditions of his parole. The last thing she needed was to spend all her time looking over her shoulder, waiting for him to find her and make good on the promises he made after she had him arrested. He'd vowed she would regret betraying him.

A shiver ran down her spine. Part of her thought his threats were just a knee-jerk reaction to the situation. But a larger part knew him and what he was capable of, and recognized his threats for the promises they were. When he said he wouldn't let her live without him or take his daughter away, he meant it.

Laughter from the kitchen drew her from her thoughts. She shook off the undercurrent of fear and put her phone away. There was nothing she could do about Lance right now. He didn't know where she was. And even if he found out, she wasn't alone. Plus, the security on the ranch was decent with the upgrades Asa made after the incident with his ex-girlfriend.

"When are the trailers coming for the wedding guests?" Sofie heard Sara ask as she walked back into the room. Her eyes strayed to Olive, who sat at the small table, tongue poking out between her lips as she concentrated on coloring her picture. Sofie's heart lurched as she looked at the girl. She wouldn't let anything happen to her daughter. If Lance came after them, she'd do everything she could to protect her. She wouldn't let Olive end up with her father. She deserved better than the abusive bastard.

"Tomorrow. Along with the first of our guests," Daisy replied. "Asa's friend, Knox, and his sister Alice are supposed to arrive sometime tomorrow afternoon. Knox wanted to help with setup."

"That's cutting it close," Marci said. "Why didn't Asa have the trailers here today?"

Daisy shrugged. "No idea. Asa and Silas both assure me they'll be ready. I guess if they're not, we'll set them up in the guest rooms. And if my family arrives before they're ready, we'll spread air mattresses all over the house until they are."

Nori groaned. "I do not want to listen to your brothers if they have to sleep on air mattresses."

That made Daisy laugh. "No one does. It'll be fine. Asa contracted with a rental company the movie and music industries use. They'll be here."

Sofie forced a smile onto her face and sat down. "Who else is coming besides them? Didn't you say something about another friend of Asa's from Colorado? Brady? Was that his name?"

Nori gave Sofie a quizzical frown. Sofie did her best to hold her smile and turned her face away. She was sure her mom would grill her about it later, but right now, she didn't want to discuss her phone call.

Daisy nodded. "Yes. I think most of the Archers are coming, not just Brady. A few of them couldn't get away from work." She blew out a breath. "But that's still like fifteen to twenty people once you include the kids."

"And how does Asa know them?" Sofie wasn't clear on the connections to all these people.

"Asa met Brady Archer through Knox. The Archers own a large cattle ranch and get most of their horses from him. They've all become good friends over the years. I haven't met any of them yet, but Asa's talked about them."

"And there are twenty of them?" Marci asked.

"Roughly. Lee and Jenny, then their five kids and all their spouses. A few of them have kids of their own. Plus, there are a few foster children in the mix."

Sofie listened with half an ear as she pulled a jar toward herself and picked up the glue gun. Her fingers still shook, so she took a steadying breath, willing them to stop. She didn't want to put a damper on Daisy's wedding in any way.

"How long is everyone staying?" Sara asked.

"The Archers will be here a couple days beforehand and are leaving a couple of days after the wedding. They're driving, so they didn't want to rush out the next morning. My family is coming mid-week. Ian said they're flying back in the evening the next day. They all have to be back at work or school on Monday. My old boss is coming. Sandrine. She'll be here the day before. She's staying in the house, though. She and Alice both."

"I'm glad I live in town," Sara said. "It's going to be crazy out here for a few days."

Sofie agreed. And was glad. All her little cousins running around, not to mention the big ones, would help distract her from the news she just got.

"Mommy, look!" Olive ran up with a picture in her hands of a princess, colored head to toe in purple, Olive's favorite color.

"It's very pretty, sweetie."

The girl beamed and ran back to the table.

"I don't remember ever being as obsessed with a color as she is," Daisy mused.

Sofie smiled. "It makes it easy to buy things for her, though. If it's purple, she loves it."

Nori chuckled. "You were like that, but with pink. Do you remember that? Everything had to be pink, right down to your underwear."

Sofie laughed. "Yes. And my room too. It looked like bubblegum. I suppose her obsession is payback for what I put you through."

"Of course it is." Nori grinned.

"I'm just glad you went with purple as one of your colors, Daisy. It made it easier to convince her to wear the white dress once she saw it had a purple sash, and she saw she got to carry purple flowers." Sofie had steeled herself for an argument with Olive when she showed her the dress Daisy wanted her to wear. Olive was not a fan of dresses, but the purple accents kept the whining to a minimum.

"Good. That wasn't my goal when I picked the colors, but it's a nice bonus."

They all chuckled as they worked, the conversation lulling as they concentrated.

Nori leaned over, laying a hand on Sofie's arm. "Honey, what's wrong? Ever since you took that phone call, your shoulders are stiff and your smile is strained."

Curses flew through Sofie's brain. She should have known she wouldn't be able to hide her feelings from her mom. No one knew her better. "It's nothing."

"Don't give me that load of bull. I know you better than that."

Sofie huffed. "I know, but I don't want to talk about it. Not here."

Nori's eyebrows winged upward before she narrowed her eyes. "Later, then. No secrets, Sofia Grace. Not anymore. You promised."

Sofie nodded. "I know. And I'll tell you. Later." Her eyes

darted around to take in the other women. Thankfully, none of them were paying attention to Sofie and Nori's whispered conversation.

Nori straightened. "Okay. I'll hold you to that."

She was sure she would. After Lance beat the snot out of her the last time, Nori made her promise not to keep secrets again. But in all honesty, she didn't want to. The only reason she kept the abuse a secret before was out of shame. Her mother cautioned her not to marry Lance. She'd never liked him. But Sofie hadn't listened. She'd been in love. Then bullied into being too afraid to leave. The next thing she knew, she was married, then pregnant. Once Olive was in the picture, Sofie had been too afraid of what would happen to her baby if she left. She only had her meager jewelry business to support them. Lance was a successful sales rep for a pharmaceutical company.

If Nori hadn't found her after the last beating, she wasn't sure she would've had the courage to leave. It was only the presence of her DNA in his class ring and the matching wound on her face that convicted him. He'd tried to claim someone broke into their apartment. She thanked God for her mother and the detective who wouldn't give up. It was because of both of them she was free of the monster.

She just hoped she stayed that way.

Two

The transition from pavement to gravel rattled the trailer Knox Duvall pulled behind his truck as he turned into the driveway for the Stone Creek Ranch. He was glad to finally be here. His ass was numb from the long drive. Pulling up to the gate, he rolled down his window. Icy wind ripped through the cab, making him shiver. Montana winters were a different animal from Colorado. They got snow back home this early in the season, but the brutal temperatures usually held off a little longer.

He darted a hand through the open window and punched the call button on the video intercom.

"Hey, man. Come on up." Asa Mitchell's voice came over the speaker a moment before the gate opened.

Knox gave him a thumbs up and rolled up the window.

His sister, Alice, who occupied the passenger seat, reached for the heater controls, turning up the fan. "Damn, it's cold. Why couldn't they wait until spring to have this wedding?"

"I don't think they were counting on subzero temps the first week of November."

"Still. I wouldn't want to walk around in a wedding dress if there was a potential to freeze my booty off."

Knox chuckled. "Maybe she's wearing pants."

Alice laughed. "Maybe."

They bumped up the ranch drive to a cluster of buildings. He pulled up to the house as Asa stepped out the front door. A tall woman using a cane and wearing a teal beanie and black coat walked out behind him. Knox rolled the window down.

"Hey, you made it." Asa walked up to the truck. He glanced at the trailer. "And you brought your horse?"

Knox grinned. "Sort of. Meet me at the barn?"

"Sure." A curious smile lit Asa's face. "We'll see you there."

Rolling up the window, Knox pressed the accelerator and headed for the horse barn.

"You didn't tell them you were bringing the horse?" Alice asked.

"What kind of present would it be if I told them about it?"

She sighed. "Only you bring a horse as a wedding gift."

He shrugged and turned onto the lane to the barn. "It's not like they need household stuff or money."

Alice tipped her head. "True. I hope they find some use for the serving dish set I made."

"That's different. It's one of a kind and not something most people use on a daily basis. I bet Daisy will love it and bring it out on all the special occasions." He glanced at his sister as he stopped in front of the barn doors. "I wouldn't worry about it."

She rolled her eyes and opened her door. "Says the man who brought a horse."

He laughed and got out, grabbing his coat, hat, and gloves from the backseat. Asa's truck pulled up behind them as he thrust his hands into his gloves and tugged his hat lower on his head so the wind didn't take it.

Car doors slammed as Asa and Daisy exited their vehicle.

"You picked the worst weather for your wedding." Knox slid open the bolt on the back of the trailer.

"It's supposed to warm up this week and be in the fifties next weekend," Asa said.

"I hope so," Daisy said. "Or you might be peeling leggings off me after you peel off my dress."

His mouth flattened. "Sexy."

She laughed, then looked at Knox. "Hi. I'm Daisy. I'd offer to shake your hand, but I think I'd rather go inside first."

He smiled at her. "It's nice to finally meet you, Daisy. This is my sister, Alice." He nodded at the woman who'd come around the other side of the trailer.

"Hi." Alice smiled.

Daisy waved. "Hi."

Knox opened the trailer door and stepped inside. He untied the horse and led him out.

"You brought the paint I looked at the last time I was at your place?" Asa said, frowning. "Why?"

"He's your wedding gift." Knox headed for the barn to get the animal out of the cold.

Daisy squealed, making him smile.

"Asa told me about him. Said if you still had him this spring, we might buy him for me to ride." She clapped her hands as she followed him into the barn. "Now we don't have to."

"You brought us a horse for a wedding present?" Asa said. He shut the door after Alice stepped inside.

Knox grinned. "What the hell else was I supposed to get you? You don't need anything."

Daisy laughed as Asa sighed. "He's got you there, babe."

Asa chuckled. "True." He stared at the horse a moment longer, then glanced at Knox, one eyebrow raised. "You're sure about this?"

"Yes." Knox's head bobbed once. "He's too docile for me to sell as a cutter. He'll be the perfect trail horse for her." He pointed at Daisy.

She beamed. "And he's perfect. I want to name him Patches."

"Patches?" Asa said. "Really?"

"What's wrong with Patches?"

He shrugged. "It's just a little..."

She put her free hand on her hip, narrowing her eyes. "It's what?"

"Not macho?" He held up his hands.

"Hmm." She stared at him another moment, before smiling and turning to Knox. "We'll table the discussion for now. Thank you for bringing him. He's beautiful."

"You're welcome. Where do you want me to put him, Ace?"

Asa pointed down the corridor. "Just find an empty stall. I'll get some hay."

With a nod, Knox walked the horse between the rows of stalls until he found an unoccupied one. He put the animal inside and removed the heavy blanket they used to keep him warm during transport. Even in the heated trailer, drafts found their way in.

"He really is a beautiful animal." Asa stepped into the stall, a bundle of hay in his arms. He dumped it into the feeder hanging on the front wall of the stall. The paint stepped forward and stuck his nose in it, taking a bite of the fresh offering.

Together, they stepped into the corridor. Asa picked up a hose and walked back inside. He flipped the nozzle open and slid the end into the bucket next to the feeder, filling it up.

"I hope you're hungry," Asa said, shutting off the hose and setting it down. "Daisy made a feast for your arrival."

Knox grinned. "I could eat."

Asa chuckled and slapped Knox's shoulder. "Good. Let's go."

They made their way back to the front of the barn where Alice and Daisy stood talking like old friends.

"Are you ready to go?" Daisy asked.

Both men nodded.

"You guys can ride with us," Asa said. "We can come back for your luggage later. I need to show you to your trailer, anyway."

Knox nodded, then braced himself as Alice opened the door. Icy wind rushed in, immediately chilling him to the bone. He stuffed his hands in his pockets and ducked his head, letting his hat buffer the wind as he hurried to Asa's truck. Grabbing the handle on the rear passenger door, he gave it a tug, then helped Alice inside before climbing in next to her. Asa started the engine, then headed back to the house, pulling into the attached garage. Knox said a prayer of thanks he didn't have to go back out in the cold to get into the house.

The group filed inside, leaving their boots and winter gear in the mudroom.

"Knox, good to see you." Asa's dad, Silas, stepped away from the counter and the woman slicing meatloaf to hold out a hand.

"Silas." Knox shook the older man's hand. He glanced past him to the woman. "This must be your new wife."

She smiled at him and put the knife down. "Yes." She held out a hand. "I'm Noreen. Call me Nori, please."

He shook her hand. "It's nice to meet you, Nori." He looked back at his sister. "This is my sister, Alice."

Alice waved at her and at Silas. "Hello."

"Good to see you again, young lady." Silas clapped his hands together. "How about we take this party into the dining room? I don't know about you all, but I'm starving. I've been smelling Daisy's meatloaf for the last hour, and I don't want to wait any longer."

Nori nudged him. "We still need to wait on Sofie and Olive."

He frowned. "Do we really?"

She glared up at him. "Yes."

He grinned. "I'm just teasing. Olive would chew me up one side and down the other if we didn't wait." He looked at the others and winked. "It's her turn to say grace."

Knox gave him a quizzical frown, then glanced at Asa. "Who's Olive?"

"My granddaughter," Nori said. "She and my daughter, Sofie, moved here with me. They live in one of the little bungalows down the lane."

The back door banged before Knox could say anything. He heard movement, then a ball of purple flew through the door.

"Olive, you left your coat on the floor!" a woman hollered from the mudroom.

The ball of purple skidded to a halt inches from Nori, black pigtails bouncing as she reversed direction and ran out again. She was only gone a few moments before she ran back to give her grandma a hug.

"Grandma!"

Nori laughed, wrapping her arms around the child. "Hi, button."

"You'd think she didn't just see you."

Knox glanced toward the door at the sound of the female voice. The air left his lungs and his heart stuttered as he took her in. Dark hair fluttered around her heart-shaped face. The rust-colored sweater and jeans she wore showed off her curvy figure to perfection. His hands twitched, wanting to touch her, and he balled his fists. He'd never been so poleaxed by a woman in his life.

She rolled her green eyes as she spoke to Nori, a sardonic tilt to her perfect mouth, then ran a hand through her hair and pushed up the sleeves of her sweater. As she stepped into the room, she noticed the newcomers and smiled. "Hello."

His lungs, still frozen, refused to allow him to take in any air to reply. Not that he could, anyway. His brain was as frozen as his lungs.

Alice elbowed him, breaking the spell. She stepped forward while he recovered.

"Hi. I'm Alice Duvall. This is my brother, Knox."

The woman held out a hand to Alice. "Sofie McAllister. The bundle of energy there is my daughter, Olive."

"It's nice to meet you."

"You too." She let go of Alice's hand and turned to Knox. By rote, he took her hand. Electricity shot up his arm, making the hair on it stand on end like he'd been zapped. He clenched his teeth and forced himself not to yank his hand back. "Ma'am. It's nice to meet you."

Her smile dimmed, and she gave him a curious frown, but nodded. "Same."

"Hi!"

Knox looked down, letting go of Sofie's hand. Olive stood in front of him, beaming. Some of the tension created by his reaction to her mother left his shoulders. "Hi." He waggled his fingers at her.

"You're tall. Like Asa and Grandpa."

"I am, yes." He was only a couple of inches shorter than Asa's six-foot-six.

"Mommy says if I eat my vegetables and fruit, I can grow big too. But I don't like vegetables. They're yucky. 'Specially broccoli. I like carrots, though. And apples! Did you eat your vegetables when you were a kid? Is that why you're so tall? I wanna be tall when I grow up. I don't like being short."

Knox's eyes widened with every word the girl spoke. He

cleared his throat, preparing to answer, when her mother scooped her off the floor with a chuckle.

"Leave the poor man alone, Liv. He just got here."

He waved a hand. "It's okay. She's fine." He offered the girl a smile. "And to answer your question, yes, I ate lots of vegetables growing up. Even broccoli."

Olive's face scrunched. "Yuck."

The adults chuckled. Silas stepped around Knox and took Olive from Sofie, tossing her in the air. "Come on, kiddo. Let's go sit down and have some of Daisy's meatloaf."

"Yay! I like meatloaf. It's better than broccoli."

"I agree, kid," Asa said. He looked at Knox and Alice, then gestured toward the hallway with his head. "Come on. Let's eat."

~

Sofie took her seat at the table between her mom and Olive, forcing the smile to stay on her face. Unwanted attraction zipped through her body at the tall blonde hunk who'd just arrived. Why couldn't Asa's best friend be a troll? A short, balding rancher with a potbelly and receding hairline. Why did he have to be the blonde Adonis before her? He could at least be married. She could stuff her attraction in a nice, tight box if that was the case.

She studied the man from under her lashes as they all settled into their seats. Maybe he was. No one said otherwise. Though she would think he'd bring his wife with him to an event like this if he were. Maybe they had a sick kid at home and she couldn't come, she mused.

"So, tell us about yourselves," Nori said as they passed the food dishes around.

Sofie could have kissed her. It saved her from having to ask about him herself.

"I know you breed horses, Knox, but what do you do for fun?"

He put a spoonful of potatoes on his plate and shrugged. "Read."

"Just read?" The words were out of Sofie's mouth before she could stop them.

Alice giggled. "Yes. He's a stick in the mud."

Knox frowned at his sister. "Oh, whatever. I do more than just read."

"Right, I forgot. You go to the Broken Bow and have a beer with Brady every once in a while." She looked at Sofie. "Knox is a genius, so his favorite pastimes generally involve things he can learn from."

Sofie's eyes widened. Did she mean that literally?

Knox rolled his eyes. "Like you're more exciting. The extent of your socialization consists of coffee with Maggie."

She shook her fork at him. "You're forgetting the craft shows. I socialize there while I sell my pottery."

"You make pottery?" Sofie asked, distracted from the whole Knox was a genius statement.

Alice nodded. "I do. It's my first love. My day job is teaching art at our local elementary. I'd love to open my own pottery store and studio. One day, maybe."

"I've been looking at a storefront in town here. I make jewelry. So far, it's been an out of the home thing, but I want to branch out. I've been thinking of opening an artisan gift shop. I know I'm not the only artist around here who'd like a place to sell things other than at farmer's markets and online."

"That sounds interesting. We don't have anything like that back home, either. I do parties sometimes at the ranch. Have people come and paint pottery. Most of it I make myself and sell online or at craft fairs. Some of it I take in for one of my classes. We're doing ornaments next month."

"We should brainstorm. Do you have any pictures of your pottery?"

Alice nodded as she picked up the gravy.

"I'd love to see them. I could use a few dishes. I left a lot of that behind." A slight frown settled over her face as she thought about the house full of things she'd left behind when she left Lance. Living at her mom's, she didn't need any of that. She didn't really want it, anyway. The few things she did want, she got. Everything else just held bad memories.

"Why would you leave all your stuff behind?" Knox asked, pausing as he slathered butter on a roll. "I mean, don't you need that here since you and Olive live alone?"

Sofie cleared her throat. "It's a long story."

He frowned, but said nothing. Sofie was glad. She didn't want to explain about her abusive ex over the dinner table. Especially where her daughter could hear.

"Daddy is a bad man. He hurt Mommy and yelled at me a lot, so we left."

Sofie sighed. Apparently, she didn't need to protect Olive; she was well aware of what her father was like.

Knox's eyes shot to the girl, then swung to Sofie, a question in their icy blue depths.

"My ex was abusive. We moved in with Mom, and I left everything behind except the essentials. It was all just stuff. Stuff he bought. And it could all be replaced."

"Oh. I'm sorry. I didn't mean to drudge up bad memories."

"It's all right. But can we talk about something else?"

"Of course," Silas said, jumping in. "Olive, can you say grace, please, so we can eat?"

The little girl nodded and folded her hands, closing her eyes. "God, please bless this food. And thank you for our guests. Amen." Her eyes popped open, and she picked up her fork, smiling.

"Thank you, button," Nori said. "Everyone dig in."

Sofie tucked into her food and tried not to look at the beautiful stranger sitting across from her. While he provided a nice distraction from thoughts of her previous life, the unwanted attraction she had to him wasn't really any better. The man could seriously be a model. Tall, with a shock of sun-kissed blonde hair and icy blue eyes, he looked like some kind of Nordic god. His sister was just as beautiful. And the worst part was she had to spend a not insignificant amount of time with him over the next week because of wedding preparations.

Again, she wished he was a pudgy, short, balding rancher with a belt buckle as big as his ego.

She forked a bite of meatloaf into her mouth. It was going to be a long week.

THREE

Knox stepped into the barn and tugged off his gloves, blowing on his hands to warm them up. It was still brutally cold, but at least the snow had stopped. He wandered down the aisle between the stalls, making his way to the indoor arena to help Asa with wedding preparations. As he got closer, he could hear the murmur of voices.

He turned down a short hall at the end of the stables and entered the arena. He glanced around, noting the divide down the middle. One end was empty, but several men milled around in the other, busy building a temporary event space. Finding the gate, Knox let himself in and wandered over, shrugging out of his coat as he went.

"Hey. You should have told me to be here earlier if you were going to start sooner."

Asa glanced up and smiled. "Sorry. I figured you'd want to get a little extra rest after driving all day yesterday. We've only been in here about an hour."

Knox waved a hand, then propped them both on his hips. "What do you want me to do?"

"You can start nailing the boards to the deck structure as Jasper and I build it out. I think we have enough done we can start that. Dad and Chet are working on cutting the pieces for the stage."

"Sounds good. Is this the wood I'm supposed to use?" He pointed to a pile off to the side.

"Yep."

Knox found a nail gun and brought it over to the edge of the floor, then retrieved several boards, setting them over the foundation Asa and Jasper had laid. The nail gun made a satisfying pfft-thwack as he nailed the boards down. It didn't take him long to find a groove, and he soon caught up to Asa and Jasper.

"Dude. Maybe you should be the one building the decking." Asa sat back on his haunches and smiled.

"Maybe." Knox smiled back and shrugged. "Or maybe you should pick up the pace. There are two of you and one of me. It seems logical you should be way ahead."

"Hey, you don't have to cut boards except the very end piece."

Knox tipped his head. "True. But you're still slow." He grinned.

Asa rolled his eyes and chuckled. "Whatever."

"Here." He held up the nail gun. "Switch me spots."

"Uh-uh. Not now. It's on."

Knox laughed. "Okay, fine. Get busy so I can kick your ass."

"You better be nice to him," Jasper said, walking up with several cut boards. "Daisy will beat you with her cane if you damage him before the wedding."

"No doubt," Knox said with a chuckle. "How's she doing, anyway? It didn't look like she was relying on her cane very much."

"Yeah, she's doing great. Her physical therapist wants her

LONER   25

to use the cane through the winter just because of the risk of slipping. She doesn't use it much in the house now."

"That's great. I'm glad to hear she's mostly recovered." Knox remembered how much of a wreck Asa was after Daisy's accident. He'd seen it on the news and called him to ask about her. Knox hadn't seen his face, but he could tell by his voice he'd barely been holding it together.

"Me too. Though she won't be happy until her hair grows out. I tried to convince her she should leave one side shaved— that it was trendy—but she looked at me like I'd lost my mind, then had Marci cut the other side to match." He chuckled.

Knox grinned. "Smart woman." He picked up another board and laid it down over what Asa had just nailed together.

They worked in tandem for the next couple of hours, getting a large portion of the floor done before they all needed a break from bending over. Knox lifted a water bottle to his lips, but stopped as a woman's voice echoed through the arena.

"Olive?"

They all turned at the sound of Sofie's voice.

"What's wrong, Sofie?" Silas called.

She hurried through the doorway. "Have you seen Olive? I was working on some new jewelry pieces, and I thought she was in her room, playing. She said she wanted to play with her dolls. When I went to ask her if she wanted a snack, she wasn't there." A frantic edge made her voice shrill.

Silas hurried forward. "Calm down. She has to be around here somewhere. We'll all look for her."

Tears welled in Sofie's eyes. "You don't understand. Lance —he—" She broke off as a sob slipped out.

Knox frowned as Silas folded her into a hug. What was she talking about? It sounded like she was afraid her daughter had been kidnapped.

"Shh, it's okay," Silas said. "He's not here. Nori told me

he's been released, but he has no way of knowing where you are. And there's no way he could have snuck into your house and grabbed her without you knowing."

She pushed back to look up at him. Swiping at her eyes, she nodded. "Yeah. Okay. You're right. Olive probably just snuck out. She wanted to help with the chickens this morning, but I wouldn't let her because it was too cold. She was pretty mad. I thought that was where she went, but she wasn't in the coop."

"Was her coat gone?" Knox asked, coming closer, having heard what she said.

Sofie sniffed and nodded. "So were her boots and hat."

"Good. She's at least dressed for the weather. And she should be easy to spot with all that bright purple." Knox walked over to the fence and picked up his coat. "Let's spread out. Hopefully, she didn't stray too far."

"Honey, why don't you go home?" Silas said. "In case she comes back."

Sofie's eyebrows dipped. "No, I want to help search."

"Dad's right, Sofie. We'll call Nori and have her come sit with you. But we don't want to be out scouring the ranch and she's sitting in the living room watching cartoons, waiting for you to come home."

Her shoulders slumped. "Fine. But I want to know the minute you find her."

"You will. And the same goes for you. If she shows up at home, call us."

She nodded. Her mouth quivered again, and she took a shaky breath. "Please find my baby." Her eyes took them all in as they gathered around her, donning their winter gear.

"We will." Silas nudged her toward the door. As soon as she disappeared, he spun around, pulling out his phone. "I'm going to call Noreen and see if Olive's there." He clicked the screen a couple of times and held it in front of his face. The ring filled the air.

"Hey, hon. What's up? I thought you were working all morning in the barn."

"I am. Sofie was just here. Olive is missing. Is she there with you?"

"What? No."

Silas cursed, echoing the thoughts running through Knox's head. He'd been hoping the girl played with the chickens, then decided to visit her grandmother.

"Okay. I sent Sofie back to her house in case Olive comes home. Why don't you head over there and keep her company? We're going to search the grounds. She couldn't have gone too far."

"Oh, goodness. Okay. Please find her, Silas."

"I will. I'll talk to you soon."

"Okay." She hung up, and Silas pocketed his phone.

He blew out a breath, then looked at them all. "Jasper, check the bunkhouse and the area around the chicken coop. Chet, saddle a horse and ride the perimeter of the buildings. See if you find any sign she left the immediate vicinity. Asa, Knox, search the barns. Maybe she ducked into one to get warm. I'm going to walk the area between Sofie's and the main house."

"Don't forget the trailers," Asa said, as they ran out of the arena.

Silas nodded. "First place I'll go after I check the houses. And let's grab the radios from the supply room. It'll be easier for us to keep track of where all we've looked."

They filed down the corridor, gathering the radios, then splitting up.

"You check this barn," Asa said to Knox, backing away. "I'll head next door. And don't just call her name. She might be hiding, afraid she'll get into trouble for sneaking out."

Knox frowned. "Has she done this before?"

"Not exactly, but Sofie's said before that she'll hide under her bed or in her closet when she's in trouble. It's a holdover from when they still lived with Lance. I'm not sure he ever laid a hand on Olive. I think Sofie might have taken the beatings for her. But I know he yelled a lot."

Knox's blood boiled as he thought of anyone hurting either of them. Abusive men were a special kind of sick he had no tolerance for. He swallowed his anger. It wouldn't help him find Olive. "Look in every nook and cranny, got it."

They split up, calling Olive's name as they went. Knox opened every stall he passed, checking all four corners for the girl. When he came up empty, he moved to the supply and tack rooms. He even opened the grain bins, but found no sign of her.

"Asa, do you copy?" He ran for the door as he spoke into his radio.

"Yeah."

"I'm headed your way. The horse barn is clear. Anyone else find a sign of her?"

"I've got tracks coming out the back door of Sofie's house," Silas said. "They're drifted over, though, once I get more than a few yards from the porch."

"Chicken coop is clear," Jasper said. "She was here, but she's not now."

"I just reached the perimeter of the housing complex," Chet said. "I'll let you know."

"Knox, start searching the RV trailers we brought in for the wedding. I'll finish the barn," Asa said.

"Will do." Knox pocketed the radio and took off through the snow for the RVs near the main house. He reached the first one and tried the door. It was locked. That didn't mean much, though. Olive could have locked it from the inside. He took out his radio again. "Silas, Asa, were these RVs all locked when they arrived?"

"Should have been," Asa said. "They lock them during transport. We didn't unlock any of them except the one you're staying in."

"Okay, thanks." He put the radio away again. That narrowed things down a bit. He cruised the line of RVs, looking underneath until he got to the trailer he slept in last night. He hadn't bothered to lock it up when he left this morning. Why would he out here?

Glancing at the ground near the steps, it was hard to tell if any of the footprints were Olive's. His boots had tamped down the snow around the stairs and a few feet past them. But past the steps into the yard, tiny, partially drifted over boot prints marred the pristine snowfall. His heart leaped into his throat and he mounted the steps, pulling open the door.

"Olive?" He walked inside, eyes darting around the small interior. It didn't take him long to find her curled up on the long bench in the sitting area, sound asleep. His breath left him on a whoosh as relief filled him. He pulled the radio from his pocket. "I found her. Someone tell Sofie she's safe. I'll bring her home."

"Hallelujah," Silas said. "I'll go there now."

Knox set the radio on the ledge behind the bench and sat down. He laid a gentle hand on Olive's back and gave her a soft shake, hoping he didn't startle her. "Olive. Sweetie, wake up."

The girl took a deep breath as sleep left her. She stretched, then froze as she remembered where she was.

"Hey, it's okay. It's me, Knox."

She sat up and rubbed her eyes, then looked at him, wary. "I'm sorry. I know I'm in your trailer, but I was cold. Please don't be mad." Her lower lip trembled.

"I'm not mad, honey. We were worried about you. Your mom couldn't find you. Why did you sneak out?"

Olive huffed. "She wouldn't let me help with the chickens. I always help with them."

"She had a reason, though, didn't she?"

The girl nodded. "Yeah. She said it was too cold. But we went outside in the cold all the time in Chicago. I put on all my winter stuff. See?" She held up the gloves, hat, and scarf that she'd used as a pillow when she laid down.

"I do, but Olive, Montana winters aren't like Chicago winters. They're much harsher. Your mom had a good reason for keeping you inside today, especially with the snow falling. It's not hard to get lost out here when it's snowy and windy like today. Do you understand?"

Olive pursed her lips and nodded.

"Is that what happened? You got lost?"

"No. I was cold."

"Why didn't you go home?"

She lifted one shoulder and looked away. What Asa said about her hiding when she was in trouble filtered into his brain.

"Were you worried you'd be in trouble?"

Still looking away, she nodded. "Yeah," she whispered.

Knox folded her small hands into his. "Honey, Asa told me your daddy yelled a lot, but I'm betting your mommy doesn't, am I right?"

"Yeah."

"Then there's no reason to hide anymore when you do something wrong. I know she's still upset with you, but it's because she cares about you and wants you to be safe. She didn't know where you were, and in this weather, that scared her even more."

A tear leaked out of Olive's eye. "I'm sorry. I didn't mean to make her scared."

"I know you didn't. And I think you've learned something from this, right? No more hiding and no more sneaking out."

She nodded.

"Good. Now, let's get your winter gear back on and I'll take you home, okay?"

She sniffed, nodding again, and picked up her hat, settling it on her head. He helped her with her gloves and scarf, then stood, holding out his arms.

"Come on. I'll carry you."

She stood up on the bench and held up her arms. He scooped her against him and headed for the door. The wind hit him as soon as he stepped outside. Olive tucked her face into his shoulder, her little hands clutched in his jacket as he hurried across the yard to the bungalows by the bunkhouse. It wasn't far, but his face felt chapped by the time he mounted the steps to the porch and stepped inside.

"Olive!" Sofie hurried out of the living room to greet them.

The girl's head popped up, and she reached for her mother.

"Oh, you scared the life out of me. Please don't ever run off like that again."

"I won't, Mommy. I'm sorry."

Sofie buried her face in Olive's hair, pressing kisses to her head. Several tears leaked from her eyes. She looked up, meeting Knox's gaze. "Thank you," she whispered around the emotion clogging her throat.

He gave her a nod and touched the brim of his hat. "Anytime. I'm glad she's safe. Olive, no more hiding, okay?"

The girl looked back and nodded, still hugging Sofie's neck. "Okay."

He smiled at them both. "I'll see you later." He took a few steps back and let himself out. The adrenaline that spiked while he looked for the girl ebbed, and he drew in a deep breath of the frigid air to regain his equilibrium. That hadn't been a pleasant diversion, but he was glad it ended well. Turning, he headed for the barn. They still had a dance floor to finish.

FOUR

Sofie wiped her hands on her jeans and hesitated at the base of the steps to Knox's RV. She raised a fist to knock, only to pull it back.

What the hell am I doing? She'd come over here to ask him if he'd like to join her and Olive for dinner tonight. As a thank you for finding her daughter. But now that she was here, she was second-guessing herself. Why would he want to eat with her and her wild child? She should just turn around and go bake the man some cookies.

She huffed. This was ridiculous. *Just knock on the damn door, Sofie.*

Before she could talk herself out of it, she reached up and knocked. Stepping back, she stuffed her hands in her pockets to keep them busy while she waited for him to answer. She knew he was here. She'd seen him come back from the barn not long ago.

He didn't keep her waiting long. The door swung open, and she was face to face with the sun god himself again.

"Sofie, hi." He smiled at her, but it quickly turned to a frown. "Is everything okay? Did Olive run off again?"

"No. She's helping Daisy with some wedding stuff."

"Oh. Well, what can I do for you, then?"

"Um." She cleared her throat. "I wanted to ask if you'd like to come over for dinner tonight."

"Dinner?"

She nodded. "As a thank you for finding Olive."

"You don't need to thank me, Sofie. I was happy to help look for her."

"I know, but I still want to. Actually, more so for what you said to her. She told me how you helped her understand what she did really worried me. She said she didn't think about that when she left. And when she stopped to think about going home, she only thought about how angry I'd be, and not that I'd be scared she was missing. You didn't have to do that."

He lifted a shoulder. "You still don't need to thank me. I was just—"

"Helping a little girl who was scared, I know. I just—please, come to dinner?" She looked at him through her lashes.

He rolled his lips in and looked past her at the landscape before nodding. "Okay. Dinner sounds nice. What time?"

Nerves assailed her again. *He said yes!* She wasn't sure what to do now. She hadn't really thought much past asking him to come. "Um, about an hour or so? Does that work?"

"Yes. I'll see you then."

She forced a smile out, hoping it didn't look as nervous as she felt. "Okay, good. See you then." She stared at him for a beat, then spun on her heel and hurried away.

God! Could she have been any more awkward? It was like she was fifteen again, with a crush on the varsity quarterback. She was so out of practice talking to men she found attractive. Not that she wanted anything from Knox. She didn't. But it didn't change the fact that he sent a flock of butterflies flapping around in her belly.

Sofie groaned. This was not good. She had to sit through

an entire meal with the man. She really should have just baked him some cookies.

Reaching her house, she walked inside, stomping the snow off her boots as she crossed the threshold. She removed her winter gear and padded into the kitchen in her stocking feet, crossing to the refrigerator and yanking it open to get the chicken breasts.

She grumbled under her breath, berating herself for being foolish, as she laid them on the counter and pulled open a drawer to get her meat mallet and the freezer paper. After sandwiching the chicken between two sheets of paper, she gave them a good whack, glad she'd picked chicken parmesan for dinner. Tenderizing the meat was cathartic.

The back door closed, and she looked back as Daisy and Olive came inside.

"Whoa." Daisy paused in the doorway, watching Sofie pound the chicken into a half-inch thickness. "What put that frown on your face?" Her expression cleared. "Was it—" she broke off and glanced at Olive, then mouthed, "Lance?"

Sofie shook her head. "No. Olive, sweetie, why don't you go watch some cartoons if you want?"

The girl's eyes lit up. "Okay!" She scampered out of the kitchen, leaving the women alone.

Daisy smiled as she watched her go, then walked further into the room. She hung her cane over the back of a chair and leaned against the counter. "Spill."

Sofie sighed and brushed a lock of her hair away from her face with the back of her hand. "I invited Knox to dinner."

Surprise widened Daisy's eyes. "You did?"

"Yep. To say thank you for finding Olive and being so good with her." She whacked the chicken again. "I should have just baked some damn cookies." The chicken took another hit, this time hard enough to tear the paper and send little pieces of meat flying outward.

"Okay." Daisy slid the mallet from her hand. "I think they're done." She set it in the sink. "Why does the prospect of dinner with Knox have you all befuddled? He's a nice guy. Although, I have to admit, I'm surprised he said yes. I invited him earlier to come to dinner tonight, and he said he'd just go to town to eat."

Sofie blew out a breath. "I don't know why he said yes. All I know is he—makes me feel things. I mean, have you looked at the man? Add in how nice he is and, well, there are parts of me that rejoice."

A giggle escaped Daisy's lips before she could smother it. "That's not a bad thing."

"It is when there's no future in it. Not that I'm looking for anything, because I'm not." She rolled her eyes. "I just got out of a long-term relationship. I don't want another."

"Who says it has to be that way? Maybe a fling would do you good. If he'd go for it, that is. I don't know that much about him, except he's a good friend to Asa, and he's a loner. I get the impression he's not much for socializing."

Sofie's eyes went wide. "A fling? No." She waved her hands. "No. That's not me. I've never slept with a man I didn't have a relationship with. And I don't really have a desire to."

"Yeah, well, I said I'd never date Asa because he was a pompous ass and look at us now." She shook her head and smiled. "He can still be a pompous ass, but he's not all bad." Her expression turned serious. "But we're not talking about me. We're talking about you and what you need to get over your asshole ex-husband."

"Oh, geez." She rolled her eyes. "I'm already over him. He killed anything I felt for him when he put me in the hospital."

"Not like that." Daisy waved a hand. "I meant get over what happened and move on. Reset your mind."

"Oh." Sofie frowned. "You think a fling with Knox would do that?"

"Honey, as you said, look at the man. Being with a guy like him would erase all the bad memories of Lance and give you something good to focus on for the future, don't you think?"

Sofie bit her lip. "Maybe." She rolled her eyes again and spun back to her chicken. "But it doesn't matter. I'm not having a fling. Not with Knox. Not with anyone." She took a canister of breadcrumbs from the cupboard and dumped them into a shallow dish, then took two eggs from the basket on the counter, cracking them into a bowl and whisking them with a fork.

Daisy sighed and watched her. "You're as stubborn as your mother."

That prompted a laugh from Sofie. "That's no lie." She dredged a chicken breast through the egg, then put it in the breadcrumbs.

"So, if you're not going to have a quick fling with him, what are you going to do?"

"Nothing."

"Nothing?"

"Nothing." She glanced at her cousin. "I'm going to pull up my big girl panties and muscle through this dinner, hoping I don't make a fool out of myself as I drool over him from across the table."

Daisy giggled, making Sofie smile.

"He really is gorgeous, isn't he?" Daisy said.

"As the sun god himself, yep." She dredged another chicken breast. Knox's icy blue eyes floated through her mind, along with the tiny crinkles that formed around the corners when he smiled. She resisted the urge to groan again as the butterflies came to life once more. Supper was going to be torture.

∼

Knox walked up the front steps to Sofie's house and rapped his knuckles on the door, wondering what the hell he was doing here. He should have politely turned her down and gone to town like he planned. After interacting with people all day—even people he considered friends—he was ready for some alone time. It opened as he stomped snow from his boots, Olive's little face smiling up at him.

"Mr. Knox! Mommy said you were coming to dinner. I'm glad. I want to show you my room!" She took his hand and hauled him inside.

"Hang on, Olive. I want to take my boots off." He tugged on her hand as he crossed the threshold.

"Olive!" Sofie came out of the kitchen, frowning at her daughter. "You know not to answer the door."

"But I knew it was Mr. Knox. I looked through the window first."

Sofie sighed. "Just don't answer it unless I say you can, okay?"

The girl nodded. "Okay, Mommy. Can I show Mr. Knox my room now?"

"If he wants to see it, sure." She looked at him.

He smiled at them both, then looked at Olive. "Of course I do." Bending down, he took off his boots and left them near the door. "Okay, show me your room." He straightened and Olive took his hand again.

"You'll love it. Mommy painted it purple."

"I'm sure she did." He glanced back and smiled at Sofie as Olive led him away.

"Come on, Mr. Knox." She pulled on his hand as she led him down the short hallway to the bedrooms.

Still smiling, he followed the little girl into her room and stopped in the doorway, his mouth dropping open as he took in the sight before him.

"It's purple, all right." And it was, from the walls to the bedding, to the canopy hanging from the ceiling over the cream-colored bedframe. Even her dresser had purple drawers.

"I know. Isn't it great? Mommy painted it as soon as we moved in. I always wanted a purple room, but Daddy wouldn't let me."

"Well, I think it's very nice." Knox would die before he would tell her anything else. Not when her own father refused to support her wishes. Painting a child's room was an easy task, and one that was easy to rectify once they changed their mind. If he ever had kids, he'd paint their rooms any color they wanted.

She hopped up on the bed and picked up a large purple unicorn, hugging it on her lap. "This is Fiona."

He waved. "Hello, Fiona."

Olive giggled. "She can't talk, you know."

"Are you sure?" He walked over to sit on the bed, then took the stuffed animal from her, holding it in front of his face. "What do you mean, I can't talk?" He pitched his voice into a falsetto. "I have lots to say."

She giggled again. "Like what?"

"Like, I need a sparkly tiara to match my sparkly horn."

The girl's eyes lit up. "I have one!" She shot off the bed to her toy box under the window and came back a moment later with a silver tiara. Tongue peeking from between her lips, she settled it on Fiona's head.

"Thank you," he said in his Fiona voice.

She let out another little giggle. "You're funny."

Knox peeked around the unicorn's head and smiled. "Nah, Fiona's funny." He schooled his face. "I'm a serious person."

She laughed, and he joined her.

"Show me what else you have in this bright purple room of yours."

Olive looked around a moment, then shot off the bed again for a dollhouse against the far wall. "Come see my dolls. Grandpa Silas made me a house for them."

Knox followed her over to kneel on the floor. "This is pretty cool." And it was. She had quite the collection. The house fit her dolls and all their accessories perfectly. Three stories, it held a plethora of furniture sets. Everything from what one would expect to find in a house, to a store set and even a clinic. Each room was painted a different color or had wallpaper. Some of the furniture looked handmade, too.

"Yep!" She handed him a small figurine.

"What's this lady's name?"

"Jessica. I named her after my friend from preschool." Her expression fell, and she stared at her lap. "I miss her."

"I'm sure you do."

"Have you ever moved away from your friends?"

"No. But I've had friends move away. You're right. It's not fun."

Her lower lip popped out for a moment before she took a deep breath and her face cleared some. Knox was impressed with her ability to compose herself. He was a little sad, too. A four-year-old shouldn't be so good at that. A slow burn of anger lit in his gut for the man who'd forced her to grow up so fast. He didn't know much about her father, but what he was learning, he didn't like.

"You wanna play?"

"Sure. What do you want to play?"

She picked up a doll wearing an apron. "They're at the store. This is the lady at the register." She held up her doll, then put it in the house behind a counter.

Knox peered inside. She had a little grocery set up. "Man, you've got everything in this thing, don't you?"

"Yep."

"Okay, so I'm the customer?"

She nodded.

"Okay."

For the next fifteen minutes, he sat on the floor and played shop with Olive. The little girl was a shrewd business-woman, negotiating a fine price for his mini apple and loaf of bread.

"Dinner's ready."

Knox glanced back to see Sofie in the doorway.

"Yum!" Olive put down her doll and stood. "Come on, Mr. Knox. Mommy made chicken parm-john. It's the best!"

"Is there garlic bread?" He let Olive take his hand and lead him from her room. They brushed past Sofie, who—looking at him funny—led them down the hallway to the small dining table at the back of the kitchen.

"There's always garlic bread," Olive announced, stopping at the table.

"And salad," Sofie said, sitting the bowl of mixed greens in the center of the table. "Don't forget that."

Olive wrinkled her nose. "I don't like salad."

"I didn't either at your age, but I ate it anyway. It's good for you."

"That's what Mommy says too." Olive plopped into a chair.

"Wise woman, your mother." He looked at Sofie and winked.

She blushed and turned away to take a plastic cup with a lid from the cupboard. "Olive, what do you want to drink?"

"Chocolate milk."

Sofie glanced back, an eyebrow raised. "Will you eat your salad?"

"Yes."

She stared at the girl a moment longer before nodding and

moving to the fridge for the milk. "Knox, how about you? What would you like?"

"Chocolate milk sounds great, actually."

"Oh. Okay." She shrugged and closed the fridge door, gallon jug of chocolate milk in hand. "I guess we can all have that."

"You're going to drink chocolate milk, Mommy?" Olive stared at her mother with wide eyes.

Knox laughed. "I take it you don't drink it much?"

Sofie smiled. "Not that she sees. Sometimes I have some before I go to bed, but I normally just drink water with dinner." She poured three glasses, putting the lid on Olive's.

Knox picked up the other two glasses and set them on the table. He waited for Sofie to sit, then sank into his own chair beside Olive. The girl said a quick blessing over their meal, then Sofie dished up their food. His mouth watered as he took his plate from her. Olive was right; it looked and smelled delicious.

"Thank you for inviting me over. This looks great."

"You're welcome. We're glad to have you. Right, Olive?"

The girl nodded, a bite of bread already in her mouth. She swallowed. "Thanks for finding me and taking me home." She ducked her head. "I'm sorry for running away."

"Hey." He touched her arm. "We talked about this, remember?"

She looked up. "Oh. Yeah, okay." Her face brightened with a smile.

"Good. Let's eat, yeah?" At her nod, Knox cut off a piece of chicken and shoved it in his mouth. Flavors burst over his tongue, and he moaned. "Oh my God." He chewed and swallowed. "Did you make the sauce from scratch?"

Blushing again, Sofie nodded. "I take it you like it?"

"It's amazing." He took another bite.

They ate in silence for several minutes before Olive spoke up.

"Daisy said you brought her a horse for her wedding."

"I did."

"She showed him to me. He's pretty. I wish I had a horse."

"You're a little young yet," Sofie said.

"Not really," Knox said. "My parents had me in the saddle before I could walk. I was riding on my own by the time I was three."

Sofie glared at him, and Knox realized he wasn't helping. He pressed his lips together. "Sorry," he muttered.

But it was too late. Olive took his words and ran with them.

"Oh! Can you teach me? Grandpa's been too busy and so has Asa. Daisy isn't allowed to ride yet, and Mommy doesn't know how."

Knox glanced at Sofie, his eyes pleading. She gave him a sweet smile and shook her head, letting him know he was on his own to get out of this one. He cleared his throat. "Um, well, I'm not sure. I don't know if your mother wants you to learn just yet. And I'm only going to be here a little over a week."

Olive put her fork down and pressed her hands together. "Please, Mr. Knox. I'll be the bestest student ever, I swear."

He caught Sofie's eye again. She frowned. He looked back at Olive. "We'll see, okay? I can't promise anything, but your mom and I will talk."

The girl's shoulders dropped, but she nodded.

"Eat your dinner," Sofie said softly.

Olive forked a piece of lettuce in her mouth, grimacing at the taste. Knox fought a smile. She was cute.

"So, tell us about yourself, Knox." Sofie speared a bite of chicken. "I've heard mention a couple times now you're a genius, but not much else."

His face reddened. "I guess technically I am. There's not much else to tell, though. I've lived my entire life in Silver Gap, Colorado, minus the years I went to college. Now, I breed and train horses."

"What did you go to college for?"

"Business and genetics. I wanted to take our operation to another level. My dad didn't have the right temperament or business sense, but he agreed with me that we could do more."

"What did you expand on?"

"The breeding part. Training horses is what we've always done, but I wanted to breed our own line, train them, and sell them. That's what we do now."

"How many horses do you have?"

"On a routine basis, about twenty. That number varies with births and sales, but not by much. If you include the animals we board, I have closer to forty."

"You have forty horses?" Olive's eyes were round.

He smiled. "Thereabouts, yes."

"Wow!"

"Do you train all of them?" Sofie asked.

"Most. Some boarders are just that. Boarded. People go on vacation and need a place for their horses, or they don't currently have a barn, so I house them."

"Do you do it all alone?"

"I have a few assistants, but I oversee everything. We rotate through the herd." Knox raised a forkful of chicken. "So, what about you? Have you always made jewelry?" He ate the bite on his fork.

Sofie nodded. "Mostly, yes. I worked a few odd jobs during college to help make ends meet, but art has always been my passion."

"You went to college for art?"

"Yes. My focus was design."

"What sort of things do you make?"

She pointed to the wire pendant hanging at her neck. "I made this. I also use semi-precious gemstones and solid metals, not just wire. I actually worked for a jeweler in Chicago before Olive was born. Once she came along, I needed more flexibility. Plus, with Lance's job, I didn't really have to work. I just wanted to, so I started a business from home. It's really grown in the last couple of years."

"Mommy makes the prettiest things." Olive smiled at them.

"Thank you, sweetie." Sofie patted her daughter's hand.

Knox wanted to ask more about her ex, but didn't dare with Olive in hearing range. He wasn't sure what all she knew about her father's actions, and didn't want her asking questions Sofie wasn't ready to answer. Instead, he focused on his food.

Sofie cleared her throat. "So, is Alice your only sibling?"

He wiped his mouth. "Yes. What about you? Do you have any siblings?"

She shook her head. "No. My parents had a difficult time having kids. I'm it."

"I want a sister," Olive said, swallowing the last of her salad. She stabbed a piece of chicken. "But not a brother." Her nose wrinkled. "Boys are a pain."

Knox coughed to cover up a laugh and reached for his milk glass.

Sofie's eyes twinkled, and she held back a smile. "Boys are not a pain, Olive."

"Yes, they are. Evan always pulled my ponytail, and Reece wouldn't stop calling me a doody-face."

Knox choked on his milk. He knew he shouldn't laugh, but she looked so indignant. He set the glass down and covered his mouth with his napkin, looking at Sofie. Her eyes were wide, her lips pressed together.

"I'm sorry they acted that way, honey," Sofie said.

Olive stabbed a piece of chicken. "Boys are dumb." She put the bite in her mouth.

They ate several more bites in silence before he spoke again. "So, how are you enjoying your first Montana winter?"

"It's cold," Sofie replied. "Colder than Chicago. Does it get this cold in Colorado too?"

"Sometimes, but not usually this early. It was warmer there when we left to come here."

She scrunched her nose, much like Olive. "I need to get some warmer clothes. My coat isn't bad, but my boots aren't going to cut it once we get into the depths of winter."

"Asa and Silas will be able to help you with that. They'll probably want to outfit Daisy and Nori, too. You guys could make a day of it in Billings."

She smiled. "I'll have to remember that. That sounds fun." Her phone rang, cutting through the conversation. She frowned and turned to look at the counter where it rested, but didn't get up.

"Aren't you going to get that?" he asked.

"No. They'll either leave a message or call back later. Most anyone I care about is on this ranch, and I doubt a phone call is how someone would inform me of a problem. They're more of a barge in the door kind of people around here."

He grinned. That summarized Asa and Silas well.

"It's probably just a client wanting to place an order. They'll leave a message and I'll call them back later."

The phone stopped ringing, and they went back to their food. A couple of minutes later, it dinged with a message. Knox ignored it and kept his focus on Sofie and Olive. They were quite the pair. Sofie was quiet but funny. Olive was much more boisterous than her mother and not afraid to speak her mind. The three of them chatted through the rest of their meal before Olive asked to be excused to watch TV.

Knox watched her scamper out of the room, then stood to

help Sofie with the dishes.

"She's something else." He picked up his plate and Olive's.

Sofie grinned. "She keeps me on my toes, that's for sure." Her smile dimmed. "Thank you again for finding her."

"We were all looking. I just got lucky."

"Well, regardless, I'm glad you did." She headed into the kitchen and deposited her plate and their glasses in the sink.

"Do you want help washing up?"

"No. I'll throw everything in the dishwasher later." She stood in front of the sink and folded her hands. Her eyes met his, then glanced away.

Knox's gut clenched as attraction flared. Those big green eyes of hers were unlike any he'd ever seen; a deep, rich emerald in color. Her plum sweater just made them pop more.

She cleared her throat and walked to the counter where her phone sat and picked it up. "I guess I should see who called earlier."

He turned in time to see her face blanch. She stilled, clutching the phone. Alarmed by her sudden change in behavior, he stepped toward her. "Sofie? Is everything okay?"

Her gaze snapped to his for a moment, and she laid the phone down. "Fine."

He frowned. "I know I don't know you well, but you're not fine." He leaned on the counter next to her. "What's the matter?" He knew he was prying, but the look on her face raised all his inner protective instincts. She looked scared.

Wide eyes met his. She held his gaze for several beats. "It's nothing. My ex. He left a text."

Knox's brows dipped. "He just got out of jail, right?" He remembered that being mentioned when she showed up in the barn earlier, looking for Olive.

She nodded.

"What happened, if you don't mind me asking?"

Sofie drew in a shaky breath and ran a hand through her

dark hair. "He was abusive. For a long time, it was mostly verbal, with a slap here and there, but a couple of years ago, that changed. My jewelry business took off. I still made our family my priority and tried to keep my hours to the time he was at work, but sometimes, I had to stretch that. He didn't like it, so the slaps turned into punches. Especially when he got mad at Olive and I stepped in front of her. It's like it doubled his rage that I would protect her from him."

She shifted, crossing her arms. "Just over a year ago, we got into a big argument about my business and Olive. I wanted her to go to preschool, but he wanted me to educate her at home. I'm not a teacher. I wouldn't know where to start to teach her how to read. He accused me of wanting her out of my hair so I could play artist. I told him that was crazy. That I just wanted what was best for Olive, but he didn't want to hear it. Told me I had to shut down my business. I refused. It was something I enjoyed, plus, I was putting a little bit from every sale into an account he didn't know about, trying to build up enough money to leave."

"Why didn't you go to your mom?"

"Embarrassment, mostly. She never liked him, and I didn't want to go crawling home. She'd never say 'I told you so,' but I'd hear it in my head that I should have listened to her from the beginning. I should have just sucked up my pride and went to her. When I told him I wouldn't stop with the jewelry, he went ballistic. I spent a week in the hospital from my injuries and the surgeries needed to fix them."

Rage flared in Knox's gut. He clenched his teeth to keep from saying exactly what he thought of her ex.

"When I woke up, I knew I couldn't go back. That the next time, I might not be okay. Or he might hurt Olive. We moved in with my mom, and Lance went to jail on my testimony. He was released a couple of weeks ago because of overcrowding."

"How long was he supposed to be in?"

"A few more months. He's also not supposed to have any contact with me or Olive. Everything is supposed to go through a court-appointed intermediary."

"And he just texted you? Sofie, you need to call the police, so they can arrest him for violating the terms of his release."

"But I can't prove he did. It's the same number that called, but he didn't leave a voice message, only text. I don't recognize the number, and he doesn't indicate who he is to me in the message."

Knox frowned. "What does it say?"

She put a finger on the fingerprint sensor on her phone, then turned it so he could see it.

You think you can hide, but you can't. I'll see you soon.

That rage burned a little brighter. He took a steadying breath. "I think you should still call the police. They might not be able to do anything, but at least it'll be on record if he does anything else you can trace back to him. And they can at least try to track the number."

She groaned and scrubbed a hand over her face. "I just want to move on. I was just beginning to feel like I was in control. Moving here was the best thing I could have done. Now I feel like I'm back at square one." She blew out a breath and waved a hand at him. "I don't know why I'm telling you all of this." She scooped up her phone and pushed away from the counter. "I'll be fine. Don't worry about me."

"Sofie." He laid a gentle hand on her arm. "I know we just met, but if you need anything, all you have to do is ask."

She offered him a shaky smile. "Thank you."

Knox nodded once and watched her walk out of the kitchen. He swiped a hand over his face, wondering why, of all the women he'd met in his thirty-eight years, she was the one to get under his skin and make him want to wrap her up and keep her from all the evils in the world.

FIVE

"Sofie!"

Pausing on her way across the yard at the sound of Knox's deep voice, Sofie bit back a groan as she turned. She'd managed to avoid him since their dinner together the other night. Embarrassment that she'd aired her dirty laundry to a man she just met kept her far away from him the last several days. That in itself was a minor miracle. Daisy had a list of things that needed to be done, and Sofie had jumped on any that she thought wouldn't include Knox. Who knew just walking across the yard would lead him to her?

"Hey. I'm glad I caught you." He jogged to a stop a few feet away. "You're a hard woman to find."

She offered him a tight smile. "I've been busy. What's up?"

His eyes narrowed a fraction at her reserved greeting, but he didn't say anything. "Olive was in the barn with Nori. She asked about riding lessons again. We never talked about it at dinner the other night. I'm fine with showing her the basics if it's okay with you."

"Oh." Sofie glanced at the barn and the horses milling in the corral.

"I'll put her on the gentlest horse here and we'll stay in the arena."

She bit the corner of her lip and looked up at him. It wasn't so much that she was worried about her daughter on a horse. She knew anyone here would keep her safe. It was more the thought of Knox being her teacher. The man seriously upset Sofie's equilibrium. He wasn't just a beautiful human being; he was also friendly and kind and had a weird ability to get her to talk about things she never talked about. It was unnerving.

"She'll be completely safe, Sofie."

Sofie took a quick breath and nodded, coming to a decision. She couldn't put her comfort in the way of Olive's happiness. "I know. And I guess that would be all right. So long as you don't promise her she can have her own horse."

He grinned, and Sofie's heart skipped.

"No promises for a horse for Olive, got it." He drew an X over his heart. "When do you want to start?"

"Um, whenever's convenient for you, I guess."

"How about after dinner tonight? I'll be free then."

She nodded. "Me too. Okay, that sounds fine."

"Good." The smile on his handsome face dimmed, and he looked at her with a low level of concern shining in his icy blue eyes. "How are you doing? Any more menacing texts from your ex?"

Sofie's heart skipped again for a different reason. "A few, yes. All from different numbers, so every time I block one, he still gets through. I might need to change my phone number, but I don't really want to. It's all over my new business cards and website."

"Which is probably how he got it."

She nodded. "It wasn't supposed to be a secret. He just wasn't supposed to contact me. I don't think he knows where we are, though. I didn't leave a forwarding address except with the post office. Mom didn't either."

His mouth pulled. "Her marriage to Silas was in the gossip papers, though, because of his connection to Asa. Maybe he saw that."

Her shoulders slumped. "I didn't think of that."

"Did you make a police report about the messages?"

"Yes. The detective I talked to said he would send the report to his parole officer, but not to hold my breath since there wasn't anything tying him to the messages."

Knox's mouth flattened. "Yeah. I figured that's what he'd say. Do the others know?"

Her eyes widened. "No. You didn't say anything, did you?" Mentally, she cursed. She should have told him not to say anything. She didn't want to worry anyone so close to the wedding. It was just text messages. And they all pretty much said the same thing.

"No. It's not my place. But I do think you should say something. Especially to your mom and Silas."

She did too. And she would. After the wedding. "I will after the wedding. I don't want to do anything to put a damper on Daisy's day. She and Asa deserve to have a wedding without my problems weighing them down."

He stared at her a moment, those icy eyes seeing more than she wanted him to see. "Okay. But if it escalates, tell me at least? You shouldn't have to deal with this alone."

To her horror, she felt tears well at his kindness. Dammit! Why did he affect her so? Her anger helped her banish the waterworks.

"Why do you care? You don't know me." Sofie's anger at herself made her defensive.

Hurt flashed in his eyes. He held up his hands. "I just want to help." He took a few steps back. "You know where to find me when you're ready for Olive's lesson." With a quick spin on his heel, he loped away.

Sofie growled, frustration mounting. She was both glad she'd put some distance between them and upset. She needed the distance to keep from melting into a pile of goo at his feet, but she felt like she'd lost an ally.

Stomping her foot, she whirled around and headed for the main house. Damn man. Who did he think he was, showing up here and messing with her emotions? He needed to take his gorgeous, friendly self back to Colorado.

~

Pulse beating a rapid flutter in her throat, Sofie knocked on Knox's trailer door after dinner, clutching Olive's hand. The little girl bounced on the balls of her feet as they waited.

"I'm so excited, Mommy!"

"I know, sweetie." She smiled at her. Sofie might not be enthusiastic about what they were doing, but Olive was over the moon.

The door swung open, sending Sofie's heart flutters into overdrive. She had a whole flock beating in her chest now at the sight of him. His eyes met hers and held for a brief moment, then he looked at Olive and grinned.

"Hey, kiddo. What's up?"

"Mommy said you're going to teach me to ride a horse."

"She did?" He frowned, but a smile teased the corners of his mouth. "Are you sure?"

"Yes! I ate all my sketti, then she said to put my coat and boots on because you were going to give me my first lesson."

"Oh, man. You had spaghetti for dinner? That's good stuff. I had a sandwich."

"We have leftovers. You can come eat some after my lesson."

He chuckled. "Well, thank you, Olive. We'll see what your mother says. Let me put my boots and stuff on and I'll meet you in the barn, okay?"

"Okay!"

Knox gave Sofie a quick nod, then closed the door.

"Come on, Mommy. I want to look at all the horses while we wait."

They trudged through the muddy yard to the barn. Sofie was glad it had warmed up, but she wasn't sure the mud was any better. She hoped it dried before Saturday, or Daisy's dress would be a mess.

Mentally, she snorted. Her cousin was getting married in a barn. With animals. There would probably be more than mud on her dress by the end of the night. Sofie didn't think she'd care, either.

At the barn, Sofie opened the man-door and let them inside. Olive ran down the aisle between the stalls to greet the first horse. Sofie took off her hat and gloves, stuffing them in her pockets. "Don't disappear. Knox will be here soon."

"Okay." The girl scratched Asa's horse, Storm, on the muzzle, then hurried to the next stall.

Sofie unzipped her coat and followed at a slower pace. She stopped in front of Storm. The horse butted her arm. "Hey, bud." She scratched his face, and he leaned into her touch. "You're a sweetie, aren't you?" She was slowly getting used to the big animals. Before they moved here, the closest she'd ever been to a horse was the pony ride at the state fair. She still hadn't ridden one here yet, but she was comfortable now being around them.

The outer door opened, and she turned to see Knox stride through.

"Mr. Knox!" Olive came running back down the aisle. "Which horse do I get to ride? The new one?"

He chuckled and scooped her up. "Probably not him. He's

a little tall for you. If I remember right, Asa has an older mare that's on the smaller side. Let's see if we can find her. Her name is Trudy."

"Okay." The girl squirmed to be put down, so he set her on the floor. She took off again, looking at the nameplates on the stalls.

Knox walked up to Sofie, smiling. "Can she read to find the right horse?"

"Sort of. She knows her letters and some of the sounds they make. She'll probably be able to find one that starts with T R."

"I found her!" Olive's voice echoed through the barn, making the adults chuckle.

"I guess you were right."

They wandered down the corridor until they found the girl standing in front of a stall, trying to reach the cream-colored horse, who'd poked her head over the door.

"She's pretty," Olive said as they approached.

"Yes, she is." Knox picked up the halter hanging beside the door and lifted the latch. He walked inside and slid the halter over the mare's head, buckling it behind her ears. "Sofie, can you hand me the lead rope, please?"

She glanced at the wall beside the stall door, then took a rope with a clip on the end of a hook. "This one?"

He nodded.

She walked into the stall and handed it to him.

"Thanks." He clipped it to the halter and led the mare to the door.

Sofie turned and put a hand on Olive's shoulder, ushering her out of the way.

"Let's go down to the arena. I can tie her to the fence and saddle her there."

She stepped back and let him lead the way with Trudy. Olive vibrated in her grasp, eager to get on the horse. As they walked, she chattered away, asking question after question about the animal, interspersing her commentary with exclamations of how excited she was. Sofie couldn't help but smile at her daughter's enthusiasm. This was why she was braving the emotions Knox provoked. Olive would never forget this.

They entered the arena, and Knox tied Trudy to the fence rail, then disappeared long enough to get her tack. He came back with a saddle propped on one shoulder and bridle and a brush dangling from his fingers.

Sofie's mouth watered at the sight. She never knew she had cowboy fantasies until he showed up. Now, all she could think about—dream about—was a golden-haired man in a cowboy hat and boots, wearing jeans that hugged his perfect ass and nothing else. Her imagination was doing a great job filling in what was under his plaid work shirts.

"Okay." He set the saddle on the ground and draped the bridle and the blanket that was with the saddle over the railing. "First, we have to brush her to make sure there's nothing in her hair that will irritate her under the saddle."

"That would be bad." Olive stared up at him, her face serious.

He nodded. "It would be like you having something inside your shirt, poking at you and digging into your skin."

Sofie's grimace echoed Olive's. That definitely didn't sound pleasant.

Knox brushed the horse's back with smooth, efficient strokes while Olive watched on, soaking in everything he did. Once he was done, he handed her the comb, then picked up the saddle blanket and positioned it over Trudy's back. Satisfied with where it was, he lifted the saddle and set it on her back, then crouched to reach the strap on her other side and pull it through the buckle on his side.

"I still don't understand how that one strap keeps the

saddle from just sliding over the horse's side and dumping the rider." Sofie tilted her head as she watched him.

He glanced up, one side of his mouth quirking. "Part of its design. The rest is making sure it's tight, but not so tight it bothers the horse." He stood, pulling on the strap and buckling it into place. After testing the saddle, he made a quick adjustment, then stepped back. He picked up the bridle from the fence and replaced Trudy's halter with it, sliding the bit between her teeth. "Okay, little miss. She's ready for you."

Olive squealed. Trudy whickered and flicked her ears.

"We need to go over a few things first. There are rules when you're around horses."

"Like what?"

"First, a horse's greatest danger lies in their feet. They can kick hard enough to kill a person, so always watch their feet. Don't walk behind a horse that doesn't know you're there. Even the most mild-mannered ones, like Trudy, could kick you if they think they're being threatened."

"Okay."

"Second, don't run up to a horse you don't know well for the same reason."

Olive nodded.

"And third, don't ever go into a horse's stall or enter the arena or corral without an adult. You always ask first."

Sofie liked that rule. And she liked that he was taking the time to teach her about how to be safe around the large animals, and not just how to sit on one.

"So, do you understand and agree to all the rules?"

"Yes." Olive bounced on her feet.

"All right. Up we go, then." He put his hands under her arms and lifted her, settling her into the saddle on Trudy's back.

Olive giggled and clutched the saddle horn. "Wow! I'm so high! Look, Mommy!"

"I see you, sweetie."

"Are you comfortable up there?" Knox asked.

The girl nodded. "Yep."

"Okay, we're going to take a lap around the arena. Ready?"

"Yep!"

Sofie leaned against the rail and watched as Knox led Olive around the arena. The girl kept up a steady stream of conversation as they went. She couldn't help but be impressed with how good he was with her. It made her wonder if he had any kids of his own. She never asked, and he hadn't mentioned any. In any case, he was great with children. At least her child, anyway.

Knox and Olive walked the arena several times until she relaxed and looked more comfortable in the saddle.

"I think that's a good start for your first lesson." Knox led her to Sofie's side and stopped.

Olive pouted. "Can't we do one more lap?"

"Olive, Knox said you were done. What do you say?"

The girl's mouth flattened, but she looked at Knox. "Thank you for the lesson."

He smiled at her. "You're welcome, munchkin." He helped her down. "Same time tomorrow?"

Sofie nodded. "That sounds good."

"Mommy, I have to pee."

"We're going home, sweetie. Can you hold it?"

"No." Olive crossed her feet and bent slightly. "I really have to go."

Sofie sighed.

"There's a bathroom right through there." Knox pointed to a doorway. "It's on the left as you go back into the barn."

"I remember," Olive said. "Can I go, Mommy, please?"

"Yes, but don't take too long."

Olive shot away, running as fast as her short, four-year-old legs would carry her. Sofie glanced away from her to look at Knox. He'd loosened the strap on Trudy's saddle.

"Thank you for giving her lessons. She had a blast tonight."

He smiled. "So did I. She's a great kid."

"Thank you."

He nodded and slid the saddle off the horse. Sofie bit her lip. Should she ask? Curiosity got the better of her, and she couldn't stop herself.

"Do you have kids?"

"No. Why?" He looked at her.

She shrugged. "You're just really good with Olive. Better than what I would expect from someone who doesn't have any kids of his own or hasn't been around little ones much."

He wagged a finger. "That's where you're wrong. Alice teaches art at the local school, which means I get roped into all kinds of fundraiser stuff for the district. I've been working with the local kids back home for about ten years now."

"Really? That's great. I spent some time with Olive's preschool class. It was a lot of fun."

"Yeah, the little ones are the best. They're the most eager to learn, and they take direction really well."

She smiled. "What kid doesn't want to learn to ride a horse? I did, but I never got to."

"Have you ridden since you've been here?"

Sofie shook her head. "I've gotten comfortable around them, but between getting settled in and the wedding, learning to ride has been low on the totem pole."

"Well, we need to change that. Looks like I'm getting that paint out after all."

Her eyes widened. "What? No. I don't need a lesson."

He grinned. "What's the matter? Scared?"

She scoffed. "What are you, like eight? I'm not scared."

Laughing, he switched out Trudy's bridle for her halter

and clipped the lead rope to her. "Here." He handed her the rope, then hefted the saddle onto his shoulder. "Let's go get your ride."

"Knox—"

He walked away, leaving her staring at his broad back, holding the horse's lead. Trudy tossed her head. "I know." She looked at the mare. "He's a turd." She sighed. "Come on."

Olive ran out of the restroom as Sofie entered the barn.

"Is it time to go?"

"Not just yet, sweetie. Knox decided Mommy needs a riding lesson too."

The girl's eyes lit up. "We get to learn together!" She clapped.

Sofie smiled. "I guess we do. Let's put Trudy back in her stall, okay? Can you make sure the door is open?"

Olive ran ahead to the horse's stall. "It's open."

"Good." Sofie led the horse inside and unclipped the lead rope, then joined her daughter in the aisle, shutting the door behind her.

A sharp whistle from down the corridor drew her attention. Knox stood between the stalls with a black and white horse on a lead. He tipped his head toward the arena. "Come on."

Grumbling under her breath, Sofie walked toward him. Olive ran ahead, but after several steps, remembered Knox's admonishment about running up on a horse and slowed to a fast walk. She stayed several paces back and to the side as she chattered to him about how excited she was that Sofie got to ride, too.

They repeated the process of saddling the horse, but this time, he made her participate.

"You never know when the knowledge will come in handy, Sof." He stepped back after hefting the saddle onto the horse's back and gestured for her to take over.

Sofie blew her bangs out of her face and crouched beside the horse, reaching beneath him to grasp the strap. She threaded it through the buckle and stood, pulling. Latching it, she stepped back. Knox checked the fit, then helped her with the bridle.

"All right, he's set. Up you go." He pointed to the stirrup.

Feeling a little silly about getting a riding lesson after her four-year-old, Sofie ducked her head and stuck her foot in the stirrup, avoiding his gaze. She mounted the horse the way she'd seen Asa, Silas, and the hands do it, settling her butt in the saddle. The horse was much wider than she expected.

"Comfy?"

She looked down at Knox. "As I can be, I guess."

"Good."

Sofie clutched the pommel as he took the reins and led the horse forward. Once the horse settled into his gait, she loosened her grip.

"Mommy, you're riding!" Olive skipped along beside them.

"I know."

"Is it fun? I had fun."

"It is." And it was. So long as the horse maintained a steady pace, she didn't feel like she was going to fall off.

"You're a natural. Wanna step it up a bit?"

"What?" She stared at Knox with wide eyes. "No. I'm happy at a walk for now."

He shrugged. "Suit yourself."

She rolled her eyes and sighed, a smile quirking one side of her mouth.

They made several turns around the arena, much like Olive did, but he showed her how to use the reins to steer the horse. When Sofie noticed her daughter's energy flag, and she trailed behind, she leaned over and nudged Knox's shoulder.

"I think she's done."

He glanced back and nodded, then led her back to where they started.

"Do you know how to get down?"

"I think so." She swung her right leg over the paint's back and reached for the ground. It was further away than she thought and she went too fast, stumbling as she touched down.

"Whoa, there." Knox's arms wrapped around her middle, and she sagged into his chest with a squeal. "Are you okay?"

She nodded. As the shock of falling wore off, awareness of the hard wall of muscle at her back crept in. Heat spread through her body. She looked back, and her eyes caught his. He stilled, staring at her. Sofie cleared her throat and forced her legs to stiffen and pushed away to stand on her own.

"Thanks for catching me."

He nodded. "Of course." His tone was gruff as he looked away. Olive stood in front of the animal, scratching his nose. "You want to go for a quick ride with me, Olive?"

Her eyes lit up. "Really?"

"Sure. If it's okay with your mom?" He glanced at her.

Sofie nodded. It was fine with her. She needed a moment anyway to settle herself after being in his arms. She'd never had such an innocent touch affect her so much.

Knox readjusted the stirrups on the saddle, then mounted the horse. He leaned over the side and picked Olive up, settling her in front of him on the saddle. "Ready?"

"Yep!"

He turned away from Sofie, then nudged the paint into a slow trot. Sofie heard Olive giggle, then shout at him to go faster. He kicked the horse into a slow lope. Olive's laughter rang through the arena, making Sofie's heart soar. It was so good to know her daughter was happy. Sofie tried to shelter her from the worst of her father's temper, but she wasn't always successful. It had an impact on Olive's behavior. Since they moved in with Nori, there'd been a gradual shift to a happier, more carefree child, and Sofie was glad to see it. Lance's influence on their lives was slowly lifting.

Her smile dimmed some as she thought about the text messages she'd received. She hoped he stayed away. Or went to therapy like the court ordered and got his anger under control. Only then would she consider allowing him unsupervised contact with their daughter.

She sighed, grinning at Knox and Olive as they passed. For now, that was one worry she didn't have to think about. The judge assured her he wouldn't even get supervised visits until he completed some therapy and kept his nose clean. He wasn't helping his case with the messages, even if she couldn't prove it was him.

Knox sped up, and Olive squealed in delight. Sofie's heart leaped into her throat at how fast they were going, but she knew her little girl was in good hands. Knox rode like the expert horseman he was. He'd never let anything happen to the child in his arms.

They came to a halt in front of her. The paint snorted out a breath and shook his head, clearly still wanting to run. Sofie held her hands up and helped Olive down.

"Did you see me, Mommy? Did you see? We were flying!"

"Yes, you were. Let's help Knox put things away, then we need to get going. You need a bath yet before bed."

Olive's little brows dipped. "I don't want to go to bed."

"You never do."

"It's close to my bedtime too." Knox dismounted and led the horse to the fence to switch out the bridle for the halter and lead rope.

Sofie took it from him so he could take off the saddle and brush the horse down. He worked quickly, brushing out the horse's coat.

"There. I think that's it. Let's put this stuff away, then I'll walk you two home."

"You don't have to do that. We made it here on our own just fine."

"Yes, but there was still some light. It's dark now."

"There's this thing called a flashlight app... It's on every cellphone nowadays."

He grinned. "Humor me. I just want to make sure you don't step in a hole or run into a bobcat or something."

"But then, who will protect you on your way home?" She smirked.

"I'll sprint. Over the same path we take to your house, so I avoid all the holes."

Sofie laughed.

They headed back into the barn and stowed the tack and sequestered the paint in his stall before venturing back out into the night. Sofie tugged Olive's hat further down over her ears. It hadn't taken long for the temperature to dip. Olive tripped, looking up at her, and Knox scooped her into his arms to carry her across the yard.

Sofie tried not to notice how much of a natural he was with her. They'd become instant friends. She knew she should be worried about how Olive would react when he left, but she also knew her daughter needed the male influence in her life.

She looked out over the yard, trying to distract herself, and her eyes landed on the horde of RVs parked near the main house. "Do you stay warm in that RV?" she asked.

"Mostly. It got a little drafty with that wintery weather we had, but it's not bad."

"That's good. Daisy's brothers and their families arrive tomorrow. Some of them aren't the outdoorsy type."

"I think they'll be comfortable."

"I just hope they behave. Kyle especially. It took him the longest to warm up to Asa, even with Ian's blessing."

"Asa told me about her family." He shook his head. "I don't know how she stayed there so long."

"The same way I stayed." Her voice was quiet. "It's familiar. And change is scary. Even if it might be better for you."

"I guess that makes sense. I'm just glad they've worked things out. I can't imagine not having Alice in my life."

They reached her doorstep. Sofie climbed the steps and opened the door. Knox walked in behind her and set Olive down on the mudroom floor. The little girl immediately shucked her winter clothing.

"Head into the bathroom, sweetie. Mommy will be there in a moment."

"Okay."

"Say goodnight to Mr. Knox."

"G'night. Thanks for the horse lesson."

"You're welcome, Olive. I'll see you tomorrow."

She beamed, then ran into the house.

"She's really a great kid. Thanks for letting me give her lessons."

Sofie waved a hand. "Oh, don't mention it. I appreciate you taking the time to do it. And for teaching me. I wasn't counting on that when we showed up this evening."

He smiled. "You live on a ranch. You should know how to ride a horse."

She chuckled. "I'd have gotten there, eventually."

"I'm sure." He hooked a thumb toward the door. "I should be going." His eyes held hers for a moment, and Sofie felt that heat build again.

"Thanks again, Knox."

"Sure. We can try again tomorrow. If things aren't too hectic with all the new arrivals."

"Yeah. Sounds good." She made no move to venture further inside.

He hesitated a moment longer before inhaling a breath and taking a step back, breaking the spell. "Goodnight."

"Goodnight." She watched him spin on his heel and walk outside, shutting the door. The breath she didn't realize she was holding escaped her, and she bit back a groan. Tonight hadn't gone at all how she planned. She'd wanted to keep her distance. Instead, she found herself liking the man. He was kind and funny. Sweet. And so good with Olive.

Sofie growled and spun away from the door. She wasn't going to think about what could be, no matter what he made her feel or want. This time next week, he'd be back in Colorado.

"Mommy! Are you coming? Can I use my bath crayons?"

Shoving thoughts of the handsome-as-sin horse trainer from her mind, she went to give her daughter a bath.

SIX

"You sure you can carry that?" Sofie glanced down at her daughter as they crossed the yard to the small goat barn. Normally, Nori fed the goats, but with so many extra people on the ranch, she was tied up, so Sofie offered to help. Olive insisted on carrying the bag of treats, even though her little arms barely fit around it. Once she realized it wasn't too heavy for her, she was determined to carry it.

"Yep."

"Okay. Let me know if you need help."

Olive's brow dipped in concentration, but she nodded. Sofie smiled and continued to the barn. She let them in through the main doors and headed for the hay stores.

"Let me have that." She took the bag from Olive and set it on the hay bales. "We need to give them fresh hay and water, then we can feed them some treats, okay?"

"Okay."

Sofie took the wire cutters off the wall and broke open two bales of hay. Olive grabbed a cake and headed for the gate in the wooden fence, separating the goats from the rest of the barn. Wrapping her arms around several more sections of hay, Sofie followed her. She fiddled with the latch and let them through the gate, then they dumped their load in the hay trough. After repeating the process several times to fill both the indoor and outdoor troughs, they made sure the goats had plenty of water, then retrieved the treat bag.

Goats swarmed them as they stepped into the outdoor pen, baaing and trying to take the bag from Olive.

Sofie laughed. "Maybe you should let me hold that before they mow you over."

Olive giggled and handed her mother the bag. She opened it and passed the girls some treats. The goats snatched them from the girl's hands.

"Boy, they like these, don't they?" Sofie tossed some treats away from them, trying to spread them out.

"They sure do. Can I have some more?"

Sofie passed her some. "Just a few. Grandma said not to give them each more than three." She did her best to monitor which goats took treats from Olive and keep them from getting extras. She knew one or two wouldn't hurt, but she didn't want to cause any of them any problems.

Feeding the smallest goat one last treat, she closed the bag. "Okay. I think that's it."

Olive giggled as one of the goats, a black one with icy blue eyes that reminded Sofie of Knox, tried to take her mitten.

"That's mine, silly goat."

The goat bleated, then stared at the girl.

Sofie smiled and took Olive's hand. "Come on. Let's head home and get some breakfast."

"Can we have some of the eggs we collected?"

"Sure. And a waffle."

"Oh, yum!"

They walked over to the gate, and Sofie unlatched it to let them out. Olive ran through, and Sofie stepped out, turning to close it. As she did, the goat that tried to steal Olive's mitten charged, head-butting the gate.

"Oh!" Sofie lost her grip on the gate and it swung wide. The goat ran through into the yard. "Crap!" She pulled the gate closed, latching it, then turned to see the goat standing ten feet away. It stared at her, then baaed.

"Uh-oh," Olive said. "The goat got out."

"I see that, sweetie. We need to catch him and get him back in the pen."

"How?"

That was a great question. Sofie sighed and glanced at the sky. Chasing a goat at seven in the morning was not how she wanted to start the day. She looked at Olive. "Get behind it and try to chase it this way. Maybe we can get it to run through the gate."

Olive nodded and circled behind the goat. Sofie kept its attention so it wouldn't scare away. Once behind it, Olive ran at the goat.

"Let's go, goat!"

The goat sidestepped, looking at the girl before it took off. Away from the pen.

"Dammit!"

"Mommy, you said a bad word."

"I know, I'm sorry. I think we might need help."

Olive looked around. Her face brightened. "There's Mr. Knox. Hey, Mr. Knox!" She waved.

Sofie glanced over, stifling a groan. Did it have to be him? She'd finally managed to stop thinking about him all the time.

∼

Stepping out of the horse barn, Knox glanced up when he heard Olive call his name. She jumped and waved her arms. He smiled and waved back.

"We need your help!" the little girl yelled. She pointed to his right.

He looked over to see a black goat standing in the yard, pulling at the frozen grass, and groaned. He hated catching goats. They were cagey animals, adept at evading capture.

But it needed caught and put back where it belonged, so he jogged over. "Lose a goat?"

Sofie nodded. "He head-butted the gate when we were leaving. I lost my grip and out he went."

"Keep an eye on him. I'll get a rope." At her nod, he ran into the goat barn and found a rope, then ran back outside, tying a lasso knot into it as he walked.

"So, how do we do this?" Sofie asked.

"I need you two to herd him toward me. We need to do our best to keep him between the barns. If he gets out into the open yard, it'll take more than just us to catch him. Circle around him, but keep a wide berth. We don't want him to spook."

"Okay." Sofie motioned for Olive to start walking while she went around the goat's other side. Once they were both behind it, they paused, looking at Knox.

"Olive, you start. Don't stay directly behind him. Try to stay on his left, so he runs toward your mother and the barn, okay?"

The girl nodded.

"Okay, start coming this way. Wave your arms and make some noise."

Olive ran forward, waving her arms and yelling at the goat. As he hoped, it ran to the right.

"Sofie, come up behind it. But try to stay behind Olive. We want it to feel like it can't go her way."

She nodded and ran up behind the goat. It changed direction, running toward Knox. He advanced, closing the circle. The wily animal bleated and turned left. "Cut it off, Olive."

The girl ran forward, and the goat turned back. Knox hurried toward it, diving at it. It saw him and changed direction at the last second. He landed on his belly in the grass.

Sofie shrieked. He looked her way in time to see her dive at the goat and land on it.

"I got it!"

Knox scrambled to his feet and ran over with the rope.

"Hurry! I'm losing it!"

He slid the lasso loop over the goat's head and pulled. "You can let go."

She rolled away. The goat tried to run, but the rope around his neck wouldn't let him. He bleated, tugging against it, before he finally stopped.

"Good job, Mommy. You caught him."

Sofie sat up, then stood, brushing dirt off her pants. She smiled at Olive, then looked at Knox. "That was much easier than I expected."

He grinned. "We got lucky. If he'd been out beyond the barns, we'd need a whole team." He glanced down at the goat. "Come on, Houdini. Let's put you back with your friends." Leading the goat to the gate, he opened it far enough to get himself and the goat through. Inside, he released the animal, then slipped back through the gate. The goat looked up at him, bleating once more, before it ran over to the hay trough.

Olive giggled. "Goats are funny."

He smiled at her. "They are that."

"Thanks for helping us catch him. Next time, we'll go through the barn gate, so if he gets out of the pen, he won't get out of the barn."

"Live and learn. And don't feel bad. I've had to chase a fair number of goats before. They're crafty."

She smiled. Knox found himself smiling back, staring. She looked lovely this morning. Her face was scrubbed free of makeup, and the exertion of catching the goat had put twin pops of color on her cheeks. Her emerald eyes sparkled in the early morning light. He could get lost staring into her face.

A tug on his jacket made him look down. Olive stared up at him.

"Mommy's making scrambled eggs and waffles for breakfast. Do you want to eat with us?"

"Oh." He glanced at Sofie. Her eyes were wide, but she didn't rescind the offer. It didn't matter, though. Spending time with these two was dangerous to his mental state. "Um, sure." *What the hell? That was supposed to be a no.* Knox cursed his subconscious. Apparently, it was in control this morning. It was too late to take it back, though. Bending, he picked up Olive and set her on his shoulders. "Come on. Let's eat."

The girl chattered all the way across the yard, saving him from having to make conversation. They entered the little bungalow Sofie and Olive called home and took off their outdoor clothing. Sofie stowed the goat treats in a cabinet, then they entered the kitchen.

"Can I watch cartoons, Mommy?"

"Sure. Just wash your hands first."

She took off down the hallway, and Knox heard the faucet in the bathroom turn on. He shook his head and stepped over to the sink. "I don't know how she has so much energy. I require several cups of coffee to start my day and don't have a tenth of that."

Sofie laughed, stepping up beside him to wash her hands. "It's called being a child. She crashes just as hard." She squirted some soap on her hands and lathered them. "You don't have to stay, you know."

He glanced over to see her look at him sideways.

"I know you said yes to make her happy. I can tell her you had to go."

He rinsed the soap off his hands. "Do you want me to

leave?" Grabbing some paper towels, he found himself holding his breath. Part of him wanted her to say yes and quash this crazy attraction right now. But the other part wanted her to say no. To see where things could go between them.

She sucked her lip in and shut off the water. "You can stay if you want to."

Knox narrowed his eyes and stepped closer. "That was a non-answer. Do you want me to stay?"

Her cheeks colored, deepening the pink already there. She searched his eyes, then nodded once. "Yes."

A fierce desire flared in Knox's gut at her admission. Unable to help himself, he reached up and wove a hand into her dark hair at the side of her head. Her damp hands landed on his chest. He felt the moisture seep through to his chest. It didn't cool him off.

She swayed into him. Knox took a deep breath, pulling her scent into his lungs. Need made his head dip toward her. Her eyes flicked to his mouth, then to his eyes and back down.

"Mommy! The TV froze!"

She jumped back, putting a hand on her chest as she looked toward the living room. "Excuse me," she muttered, and scurried away.

Knox put both hands on the counter and blew out a breath. A few more seconds, and he would have found out what those pretty pink lips of hers tasted like. Straightening, he ran a hand through his hair. Maybe it was better he didn't know. He was leaving in a few days.

His eyes strayed to the doorway, where he could hear Sofie talking to Olive.

Why did that thought make him so sad?

SEVEN

"How did this thing break?" Tears welled in Daisy's eyes as she held up the small tiara with her veil attached. The crown of it was snapped, and it sagged with the weight of the veil. "It's literally been in the box since we picked it up. And it was fine then, because I opened the box to look at it before we left the bridal shop."

Sofie took the piece from her and examined it. Some of the crystals and pearls had popped off, too. "I think I can fix it. Or make you a new one to wear." She glanced in the box, but didn't see any of the missing pieces.

"By tomorrow? The rehearsal is in two hours. That will last most of the night."

"I'll just work late. We can't have you getting married, not looking how you want."

Daisy snorted. "I already don't look the way I want." She tugged at her short hair. "But I can't do anything about this, and I refuse to wait until it grows out to marry Asa. He doesn't care about my hair. He misses it like I do, but he doesn't care." She sank onto the bed and covered her face.

Sofie sat next to her. "Hey. I'm going to fix this. You will look exactly how you envisioned yourself—minus the hair."

That drew a soft giggle from her cousin, and she looked up. "You're sure?"

"Yes. Olive can stay here with Mom and Silas if need be. We'll get you fixed up."

"Thank you." Daisy gave her a tight hug.

"You're welcome." She pulled back to look at the broken veil piece again. "Now, if I'm going to do this, I should get started. I need to go to town and see if that craft store has any crystals and pearls in the right size to replace the missing ones." She held the piece closer to her face, looking at the break. "I think I can just solder this back together and replace the missing stones." She glanced at Daisy. "The colors may not be a perfect match, but I'll get it as close as I can."

"That's fine. From a distance, you won't be able to tell."

"Nope."

Daisy squealed and stood. "Wonderful."

"I'm going to find Olive and head to town." She rose, still holding the veil, and headed for the door, Daisy trailing behind.

They descended the stairs to the living room, where Sofie had left the little girl. She rounded the corner to see an empty room. "Where did she go?" She glanced back at Daisy.

"I don't know." She stepped back into the hallway. "Aunt Nori?" There was no response.

"Did they go outside?" Sofie wondered.

"Maybe. I can't imagine why, though. It's chilly."

"I'm going to try calling her." Sofie took out her phone and called her mother.

"Hello?"

Relief took some of the tension from Sofie's shoulders. She didn't know why she thought the worst. "Hey. Where are you? Is Olive with you?"

"She's fine. We're in the barn. She got tired of coloring, so I took her to see the horses. Knox was here, so he put her on Trudy while they had some time."

Her heart skipped at the mention of Knox's name. "Oh. Well, I need to head into town to get some things to fix Daisy's veil. Can she stay with you until I get back?"

"Of course."

"Great. Thanks. I shouldn't be too long."

"Take your time. I might even stop by your house and pick up her outfit for tonight, then you can get straight to work and not have to worry about her."

"That would be great. Thanks, Mom."

"Not a problem. We'll see you later."

They said goodbye, and Sofie hung up. "They're in the barn. Knox is giving Olive another riding lesson."

Daisy waggled her eyebrows. "Oh, really? He sure has taken a shine to the two of you, which surprises me. From what Asa's said about him, he's a bit of a loner."

Sofie frowned, ignoring the comment about how Knox felt about her and Olive. "Really? He doesn't seem very loner-ish."

"He's friendly enough. Asa said he just generally prefers the company of his horses to people. I guess he's super smart, so people don't always understand the way he thinks or stuff he says."

"Hmm. That's understandable. I haven't seen it, though. He's been good with Olive."

"I've noticed. She's really taken to him too. Are you a little worried about how she'll handle it when he leaves?"

"Some. But I think it'll help, knowing he and Asa are friends. He won't stay away forever."

Daisy nudged her. "Does that help you too?"

Sofie blushed, making Daisy laugh.

"Would you stop?" Sofie gave her a discomfited smile. "I'm not looking for anything, except maybe a friend."

"Yeah, well, that's what I said, too, and look where I am."

Sofie laughed. "You didn't even want a friend."

"No, I didn't," Daisy said with a laugh. "But I'll quit teasing."

"Thank you." She turned to the sink and opened the cabinet beneath to get a grocery sack for the veil. After folding the gauzy material and placing it in the bag, she looked at Daisy. "I'll see you in a couple of hours."

"Okay. Be careful going into town. And thank you again."

"No problem. I'll be back soon." She waved and headed into the kitchen to get her coat and boots from the mudroom. Properly dressed for the weather, she hurried outside and across the lawn to her house, where she picked up her purse and keys, then got in her car.

Humming along to the radio, she made the thirty-minute drive into Pine Ridge without incident. She found a parking spot near the craft store and got out. Sofie hoped she could find what she needed here. She didn't have time to go to Billings.

The bell over the door tinkled as she entered.

"Hi, Sofie." The proprietor, Ellen Wendell, greeted her with a smile. "What brings you in? Isn't Daisy and Asa's wedding rehearsal tonight?"

"Yep, but Daisy's veil broke. I'm hoping you have what I need to fix it."

The older woman's brows drew down, and she climbed off her stool behind the counter to come look. "Let me see."

Sofie took the tiara portion of the veil out of the bag and showed it to her.

Ellen took her glasses off the top of her head and perched them over her nose. "Hmm. I might have something. Let's go look."

They headed to the bead section on the far wall. Ellen paused, looking at what she had in stock. "This one might work for the pearls." She reached for a strand of small seed pearls, then held it against the headpiece. They were a near perfect match.

"Those are great. Now we just need the crystals."

"That's going to be a little harder. That tiara is more high-end than anything I carry." She stepped closer to the display. "Let me see that." She held out a hand for the veil, and Sofie handed her the bag.

"What about those?" Sofie pointed at a strand to Ellen's left.

"Maybe." She picked up the strand and held it against the tiara. "It's not bad." She tipped the bag so Sofie could see it. "But I think these might be better." She reached for a different strand not far from the first one, then held it against the tiara.

"The cut and color are better, but they're a little large. Do you have those in a smaller size?"

Ellen turned back to the wall. "I think I do. Let me—ha! Yes, here they are." She picked up another strand and laid it on the veil.

"Perfect." Sofie smiled.

"Wonderful. I'm glad I had what you needed." She hung up the rejected strands and turned to the register. "Did you need anything else while you're here?"

Sofie shook her head and took her wallet from her purse. "No, that's it. I'm going to solder the tiara back together. I have what I need for that at home."

"Okay. Let me get you checked out so you can get back there. I know you have a busy night."

"Thanks, Ellen. I appreciate it." Sofie smiled at the older woman. She was just one of the many things Sofie loved about Pine Ridge. She'd come in here for the first time a week or so after they arrived, just to browse, and they hit it off immediately. Now, Sofie bought as much of her supplies here as she could. Ellen had even special-ordered some things for her, so she didn't have to go to Billings.

While she waited, a new display near the window caught her eye. It was full of Christmas crafts. Olive would love them. She stepped over to look. "When did you get these in?"

"A couple of days ago. Aren't they great?"

"Yes. I need to stop in early next week and bring Olive. She'll have a lot of fun with some of these."

"Oh, that would be wonderful. I'd love to see the little rascal." Ellen chuckled.

Sofie glanced back with a grin before looking at the display again. As she turned to walk back to the counter, someone near her car caught her attention, and she paused. A man stood near the driver's door, head bent, staring at the vehicle. She stepped closer to the window to get a better look. What was he doing?

As she watched, her door swung open, and he tossed something on the seat, then quickly shut the door.

"Oh my God!"

"Sofie?"

"Someone just broke into my car." She didn't turn around, keeping her eyes on the man instead, hoping he'd look up so she could give a good description to the police.

The man kept his head down as he rounded the hood, but as he paused to check for traffic before he crossed the street, he raised his head. Sofie's heart stopped as she got a good look at his face. It was Lance.

"No," she whispered. How did he know she was here? She didn't remember anyone following her into town. But she could have just not noticed. She hadn't really been paying attention.

She was now, though. He ran across the road and climbed into a white sedan, then pulled into traffic and drove away.

"Hey."

A hand on her arm made Sofie jump. She glanced back at Ellen. "Sorry."

"No, you're okay. What's wrong? You said someone broke into your car?"

"Um," she cleared her throat. "Yeah. I think it might have been my ex. Can you wait just a moment while I go out and check?" She needed to see what he threw inside.

Ellen frowned. "Is he gone?" She looked outside.

Sofie's gaze followed hers. "I think so. He crossed the street and got into a car, then drove off that way." She gestured to her left.

"If you're sure it's safe. I remember you saying your divorce wasn't amicable."

"I'll be okay." She headed for the door. "I'll be right back." Sofie stepped outside, head on a swivel as she hurried to her car. She glanced through the window to see an envelope on the seat before pulling on the now unlocked handle to retrieve it. Snatching it off the seat, she went back inside the store.

"What is it?" Ellen met her at the door.

"I'm not sure. I haven't looked at it yet." It looked and felt like a greeting card, but she doubted that's what it was. Part of her hoped it was a card for Olive, but deep down, she knew it wasn't.

"I have a letter opener. Hang on, I'll get it." Ellen jogged away, disappearing through a door at the back of the shop and reappearing a moment later with the tool in hand. "Here."

Sofie took it and sliced through the envelope. She handed the opener back to Ellen and withdrew the card. The front had a bouquet of colorful flowers on it and read, "Thinking of You." Sofie's stomach rolled with dread. She opened it, and Lance's bold, blocky handwriting stared back at her.

Montana, really? I can't say I'm surprised you'd follow Noreen out here. But don't think you can hide behind your new stepbrother's money and influence. How's Olive? Staying warm in that puffy purple coat of hers, I hope. She won't need it, though, soon. I have a lovely purple sundress waiting for her.

"Dear God." Her voice was little more than a harsh whisper. Did he mean what she thought he did? She needed to get home. Now. With numb fingers, she put the card back in the envelope.

"Sofie? What did it say? Is everything all right?"

Sofie did her best to give Ellen a smile. "It's nothing."

Ellen frowned. "That expression on your face doesn't look like nothing. Should I call the police?"

"No." Sofie waved her hands. "I'll take care of it. Are you ready to ring me up for those beads? I should be going."

The older woman stared at her a moment longer, then nodded. "If you're sure everything is okay."

"It is."

"All right. I've got your check written up." Ellen walked behind the counter, then read the total off the receipt.

Sofie opened her wallet and handed her a debit card. She swiped it and gave it back, along with the handwritten receipt and the bag containing the veil and two strands of beads.

"Thank you." Sofie took the items.

"Anytime. I hope everything turns out okay. With Daisy's veil and with your ex."

"I'm sure it will. Thanks." Sofie pasted a smile on her face and left with a quick wave. Outside, she climbed in her car and started the engine, backing out of her space and heading for home. As soon as she was out of town, she called her mom.

"Hi, dear. Did you get what you needed?" Nori said when she picked up.

"I did. I'm on my way back. Is Olive still with you?"

"She's with Knox. I had a few wedding things to do."

"Can you go check on her?"

There was a beat of silence. "Why? She's fine."

"Please, Mom." Sofie's voice turned watery as tears threat-ened. She drew in a steadying breath, blowing it out slowly. "I just need to make sure she's safe. Once you find her, whatever you do, don't leave her alone. Not even in another room."

"Sofie, what's going on?" Alarm sharpened Nori's tone.

"I saw Lance," she whispered.

"What? You're sure."

"Yes. Now, please, go make sure she's safe."

"Honey, if you just saw him in town, then she's fine in the barn."

"Logically, I know that, but I don't know if he's here alone. I would just feel better knowing she's still where you left her. If I had Knox's phone number, I'd call him."

Nori blew out a breath. "Okay. I will check on her. Can I tell Knox what's going on so he can keep an eye out for trouble?"

Sofie's first instinct was to say no. She didn't want to bring anyone else into her disaster of a marriage, but Olive's safety overrode her embarrassment. "That's fine."

"Okay. If you don't hear from me, she's fine. I don't want to distract you while you're driving."

"That sounds good. Thank you, Mom."

"Yep. We'll see you when you get here. Don't speed."

That drew a quick smile from Sofie. "I'll try not to."

"Good. See you soon."

"Bye." Sofie disconnected the call and edged the speedometer just a smidge higher. She wouldn't speed much.

Eight

A bang echoed through the arena as the outer barn door slammed shut. Knox drew his horse down to a walk, knowing it was probably Sofie arriving home. After Nori stopped in to tell him what happened in town, he'd kept an eye on the clock.

"I think that's your Mom," he told the girl sitting in front of him.

"But I want to keep riding." She pouted up at him.

He grinned. "I know, but my butt's getting tired. Plus, we all need to get ready soon for the rehearsal."

She huffed. "Fine."

Chuckling, he rode to the fence near the door, reaching it just as Sofie ran through. Her body visibly sagged when she spotted them.

"Mommy! Mr. Knox taught me how to turn the horse today."

Sofie climbed through the fence and held her arms up. Knox helped Olive down. Sofie folded her into her embrace and clutched the girl in a tight hug.

"Mommy. Mommy, you're squeezing me."

"Oh, sorry." She loosened her hold, settling the girl on her hip and brushing her dark hair away from her face. "So, you learned how to turn, huh?"

Knox climbed off his horse to stand in front of them. "She did great. Picked it up right away."

Sofie's eyes flitted to his. Pink colored her cheeks, and she looked away again. "Thank you for looking after her. I appreciate it."

"Not a problem. We had fun, didn't we, kid?"

Olive gave him a big smile and nodded. "Yep! Can we ride again tomorrow?"

"Probably not. Tomorrow's the wedding. But maybe we can squeeze one last lesson in before Alice and I go home Monday."

She sighed. "Okay."

"Can you tell Knox thank you? We need to go find Grandma. Mommy still needs to fix Daisy's veil."

"I can take her to Nori, so you can get started," Knox said.

"Oh, thank you, but I can—"

"It's no problem. Really. She can help me take care of Ajax, then we'll head up to the main house." He laid a gentle hand on her arm. "Let me help." She had a deer-in-headlights look in her eyes he wanted to take away. He knew watching Olive wouldn't fix it, but it might help some. Besides, he truly didn't mind.

A slight frown split her brow, but she nodded. "Okay." She looked at Olive. "Is that all right with you? Do you want to help Knox, then find Grandma?"

Olive nodded. "I like helping with the horses."

"Okay, then." Sofie placed a firm kiss on her daughter's cheek, then leaned her toward Knox. He took the girl from her.

"Don't worry about us, Mom. We'll see you at the rehearsal." He offered Sofie a bright smile.

Sofie ran a hand down Olive's arm. "Okay. You be good for Knox and Grandma, okay?"

"I will."

With a nod, Sofie took a reluctant step toward the door.

"Don't worry, Sof. I'll keep her safe." And he would. No one would come near Olive without going through him first.

She rolled her lips in, nodding once more. "I know." With one final look, she retreated into the barn.

Knox watched her go. He wanted more details, but knew he would have to wait. And in all honesty, she didn't owe him an explanation at all. It was her life, and he barely knew her. It didn't stop him from wondering and wanting to help, though.

"All right, kiddo. Let's get this horse put to bed, then you and I need to find your grandma."

"Okay."

He set Olive on her feet, then took Ajax's reins. "Come on, Olive. You can get the gate for me."

She took off for the gate. Knox clicked his tongue to get the horse moving and followed her, smiling. He loved kids. Most people were surprised to learn that, because he didn't have many friends, preferring his own company and that of his animals. But kids were fun. They saw the world with such innocence. It was refreshing, and he wanted to do all he could to preserve that innocence as long as possible with as many kids as he could. It was why he spent so much time volunteering to help local youth. Why he wanted to help Sofie with Olive. She deserved to be a kid and to not have to worry about whether her dad would show up and snatch her away.

The little girl reached the gate and jumped, trying to reach the latch. After several tries, she finally climbed the gate and flipped it open.

"I got it!" She turned, beaming at him at her accomplishment, before jumping down to push the gate wide.

"I see that. Thank you." He led Ajax through. "Can you get it closed too?"

"Um, maybe." Her tongue poked out from between her lips as she pushed it closed and climbed it again. Like a monkey, she wrapped her legs around the rail and reached for the post, pulling the two together.

Knox was impressed with her ingenuity. She was a smart kid. He waited on her while she secured the latch, then climbed down.

"Ready?"

"Yep."

He headed deeper into the barn and led Ajax into his stall, where he took off his saddle and brushed him down.

"Can you get him some hay while I fill his water bucket?"

Olive nodded and ran down the aisle to where they kept the fresh hay. He had to stifle a laugh as she walked back, losing chunks of it as she came. She looked so proud of herself.

"Thank you." He shut off the hose and took the bundle from her, stuffing it into Ajax's feeder. "We need a little bit more," he said, assessing how full it was. "I'll help you." He led her down the corridor for more hay, and they finished settling the horse in. Knox made sure the stall door was latched, then bundled Olive in her coat and picked her up. "Let's go find your grandma."

"Do you think she has cookies? I need a cookie."

Knox laughed. "I could eat one too. And I bet we can convince her to give us some. You give her your best puppy eyes, and I'll pout, okay?"

Olive giggled. "Okay."

He hefted her onto his shoulders and crossed the yard to the main house.

∿

Laughter rang throughout the arena, the rehearsal dinner in full swing, but Sofie barely registered it. Her mind kept going to the note in her car. She still didn't know what to do. She doubted he could get to Olive on the ranch. Security was too tight. But they couldn't stay sequestered here forever, and she wasn't sure how long Lance would wait in the area. He didn't have the best patience. Though the tone of his messages was vengeful, so he might be willing to bide his time. The man threatening to kidnap their daughter was not the same man she married.

"Hey."

Sofie glanced up from her drink to see Knox approaching. He came to a stop a few feet away and leaned against the wall.

"How are you holding up?"

She shrugged and sipped her wine. "Okay."

He arched a brow.

She narrowed her eyes at him, her defenses rising as the female part of her registered his dressier attire. That jacket made his shoulders look a mile wide. "Don't pretend you know me."

His friendly expression hardened slightly. "I'm not. I'm just offering you a shoulder to lean on."

"Why?"

He frowned and looked out over the crowd of their friends and family. "That's a good question. A lot of it has to do with her." He tipped his head toward Olive, who sat on her cousin James's shoulders, a broad smile on her face while he danced. "But not all of it." His eyes met hers.

Heat crept into Sofie's cheeks and lower, making her pulse quicken. She looked away.

"Look. I know we just met, but—" he paused, collecting his thoughts before continuing. "I'm a loner. Asa is, too, which is why we get along so well. I'm not normally quick to let anyone in, but you—there's something about you."

Her eyes widened, and she opened her mouth to speak, but he held up a hand.

"I'm not angling for a date or anything. I just... want to be friends."

"Friends?"

He nodded.

"For real?" Her eyebrows shot up.

He chuckled. "Is that so hard to believe?"

She shrugged. "I'm not used to having friends. Lance didn't like me hanging out with others outside of work. Once Olive was born, I worked from home, so my only friends were my family. I've been so busy trying to rebuild my life, I haven't had time to make new ones."

"Maybe it's time."

A warmth gripped her as he smiled. "Yeah, maybe."

His smile grew. "Good. And as your friend, I want you to know you can talk to me. I might not have the answer, but I'll always listen."

Some of the warmth faded as her problems crept back in. She sighed, debating whether to unload on him. The timing of all this was terrible. Daisy was one of the few people she talked to about her life, but she didn't want to put a damper on her wedding by telling her about Lance. She could talk to her mom, too, but Nori would only urge her to stay at the ranch and let the authorities take care of things. She wasn't sure she could do that. She'd spent years living under Lance's thumb and just wanted to be free of him.

What Knox offered was appealing. As an outsider, he had a unique perspective and might have some insights the rest of them wouldn't think of.

She bit her lip, then dove in headfirst. "What did Mom tell you about what happened this afternoon?"

He straightened, the openness on his face leaving as a seriousness took its place. "She just said you spotted your ex and wanted to make sure we kept a close eye on Olive. I told her not to worry; I wouldn't let her out of my sight." He frowned. "What really happened?"

Sofie ran her tongue over her bottom lip, biting it briefly. "I was at the craft shop, waiting for the owner to ring up my purchases. She had a display of Christmas crafts near the window, so I stepped over to look at them. I saw a man near my car, and as I stood there, he opened my door—my locked door—and tossed something inside, then shut it and stepped away. As he waited to cross the street, he turned his head, and I saw his face. It was Lance."

His brows dipped. "You're a hundred percent certain?"

"Yes. His face still haunts my nightmares. I'd know it anywhere."

"Damn, Sof." His mouth flattened. "Okay. So, what did he put in your car?"

"A card. It was a thinking of you card. Inside, he said he hoped Olive was staying warm in her puffy purple coat, but that she wouldn't need it for long. He had a purple sundress waiting for her." She took a steadying breath. "I bought her that coat this fall. He's never seen it."

He cursed. "You think he's been watching you." It wasn't a question.

She nodded. "And that he's planning to take her from me. Her well-being was part of why I stayed. I didn't know where we would go if I left, or what would happen to us. I knew my mom would take us in, but if Lance challenged custody in court, I'd lose because I didn't have the income he does."

"You couldn't prove the abuse?"

She shook her head. "Before he put me in the hospital, he never hurt me enough to send me to the doctor. It was just bruises I could cover with makeup or sleeves. Or it was mental and emotional abuse." She looked down and tapped the toe of her shoe on the floor. "I know I should have left. But it's not easy to give up your life. Your whole world. Especially when you've been told you're worthless for years and that it's all your fault."

Knox's chest rose as he inhaled a breath. The muscles in his jaw twitched.

"I just don't know what to do. I know the ranch is safe, but we can't stay here all the time. There is a world outside of the gates. Eventually, I'll have to go into town. Olive will start school. What do I do if he doesn't leave?"

"Do you really think he would take Olive and run?"

That was the million-dollar question. Lance never showed a lot of interest in their daughter. To him, she was just something that was expected of a man his age who was married. But to get back at Sofie, she didn't think he was above anything. She'd ruined his life by testifying. "I do, yes. He doesn't care about her. Not the way he should. But he'd take her to torture me. I've thought about leaving." She glanced at him as she said that last part, wanting to gauge his reaction. His eyes widened.

"Where would you go?"

She shrugged. "No clue. But if he can't find me, she's safe."

"But what if he finds you and you're all alone?"

"Sofie, there you are!" One of Daisy's sisters-in-law, Terry's wife Lynn, ran up. "We've been looking for you. I was telling Brian about the necklace you made for my co-worker. He wants to know if you can make something similar for Patricia," she said, mentioning his wife, and paused to glance between Sofie and Knox. "Sorry, am I interrupting?"

"No," Sofie said. "We were just talking." She knew she was chickening out of a difficult conversation, but she just wanted to forget the whole thing for a while.

"Oh. Do you mind if I pull you away, then?"

"That's fine. Just give us a minute?"

Lynn nodded. "We're over there." She pointed to the cluster of tables set up for the rehearsal dinner.

"Okay. I'll be over in a minute."

Lynn nodded and walked away.

Sofie looked at Knox. A frown marred his handsome face.

"I know now isn't the time for us to talk about this, but will you promise me you won't do anything until you talk this over with your mom and Silas? I just don't want you to make a rash decision you might regret when there could be an option you haven't thought of."

He made a valid point. And she hadn't planned to run away in the middle of the night without telling anyone. "I promise."

"Good."

"I better go see what Brian wants me to do." She gestured to the tables.

"You should, yes."

Sofie took a couple of steps away. "Thank you, Knox. For being my friend." She took a deep breath, trying to hold back the tears that threatened. It made her both happy and sad that his kindness affected her this way. She shouldn't cry because someone wanted to be her friend. That she'd made a friend. But her response also made her recognize how much she appreciated him.

He smiled. "You're welcome. I'll see you later?"

She nodded. "Later." Spinning on her heel, she walked away, smiling.

NINE

"Sofie, you did such a great job with the tiara." Ian's wife, Shelly, leaned in to take a better look at the aforementioned headpiece perched on Daisy's head. "I can't even tell where you fixed it."

"Right?" Daisy said, touching the headpiece. "It's amazing."

"Thank you. It didn't take long. I'm just glad Ellen had what I needed." Sofie smiled. She was good at what she did, and she enjoyed it. Fixing Daisy's veil was easy.

"Me too." Daisy gave the veil one last pat, then picked up her bouquet. "Are we ready to get this show on the road?"

"We're just waiting on Ian," Nori said. Daisy's oldest brother was walking her down the aisle.

"Where did he go? We all left the house at the same time."

"He said he needed to talk to Asa," Shelly said.

"Oh, dear God." Daisy turned to look at her sister-in-law. "What could he possibly have to say to him at this late hour?"

Shelly chuckled. "I think he just wants to tell him again that he's glad you picked him, but that if he hurts you, they'll all crush him."

Laughter rang through the small office where they waited.

"They'll have to get in line. I can handle myself just fine."

"I think he's finally seeing that," Shelly said. She straightened Daisy's veil around her face. "I'm glad you left. I knew your relationship with your brothers was dysfunctional, but I didn't know how to fix it. It's nice to see the seven of you interacting like adults."

"It's nice to be treated as one."

There was a knock on the door. "Everyone decent?" Ian's voice came through the wood.

Shelly was closest to the door and opened it. "It's about time you showed up. Daisy's champing at the bit."

Ian grinned. "That's an appropriate metaphor." He gestured to the barn around them.

Shelly giggled and smacked his arm. "Are you ready?"

He nodded, turning his gaze to his sister. "Daisy, you look beautiful."

"Thank you."

"Shall we?" He held up an arm.

Daisy beamed. "Yes."

Filing out of the room, the group congregated in the aisle just outside the door to the arena, where their family and friends waited. Sofie took her place as maid-of-honor just ahead of Daisy and Olive. The little girl looked adorable in her white satin dress and double French braid. Sofie did her best to keep Olive calm and quiet before the ceremony, so she didn't ruin her look. It wouldn't take long for her baby-fine hair to slide free of the braid and look a mess.

The music pumping through the arena changed, and the first bridesmaid, Marci, walked out onto the runner covering the dirt. Sara followed, then it was Sofie's turn. She stepped through the door, and her gaze wandered over the crowd of family and friends. She smiled, happy to be part of Daisy's day.

Sofie's smile froze on her face as she turned her eyes

forward and spotted Knox standing in line behind Asa's best man, Chet. His blonde hair was combed into a perfect wave. The dark blue western cut suit he wore highlighted his muscular, working man's frame and accentuated his height.

The memory of his arms around her as she pressed her hands into his hard chest the other day distracted her, and she caught the toe of her shoe on the runner and stumbled. She shot a hand out to steady herself. Her cousin, James, was the closest to her and rose part of the way from his chair, but she waved him off and kept going.

Get a grip, Sof.

Determined not to embarrass herself further, she kept her attention on the path forward and not on the blonde god standing at the altar. Reaching the end of the aisle, she took her place and turned to see Olive skipping down the runner, tossing handfuls of red rose petals as she went. The crowd chuckled.

Sofie grinned and held out a hand to her. Olive ran up to stand beside her.

"You did great," she whispered into the girl's ear.

Olive beamed as the music changed again and Daisy appeared in the doorway.

A murmur ran through the crowd, and Sofie cast a quick glance at Asa. Eyes wide, he stared slack-jawed at his bride. And for good reason. Daisy's beaded, white, mermaid-style gown showed off her curvy frame to perfection. Cowboy boots peeked from beneath her skirt, and a bright smile lit her face beneath her veil.

Ian led her up the aisle, then lifted her veil to place a kiss on her cheek. "I'm so happy for you, Daisy."

She smiled at him. "Thank you."

He squeezed her hand, then went to sit with his wife and kids.

Sofie stepped forward and took Daisy's bouquet, then

watched on as her cousin married the love of her life. The ceremony was beautiful. Asa and Daisy wrote their own vows, their love for each other evident in every word. Sofie had longed for that kind of love once. She still did, but didn't see it happening for her now.

Unbidden, her gaze went to Knox. He was watching her. She blushed and glanced away, but couldn't keep her eyes from straying to him again. The world faded around her until clapping drew her attention. Asa bent Daisy back as he kissed her for the first time as her husband. Sofie pushed Knox from her mind and did her best to clap with two bouquets in her hands.

The newly minted couple broke apart and faced forward as the minister introduced them. Daisy took her bouquet, and they walked up the aisle holding hands.

As Sofie took Chet's arm, she couldn't help but cast one last look at Knox before she followed the bride and groom.

∼

Conversation flowed around Knox from where he leaned against a post, watching the dancers. His eyes strayed to the tables and caught on Sofie, where she sat alone. Before he knew what he was doing, he pushed away from the post to make his way to her.

This was a bad idea. The last time he held her in his arms, he nearly kissed her. But he'd be damned if he didn't want to hold her again.

He stopped next to her chair and held out a hand. "Dance with me?"

Sofie looked up, a frown creasing her brow. "Oh, um, sure." She laid her fork down and took his hand, standing.

"Enjoying the cake?"

She smiled. "Yes." She blushed and chuckled. "That was

my second piece. Olive ran off to play with her cousins, so I took advantage of the quiet."

"No shame in indulging every once in a while. It's good cake." He stepped onto the dance floor and gave her hand a tug, pulling her into his embrace.

A shiver ran down Knox's spine. This definitely wasn't the best idea. She felt and smelled amazing.

She looked out over the arena. "Everything turned out really nice today."

"It did. I don't think I've ever seen Asa so happy."

"How long have the two of you been friends?"

Knox glanced around, getting lost in his memories. "Ten years or so. He came to me, looking for some new cutting horses after he and Silas expanded the business. We'd just expanded into our breeding program, and he came to us, saying he'd heard good things. He's a good man, but he needed a little direction back then. I could see he was struggling, trying to merge his fame with the life he wanted." He shrugged, remembering the gruff, lost man Asa had been when they met. "I offered him something similar to what I offered you. A friend he could talk to."

She arched an eyebrow. "Are you trying to save the world, one friend at a time or something?"

He laughed. "Maybe." His eyes roved over the crowd, then her face. "I think it's more that I saw myself in Asa, and in you."

Sofie frowned. "What do you mean?"

"I know what it's like not to have many friends. In high school, I took a bunch of advanced classes. I was often the only freshman in a class full of seniors. Kids my age—even though I grew up with them—thought I was a nerd. The seniors wanted nothing to do with me because I was only a freshman. I was caught between two worlds. Brady Archer was about the only friend I had. Him and his siblings. I actually graduated with his older brother, even though I'm Brady's age." He shrugged. "Eventually, my smarts and my age no longer mattered to people, but the feelings lingered. I still keep to myself, but I can't help but want to befriend people who need it."

"So that's why you offered to be my friend? Because you think I need one?"

"No. It's what initially drew me to you. The way you seemed alone, even surrounded by your family. That and your beauty. But I want to be your friend because I think you'll make a great friend. Not just so you don't feel alone."

She studied his expression, and Knox tried to let his emotions show. He wanted Sofie to trust him. He'd never wanted anything more. This woman spoke to him in a way no other woman ever had. Her vulnerability set off his protective instincts, even though he recognized she wasn't as vulnerable as she seemed. There was a strength running through her slight frame that belied her quiet persona.

"How did you get to be so perceptive?"

A smile quirked one side of his mouth. "When you don't have anyone to talk to at school, you spend a lot of time people-watching. I learned to notice things." His smile disappeared, replaced by a frown. "Like the men in dark suits, who just walked in." He stopped dancing.

Sofie pulled back in his embrace to look toward the door. Two men entered. One stayed at the door, while the other headed for Asa. "Security?"

"Yeah. Let's go see what's going on." He didn't give her a chance to protest, taking her hand to lead her off the dance floor. He had a bad feeling about why they were here. The men wouldn't interrupt if it wasn't something serious. They had the paparazzi and fans corralled outside the gate. As they neared Asa and the security officer, who held a phone in his hand to show Asa something, Asa turned to look at Sofie. That bad feeling he had got worse.

Asa tipped his head toward the door. "Office, now."

Knox changed direction.

They hurried through the door and into the barn office. Their exit didn't go unnoticed. Daisy joined Asa and the security officer, as did Silas and Nori. Knox's sister brought up the rear.

"What's going on?" Sofie asked once they were all crowded into the room with the door shut.

"Miles, show them what you showed me," Asa said.

"Fifteen minutes ago, someone tripped the perimeter alarm. Cameras near the houses caught this man." Miles turned his phone around to show them.

Sofie gasped. "That's Lance!"

"Did you catch him?" Knox asked.

Miles shook his head. "He evaded us in the darkness and slipped back through the fence in a different place. The sensors went off again. I sent men to look for a vehicle, but he must have stashed it near his exit point and walked to the entry, because we found nothing."

"Why would he show up tonight?" Sofie asked. "He has to know there are a bazillion people here for the wedding. He'd never be able to get to me or Olive."

"Maybe he was going to lie in wait," Knox surmised. "Until everyone left, and you went home. Your guard—all our guards—would be down, because the big event was over. We wouldn't be expecting anything then."

"You have a valid point, Mr. Duvall." Miles turned to Sofie. "Can you tell me how you know this man?"

"He's my ex-husband. He's not supposed to be here. The judge ordered him not to have any contact with us except through an attorney."

"Sofie put Lance in jail earlier this year for assault. He was supposed to serve a one-year term, but got out early," Nori said. "She saw him yesterday in town."

"And he's been leaving me cryptic text messages."

Nori gasped.

"Why didn't anyone tell me this?" Asa asked. He looked at his wife. "Did you know?"

She shook her head.

Sofie glanced at Knox. He gave her an encouraging nod.

"I only told Mom and Silas because I didn't want to worry you and Daisy. I figured it could wait. I did call his parole officer in Chicago and report the messages and then the sighting yesterday. He said he'd contact local authorities and try to get a bench warrant for him, but that was all he could do. I was going to tell you everything tomorrow." She looked at her mom. "And I didn't say anything to you about the messages because I didn't want to worry you. There was enough going on here."

"We could have been looking out for you," Silas said.

"And how did you keep all that bottled up inside?" Nori asked.

"She didn't, I'm guessing." Asa nodded at Knox.

"Only because he's persistent. And insightful." Sofie held her hands up in supplication. "And the point right now isn't why I kept secrets. It's what we're going to do about the fact Lance trespassed on the ranch. What it is he's doing here at all."

"To get to you, of course," Nori said.

Sofie looked at Knox again, and he frowned. His thoughts echoed the ones he could see in her eyes.

"Maybe not." Sofie took a deep breath and let it out. "When I saw him in town, he broke into my car and left a note. He said he hoped Olive was warm in her puffy purple coat, but that she wouldn't need it for long. He had a purple sundress waiting for her."

Nori's eyes widened, and she sagged into Silas.

"Jesus." Asa pressed a hand to his forehead. "So, do we think he was here to kidnap her tonight?"

"God, I don't want to think that, but it certainly sounds like it," Silas said.

"We can't let that happen," Daisy said.

"But how do we prevent it? Lock her up and keep a guard on her twenty-four-seven?" Asa glared and tossed up a hand. "That's no way for a kid to live."

"What if she left?" Alice interjected.

"No." Knox waved a hand. "If he finds them and they're alone—"

"You didn't let me finish. What if Sofie and Olive come home with us? They could circle the wagons here, make him think they're sticking close to home, and have all kinds of protection. By the time he figures out they're gone, he won't know where to look."

Knox stared at his sister for several beats. Her plan held a lot of merit. But would Sofie go for it? He looked at her and raised an eyebrow.

A frown creased her forehead. "I don't want to run. He's stolen enough of my life."

"Being confined to the ranch won't be any kind of life, sweetie." Nori reached out and stroked Sofie's arm. "For you or for Olive. And it won't be forever. Just until the police can find Lance and arrest him."

"Where he'll get a slap on the wrist for violating the protection order." Sofie huffed and pinched the bridge of her nose. "I just wish he'd leave us alone." Her voice thickened with unshed tears.

"Come home with us," Alice said. "You'll be safe and free to move about."

Knox reached for Sofie's hand. "It's a good plan. Let us help."

Her eyes shimmered as she stared up at him. "Why do you want to help me?" She shook a finger in his face. "And don't you dare say it's because you want to be my friend."

He smiled. "You already are. I just can't stand to see you scared. Or to think of Olive being forced to stay under lock and key. She might just run off again because she's tired of not getting to go anywhere or do anything."

Sofie bit her lip. "Dammit. I don't want to run." Her shoulders sagged.

"Then don't think of it as running. Think of it as living. It'll be an adventure."

She snorted. "An adventure in running." She sighed and smoothed her hair back. "Fine. We'll leave with you, but only because I think you're right. Olive will have a harder time being cooped up and watched than leaving here."

"Then we need to start planning," Asa said. "Miles, I need you and several of your men to stay behind after tonight to provide security for Sofie and Olive."

"Of course."

"Once the guests clear out, including Knox and Alice, we need to make it look like we're still concerned about their safety."

"That can be arranged. I'll leave several of my men here," Miles said.

"Good. We also need to pack up Sofie and Olive's things as quietly as possible. If Lance is watching, we don't want him to get suspicious."

"How are we supposed to get out of here without him noticing?" Sofie glanced around at the others. "If I drive my car through the gate and he sees, he'll know I'm leaving."

"You're not." Knox squeezed the hand he still held. "I have an empty horse trailer now. You and Olive can hide in it until we get several miles down the road. Once I'm sure we're not being followed, I'll stop and you can ride in the cab with us. I have plenty of vehicles on my ranch you can borrow to get around in while you're staying with us."

"As much as I don't want you to leave, I think this is the best plan for right now." Nori said.

A single tear tracked down Sofie's cheek. "I know," she whispered. She took a shaky breath and looked at Knox. "Fine. Olive and I will go to Colorado with you."

TEN

"Do we have to go, Mommy? I don't want to leave Grandma." Olive sat on the edge of her bed, her lower lip quivering as Sofie packed the last of the toys they were taking.

"Oh, sweetie." Sofie set the tote down and crouched in front of her daughter, putting her hands over the little girl's legs. "I know you don't want to, but we need to."

Olive looked up through her lashes. "Can't you just talk to Daddy?"

"I wish it were that easy, Liv, but your daddy doesn't want to talk to me. He wants to get back at me for putting him in jail by taking you away. I can't let him do that."

"I don't want to live with Daddy. He yells. And he hurt you."

"I know, which is why we're going to Colorado with Knox and Alice." She smoothed back a lock of Olive's hair. "It won't be forever. Just until the police can catch him. We might not even be gone very long. Think of it as an adventure, okay?"

"Or a vacation?"

"Exactly. It's a vacation. You'll get more riding lessons, and

Alice said you can paint pottery. Maybe you can make some gifts for Grandma and Grandpa while we're there."

The little girl's face lit up, and she nodded. "Cause Santa will come soon."

"That's right." She patted Olive's legs. "Now, how about you help me with the last of these toys? It's almost time to go."

Olive sighed, but climbed off the bed. "Okay."

They gathered the last of the items the girl wanted to bring, and Sofie took the tote out to the living room with the rest of their luggage.

"Why don't you watch some cartoons for a few minutes? I'm going to call Knox and let him know we're ready."

Olive plopped onto the couch and picked up the remote. Sofie took her phone from her pocket and walked into the kitchen to call Knox, but the back door opened as she entered, and he walked in.

"I was about to call you."

"You ready?"

She nodded. "Yeah. All our bags are in the living room. Where's Alice?"

"She's waiting outside to load your things. I pulled the truck up right outside the door." He motioned behind him.

"Okay." Sofie took a deep breath and turned. Time to get this show on the road. She knew once they settled in, she'd feel better about it all, but right now, she was uprooting her life, and her daughter's life, for the third time in a year. She was about done changing her life because of Lance.

Olive looked up as they entered the living room. "Mr. Knox!" She got up on her knees on the couch. "Is it time to go?"

"Hey, kiddo. Just about. Your mom and I are going to load up. You keep watching TV, okay?"

"Okay." She sank onto her butt and turned back to her show.

Sofie shook her head, a smile quirking her mouth. Kids were so resilient. She hoped Olive stayed that way.

It only took them a few minutes to buckle Olive's car seat into the back and load the four suitcases and two totes of toys into the trailer.

"That it?" Knox held the trailer door as Alice shoved the last tote into place.

"Yeah. I have a smaller bag with some of her favorite toys and coloring books, as well as some snacks."

"Okay, let's get going, then. It's a long drive."

"I hope you're prepared to stop more often than normal. She has a bladder the size of a pea." Sofie giggled as his shoulders fell.

Alice patted her brother's shoulder as she walked around him to the passenger side of the truck. "Now you won't have to listen to me pleading with you to find a rest stop so I can pee, because I waited too long. I'll have plenty of opportunities."

A corner of his mouth lifted. "So long as you go when we stop and don't wait until your bladder is about to burst, like you normally do."

She shrugged. "I hate stopping. Sue me."

Sofie's mouth pulled, and she headed for the house. "Well, you're going to hate this trip, then, because we'll be stopping a lot."

Alice smiled and stepped onto the running board. "Nah. Not for her, I won't."

Sofie smiled at the other woman, glad Alice was a good sport. Walking inside the house, Sofie wiped her feet on the mat as she entered. "Olive! Time to go." She walked through the kitchen to see the girl climbing off the couch. "Let's go get your shoes and coat on."

"Okay." Olive turned off the TV and put the remote on

the table, then followed Sofie into the kitchen to the mudroom.

Sofie helped her with her boots, then zipped her into her coat. They locked the door behind them as Silas's truck pulled up. Nori was out the door as it came to a halt.

"Mom." Sofie paused near the trailer. "What are you doing here? We said our goodbyes."

Nori rolled her eyes. "If you thought I was going to let you get away with a hug last night and nothing this morning, you're sorely mistaken." She held out her arms to Olive. "Come here, button." She picked the girl up and hugged her tight. "You be good for your mama, you hear? Do what she says?"

"I will, Grandma."

Silas took her from his wife, hugging the girl, while Nori sniffed and wiped away a tear.

"Mom—"

Nori waved a hand. "Don't. I'll be okay. This is temporary."

Sofie folded her mom into a hug. "Definitely temporary. We'll be back before you know it." She leaned back to look into Nori's eyes.

"I know." Nori sniffed again and let go. "You should get on the road. It's a long trip."

She nodded and stepped over to Silas, wrapping her stepdad in a tight embrace. "Take care of her," she whispered into his ear.

He hugged her tighter. "I will. You take care of yourself and that little girl. And if you decide to stay, we'll come visit."

Sofie pulled back to stare up at him, surprise on her face. He winked at her and smiled. Unbidden, her gaze strayed to Knox. She cleared her throat and stepped back.

"We should go. Come on, Olive." She took her daughter's hand and led her to the man-door on the side of the trailer, helping her inside, then stepped up behind her. Turning, she gave her mom and Silas one last wave.

"Have a safe trip. Let us know when you get there."

"We will. Love you."

"Love you too."

Sofie stepped back, her eyes connecting with Knox's as he picked up the lantern sitting on the floor, turning it on. She took it from him, and he closed the door. She blinked several times to hold back the tears. She knew this was only short term, but after all they'd been through in the last year, it was hard to leave.

She sniffed once, then pasted a smile on her face for Olive's benefit. "Let's get comfy, okay? We have to ride back here for a few miles until it's safe to move up front." She sat down on the floor between the cupboards and the wall separating the stall from the storage area. Olive sat in her lap, huddling close.

"It's scary in here, Mommy."

"It's just a little dark, is all. We'll be out of here before you know it." The truck rumbled to life, and after a moment, started to move. She braced herself, so they wouldn't topple as Knox steered them down the drive and made the turn onto the highway. The road hummed under the trailer tires as they left the ranch. Sofie wasn't sure how long they'd have to ride back here, but she hoped it wasn't too long.

Several minutes passed, and the vehicle turned a few times before it finally came to a halt.

"Are we getting out?" Olive asked.

"I think so." Sofie heard the driver's door shut, then the trailer door opened and Knox stood in the doorway.

"We're clear."

Olive scrambled off Sofie's lap and launched herself at him, eager to be out of the dark trailer. He caught her and set her on his hip, then offered Sofie a hand. She let him help her out, then got into the backseat of the truck. Once Olive was buckled into her car seat, he got back behind the wheel and they were on their way.

As Olive chattered, asking questions about the Duvalls' ranch, Sofie stared out the window, watching the scenery pass. Silas's words played in her head. Would she want to come back? What if she didn't? What would Olive think? Would she be just as eager to stay?

Sofie's gaze traveled to the back of Knox's blonde head. Was he where she was meant to be? She'd been looking for a new home—a new start—when she moved out here with her mom. What if that new start was with Knox?

She rolled her eyes at herself. What if that was all crazy talk? Her mind wasn't exactly in the best place right now.

Sighing, she looked out the window. She didn't have the answers to any of those questions yet. She just prayed she'd get some soon.

≈

Sofie jolted awake as the truck dipped and bounced. She sat up and looked out the window to see that they'd turned onto a dirt driveway. In the dark, that was about all she could see. Ahead, pole lights cast a glow over a large white house and several barns.

"Are we here?" She kept her voice low in deference to Olive sleeping beside her.

"Home sweet home." Weariness etched Knox's voice. He pulled up in front of the house and cut the engine. "Leave her there." He motioned to Olive. "I'll come around and get her."

"Oh." Sofie withdrew her hands from Olive's buckle. "All right." She wouldn't argue about not having to carry the nearly forty-pound child into the house. Instead, she opened her door and slid out of the truck, sighing as she stretched her legs. Knox's truck was roomy, but it was still a car seat. And she'd been sitting much too long. Her butt was numb.

She reached back inside to grab the small bag she'd packed as Knox opened the rear door on the other side and removed Olive from her seat. The girl grumbled and gave a little whimper at being awakened, but settled back to sleep on Knox's shoulder. Sofie tried not to stare at the picture the two of them made.

Alice led the way into the house, unlocking the door to let them inside. Knox headed for the stairs, and Sofie followed him to a room on the second floor with a twin bed made up with a purple comforter. Sofie's eyes widened.

"Did you—?" She motioned to the bed.

He nodded. "I called my foreman before we left Asa's and asked him to pick it up. His wife bought it and the sheets." He drew back the comforter to expose white sheets with purple unicorns on them.

Tears welled in Sofie's eyes. "You didn't have to do that. I'll pay you back for them."

"Nonsense. I did it because I wanted to. She deserves to feel comfortable here. You both do."

Sofie sniffed and nodded, stepping over to help him take off Olive's shoes and sweatshirt, then tuck the blankets around her. She kissed her daughter's forehead and followed Knox from the room.

"Come on, I'll show you your room."

He led her down the hall to the next room. She stepped inside and immediately felt at home. A blue and white duvet covered the full-size bed, a pretty contrast to the maple frame. A matching dresser sat against one wall, and gauzy white curtains covered the window. The room was painted a soft gray, and the rug covering the dark hardwood floor was the same color as the walls.

She turned to look at him. "This is nice, thank you."

"You're welcome. If you need anything, I'm in the next room down. Alice is staying in the room across from mine tonight, but tomorrow, she'll head back into town."

"Wait. She doesn't live here?"

He shook his head. "No, she has a small house in town. She moved there several years ago. The drive to school every day got to be too much, especially in the winter."

"Oh. I guess I just assumed she lived here."

"No, it's just me."

"Wow, you really are a loner." A smile tipped her lips, softening her words.

He smiled back. "To the core. I'll bring in your bags in the morning, if that's okay?"

She nodded. "I have everything we need in this little one." She wiggled the strap of the bag on her shoulder.

"Okay, I'll let you get to bed, then." He stepped back through the door. "Goodnight."

Sofie grasped the doorknob and gave him a soft smile. "Goodnight."

With a nod, he retreated down the hall. Sofie closed the door and leaned against it, sighing. Emotions churned in her belly, overwhelming her. A tear escaped, and she dashed it away. She wasn't normally so weepy, but the events of the last few days, plus the late hour, had her defenses down. She just needed some sleep.

Pushing off the door, she crossed to the bed and set her bag down, rummaging for her pajamas and toothbrush. She changed and brushed her teeth in the attached bathroom, then crawled between the covers on the bed, the starch leaving her muscles as her head hit the pillow. It felt nice to lie down. She closed her eyes, but the moment she did, her mind raced, keeping her exhausted body from falling asleep.

"Dammit." Her eyes popped open, some of the tension coming back. Part of her problem was Olive was next door.

She was worried the girl would wake up in the middle of the night and not know where her mother was. She didn't want her wandering around the house in the dark by herself. Not when she didn't know where anything or anyone was.

Knowing she wouldn't fall asleep worrying about Olive, she got out of bed, pulling the comforter free from the mattress and grabbing a pillow. She left her room, going to Olive's, and laid down on the floor next to the bed. It wasn't the most comfortable place to sleep, but she'd rest easier in here tonight than next door in her bed.

Sofie tucked the blanket under her chin and closed her eyes. Her body sagged as exhaustion took hold and sleep claimed her now that her mind was at ease.

ELEVEN

"Mommy, look!" The back door banged as Olive came running in. "Mr. Knox let me help with the chickens. I got lots of eggs!" She held up a basket.

Sofie set her coffee cup down on the table where she sat and took the basket. It was full of eggs. "I'll say. How many chickens are there?"

"Way too many." Knox came through the door, smiling.

She smiled back. "Thank you for taking her out with you this morning. She was wound up from the second she woke."

He took off his jacket and hung it on a peg by the door. "No problem. We had fun, didn't we, Liv?"

"Yep! Mommy, can I have scrambled eggs for breakfast?"

"Sure, I don't see why not. Knox, would you like some eggs?"

"Sounds good to me. I think there's some bacon in the fridge too. Denny was supposed to stock it for us, so we didn't have to go into town right away. I'll help you cook." He stepped to the refrigerator and opened it.

Sofie stopped halfway out of her chair. "You cook?"

He arched a brow. "I live alone, remember?"

She chuckled. "Right. That didn't stop Silas from living off TV dinners until he hired Daisy."

"What can I say? I like food without so much salt." He paused, staring at the package of bacon in his hand, and laughed.

Sofie giggled. "Sure you do."

"Can I help?" Olive asked.

"You sure can." Sofie pulled a chair up to the counter. Olive climbed onto it. "Crack these eggs into a bowl." She opened a cupboard, looking for a mixing bowl, but found plates instead.

Knox leaned in front of her and opened a cabinet.

"Oh, thanks." She tried not to breathe in the intoxicating scent of man and outdoors that was all Knox. One whiff threatened to derail her thought processes.

"Yep." He found a skillet and set about layering strips of bacon into it.

Sofie shook off her thoughts and helped Olive crack eggs into the bowl, then mix them up. She found another skillet and set it next to the bacon pan on the stove and turned on the heat, melting some butter in it before adding the eggs. Knox put several slices of bread in the toaster and buttered them while he waited for the bacon to cook.

"Should I make up a plate for Alice?" Sofie opened the plate cabinet.

"No, she already left. She had to teach today."

"Oh, okay." She took down three plates and spread them out on the counter, then lifted the egg pan and separated the scrambled eggs onto the plates. Knox put buttered toast and bacon on them, then they carried them to the table. Olive found the silverware and got them each a fork.

"So, what are your plans for today?" Sofie lifted her fork and took a bite.

"To get back to work, basically. I need to talk to Denny

and see if anything of note happened while I was gone, then see which horses need my attention the most and start from there." He took a bite of his bacon.

"Didn't you say your dad ran the ranch with you?"

"He used to. When we expanded ten years ago, it was right after my mom passed away. Dad needed a distraction. Hell, so did I. We'd been talking about it for a couple of years, so we just dove in. He just got to a point his heart wasn't in it. There were too many memories of her here, so he moved to Texas where his brother lives."

Sofie's eyebrows shot up. "And just left you here to run things by yourself?"

Knox shrugged. "I was more than capable. And I knew he was miserable. Mom was the light of his life." A slight frown marred his face.

Without thinking, she laid a hand over his. "I'm sorry. I know what it's like to lose a parent. My dad died around the same time as your mom."

He cleared his throat. "Yeah, it's hard. How did he die?"

"Heart attack. Your mom?"

"Cancer."

She understood better now why his dad had to leave. He probably watched his wife wither away in this house and memories of that were everywhere. Sofie withdrew her hand and went back to her breakfast.

"Can I have more bacon, Mommy?"

Sofie glanced over to see her daughter's clean plate. "You're still hungry?"

The girl nodded.

She looked at Knox. "Did she run laps while you were out there?"

He grinned. "She was all over the place."

"You must have gotten a great night's sleep." She shook

her head and scooted her chair back to get Olive a couple more slices of bacon.

The three of them finished their meal, then Knox went back out to get to work. Sofie cleaned up the kitchen, while Olive colored at the table. Once things were tidy, she turned to the girl.

"So, what do you think we should do today?"

Olive tapped a crayon against her mouth. "Ride horses?"

Sofie smiled. "Of course that's what you'd want to do. I think Knox is busy, though. What else could we do?"

She thought another moment, then shrugged. "I dunno. What do you want to do, Mommy?"

Sofie hadn't a clue. "I guess we'll just hang out. Maybe we'll see about finding you a movie to watch later, and I'll try to work on some of my jewelry orders."

"A movie? Yay!"

Olive's enthusiasm made Sofie grin. She pushed away from the counter and dropped a kiss on the top of her head, ruffling her hair. "How about right now, though, we go unpack all your toys? Knox brought all our bags in."

"Okay." Olive climbed off her chair, but as they crossed the hallway to the living room to get the totes, footsteps on the porch made them pause. A knock sounded on the front door.

"Who's that?"

"I don't know, sweetie. You go on in the living room, okay? I'll be there in a minute."

The girl took off for her toys, and Sofie headed for the door. She peeked through the side window to see a tall auburn-haired woman standing on the porch, holding a paper coffee cup.

Frowning, Sofie unlocked the door and opened it. "Hello. Can I help you?"

The woman grinned. "So, you're the cat Knox dragged back with him."

"Excuse me?" Sofie frowned.

The woman laughed. "Sorry. I didn't mean that the way it sounded. I'm Macy Archer. Brady Archer's wife."

"Oh!" Sofie stepped back. "Come in."

Macy breezed through the door. "Alice stopped in this morning before school to get coffee and told me about you. Brady said Knox was enamored by the bride's cousin, but I couldn't believe it and had to come check it out for myself." She held out the coffee cup to Sofie. "Vanilla latte."

"Oh, thank you." She took the coffee, frowning again. This woman was bold. And didn't hold back. She was not at all what she envisioned for a man like Brady. He was so quiet, and his wife was not.

Macy walked deeper into the house, entering the living room. "I'm sorry I couldn't make it to the wedding. I own the local coffee shop. My assistant manager came down with the flu at the same time as her daughters. My sister-in-law is pregnant and couldn't help take care of our sisters, so I stayed behind to help."

"Huh? Your sisters are your assistant manager's daughters?"

Macy smiled. "Yes. It's complicated. My dad is an ass." She spotted Olive sitting on the couch, who stared up at her. "Hello. You must be Olive."

"Who are you?"

"My name's Macy. I'm Brady's wife."

"Mr. Knox's friend?"

"That's the one. I came to meet you and your mama. It's nice to meet you."

"Nice to meet you too." Olive smiled, then got distracted by the TV.

Sofie smiled. "She's obsessed with that show. Why don't we go into the kitchen?"

"Actually, I can't stay. Once the rush died, I left one of my employees in charge so I could come say hello."

"You drove all the way out here just to say hi?"

Macy grinned. "And to invite you to book club Wednesday night. We used to do it the last Wednesday of the month, but now we just meet whenever we feel like it. I'm calling one this week."

"Um, okay? What book? I'll try to get a copy of it before then." She'd have to talk to Alice and see if she could help. That was tomorrow.

Macy laughed. "We don't actually talk about the book. At least, not very much. It's more of an excuse for us to get together and eat cookies and drink wine. We meet at my coffee shop at six-thirty. You don't have to drink if you don't want to. But cookie eating is a must."

Sofie smiled. "Sounds like fun. Do any of you bring kids? I'm not sure what I'll do with Olive otherwise."

"You can. Tara and London usually leave their babies at home, but she's welcome to come."

"Okay. I appreciate the invite."

Macy nodded. "Of course. We want you to feel welcome around here. No matter how long you're staying. Especially since I can't remember the last time Knox went on a date, let alone had a woman other than Alice or one of us in his house."

Sofie's eyebrows shot up. "Knox doesn't date?"

"Nope." Macy shook her head as she headed for the door.

"What's wrong with the women around here?"

Macy laughed. "Nothing. He's just not interested in any of them." She paused, hand on the doorknob. "One thing you need to understand about Knox, he's a private man, and he doesn't let many people in. He's been hurt before and it's left him wary."

"Yeah, he told me about high school."

"He did?" Macy's eyes widened. "Wow. Now I'm doubly glad I came out to meet you. You must be something for him to open up about that. He doesn't talk about it. Ever. I only know about it because of my relationship with the Archers."

Sofie didn't know what to say, so she shrugged. She hadn't done anything to make him confide in her. She still wasn't even a hundred percent sure why she was here. Not why she'd left—that was crystal-clear—but why it was Knox she left with. If she'd asked, Silas and Nori would have gone with her anywhere she wanted.

"Well, in any case, I'm glad he met you. Maybe he'll come out of his hole more often."

"Knox has a hole?"

Macy gestured around them as she opened the door and walked outside. "This ranch. He rarely leaves it. Maybe you'll get him to be more social."

"I doubt that. I'm here to hide out."

Macy's eyes narrowed. "About that. Bring a picture of your ex with you tomorrow if you have one. We all need to know what he looks like so we can be on the lookout."

Emotion squeezed Sofie's heart. Everyone of Asa's friends, and their friends, had been so good to her. She was starting to feel less alone. "I'll do that. Thank you."

"Yep. I'll see you tomorrow night." She loped down the porch steps and to her car with a wave.

Sofie returned her farewell, then stepped inside as Macy drove away.

TWELVE

K nox tried to be quiet as he let himself in the house that evening. It was late, and he didn't want to disturb Olive if she was asleep already. He used the bootjack to take off his messy boots, then hung up his coat and hat before padding quietly through the kitchen. One of his wolfhounds, Jai, padded in, his toenails clicking on the hard floor. Knox scratched his head and continued through to the dining room to the stairs. He glanced in the living room as he rounded the newel post, and Sofie's dark head popped up from where she was reading a book on the couch.

"Hey. You're back."

He smiled. "Yeah. Sorry it's so late. I had a lot to catch up on."

She shrugged. "It's your ranch. Keep whatever schedule you want."

Knox wandered closer. His other wolfhound, Maeve, looked up from her spot beside Sofie on the couch, tail thumping a greeting. "That may be so, but I don't want to neglect you and Olive. You're my guests."

She stuck her finger in her book and closed it. "We're fine

on our own. You have work to do. You don't need to entertain us."

He grinned. "That's good. My idea of a fun night is a good book or a sitcom."

Sofie giggled. "Me too."

"What are you reading?" He gestured to the book in her hand.

"Oh, it's the book for Macy's book club tomorrow night. She stopped by this morning and invited me."

"Macy was here?"

She nodded.

"How'd that go? Did she give you a choice about attending?" Macy was a force to be reckoned with. She often kept talking and before he knew it, he was agreeing to the things she wanted him to agree to.

"She's a bit of a steamroller, isn't she?" She chuckled. "But yes, she did. She even told me I could bring Olive."

"Did she also tell you they don't actually discuss the book?"

"Yes. But I figured I'd read it anyway. Your sister gave me her copy. I guess she's going too."

"Yeah. She started going a few months ago. They eat a bunch of cookies and brownies, drink a glass of wine, and call us if they have more than that."

"Does that happen often?"

"Not normally, no. Only if things are bad and they need to vent. Stuff's been pretty quiet around here lately."

"That's good. Asa told us about the craziness that went on here in the last year. I'm glad it all worked out."

Knox was too. He'd come close to losing some good friends.

He pushed away from the couch. "Well, I'll let you get back to your book. I'm going to head up to bed."

"Wait." She stood. "Did you eat?"

"Yeah. Sort of. Denny ran to the bunkhouse and made us a couple sandwiches."

Sofie rolled her eyes. "You need more than that after working all day. I made chicken and some roasted vegetables. There's still some left."

"Oh." His stomach growled.

She rolled her eyes again and laid her book on the couch, then took his hand. "Come on. I'll heat it up for you."

Heat traveled up Knox's arm at her touch. Her step faltered, and she glanced back at him before letting go.

"Sorry."

Knox renewed the connection. "About what?"

A pretty blush stole over her cheeks, and she looked away, withdrawing her hand. "Why don't you go clean up? I'll put a plate together for you."

He held her gaze for a moment, then nodded. "Okay. I'll be back down in a few minutes."

"Take your time."

They went their separate ways, and he didn't waste any time hurrying upstairs to hop in the shower. He wanted to catch her before she hid away in her room. He'd seen the desire to run enter her eyes as the feelings provoked by his touch hit her. She was scared, and he wanted the chance to show her there was nothing to fear. The woman tied him up in knots, but he wanted to unravel them all and see where the rope led. He'd never felt that way before.

He walked into his room, shutting the door, and stripping as he crossed to his bathroom. Inside, he didn't wait for the water to warm before he jumped in. The cold spray would do him some good and help calm the fire burning in his veins. Sofie wasn't the only one who felt something when they touched.

He soaped up and rinsed off in record time, hopping out to towel off and dress in a pair of sweats and a white t-shirt. In his bare feet, he took the stairs two at a time to get back to the kitchen. As he rounded the corner, he wasn't all that surprised to find it empty, except for Jai, who sat on the floor staring up at the microwave. A sticky note on the door told him his dinner was inside. He glanced at Jai and sighed. "I wasn't fast enough." The dog's eyes flicked from him to the microwave and back. Knox chuckled. "I'm sure you already ate."

Opening the door, he removed the plate inside heaped with a grilled chicken breast and vegetables.

Sitting down at the dinette, he ate his meal in silence, only this silence was worse than what he was used to. Every other night, he ate alone because he lived alone. But tonight, there was someone else in his house, but he still ate alone. For the first time in a long time, he wanted something other than his own company.

～

Sofie took a sip of her wine and glanced around at the other women. They gabbed like the lifelong friends that they were, but she didn't feel left out. They'd made a point to include her in the conversation, which had actually started with the book. Now, though, they were discussing the problem of going back to work after being off for maternity leave.

"How did you handle it?" Tara asked Sofie after complaining how hard it was to leave her twins and dive back into her restaurant.

"Going back to work?"

Tara nodded.

"I didn't. My husband never really liked me working, so when Olive was born, I quit. That's when I started making jewelry full-time. It started as a hobby; something to occupy my time, but it grew into a profitable business."

"Really? That's great," Tara said.

"You should see some of her stuff." Alice leaned forward in her chair. "She and Nori both wore some of it to the wedding. And she fixed Daisy's headpiece and you couldn't even tell."

"Hmm." Maggie took a sip of her water. "Do you have a website? I might need to check this out."

Macy rolled her eyes, then grinned at Sofie. "Declan's going to love that you came to town."

Sofie laughed. "He won't be the only husband to have ever cursed my name."

The group laughed. Sofie finished the last of her wine. As she set the glass down, her phone buzzed, and she picked it up, expecting a text from her mom, but it was a number she didn't recognize. Her stomach rolled, and she opened the message with shaking fingers.

Where did you go, Sofie? You can't hide her from me forever.

"Sofie?"

Alice's voice cut through the panic clouding her brain. She looked up.

"Hey. What's wrong?"

Sofie looked over at the corner, where Olive played with some magnetic tiles, then turned back to Alice. "Lance." She turned her phone around.

Alice read the message. Her eyes turned hard. "Ignore the bastard. He's just trying to scare you."

"It's working."

"You're safe here. He wouldn't be asking where you are if he knew."

"I know. I just wish he'd leave us alone."

Alice rubbed Sofie's upper arm. "I'm sorry."

She managed a weak smile. "Thanks."

"Do you want to head back to the ranch?"

Knox's face flashed in her mind. She wanted the safety of

his presence. "If you don't mind?" Alice drove, even though she lived in town, since it was Sofie's first time through the mountains from the ranch to town in the dark.

"Not at all." She stuffed the rest of her cookie into her mouth.

Sofie pushed away from the table. "Thank you all so much for inviting me. It was fun."

"Don't be a stranger," Macy said.

"I won't." She looked over at her daughter. "Olive. Honey, it's time to go."

The girl looked up from her toy and nodded, then reached for the plastic bag they brought them in. Sofie helped her with her coat, then put on her own.

"Thanks for the hot cocoa, Miss Macy." Olive adjusted her hat.

"Anytime, sweetie."

Sofie waved and ushered Olive toward the door, following Alice. She couldn't help but put her head on a swivel as they walked outside to the car. Lance's message had her on edge. It would be just like him to toy with her.

Her phone dinged again as they got into the car.

"Is that another one from him?" Alice settled behind the wheel.

Sofie pulled the phone from her pocket to look at it.

Running away doesn't look good for you. Someone might think you're an unfit mother.

She sucked in a sharp breath. Alice leaned over and read the screen, then cursed under her breath.

"The hell you are." She started the car and backed away from the curb. "If there weren't little ears in here with us, you'd know exactly how I feel about that statement."

Despite the dismay churning in her gut, Sofie smiled. Alice was fierce. "Thank you."

"You're welcome. Let's get home. I know you'll feel better once you're locked up tight."

She would. But it wouldn't so much be about the locks as a certain blonde man who turned her insides to jelly and made her feel like nothing bad could touch her. That he would stand between her and all the evil in the world.

The drive passed quickly, even though Sofie watched the mirrors closely. She was actually surprised when Alice turned onto the ranch drive. They pulled into the garage and Alice cut the engine. Sofie glanced into the backseat to see Olive sound asleep.

"I sure hope she stays asleep while I carry her in, or she'll be wound up for hours."

"Do you want me to go get Knox to carry her? She did all right the other night with him."

"We'd also been on the road for thirteen hours, so she was exhausted. It won't matter who carries her in. Just say a prayer." She got out and opened the back door to unbuckle the child and lift her from the seat. Sofie froze as Olive grumbled, willing her to stay asleep. It was already past her bedtime; she didn't want to add to that.

The girl quieted, and Sofie made her way into the house. As she passed by the living room on her way to the stairs, Jai lifted his head from where he was stretched out in front of the fireplace. Maeve's tail thumped on the couch.

Knox looked up from the recliner, where he sat with a book. "Hi."

Alice waved a hand at him. "Olive's asleep," she whispered.

"Oh, sorry." He lowered his voice and got out of the chair. "Do you need me to take her upstairs?"

Sofie shook her head and mounted the first step. "I'm good." She drank in his tall form, feeling a bit safer already, and went up to Olive's room. Maeve got up and followed.

Laying Olive on the bed, she tugged off the girl's boots and winter gear, then tucked her under the covers in her clothes. One day, they'd get back into the routine of pajamas and story time, but that was not tonight. The dog walked over to the other side of the bed and spun in a circle twice before lying down. She'd taken a real shine to Olive and spent most night curled up next to the girl's bed. The affection was mutual. Olive loved the dog, and Jai too. Sofie had been nervous about the dogs at first —they were the size of a small pony and much larger than Asa and Daisy's wolfhound puppy—but they were gentle giants.

Giving her daughter a kiss, Sofie tiptoed out of the room and closed the door, leaving it open far enough for Maeve to get out, then went to her own room.

With a sigh, she sat on the bed and buried her face in her hands. Old insults Lance used to hurl at her reared their ugly heads again as she remembered his most recent text message. She knew they weren't true, but it didn't stop her from sliding down the rabbit hole of inferiority. He had a way of making her feel small with little more than a few well-placed words. She'd done so much to build up her confidence in the last year, but she felt it slipping away at an alarming rate.

A knock on the semi-open door had her wiping her eyes and looking up. Knox poked his head into the room.

"Hey. Before she left, Alice said you got more messages from Lance. When you didn't come down, I thought I should look in on you. Are you all right?"

Sofie nodded. "I'm good."

He cocked a brow. "Sure."

She huffed. "Okay, so I'm upset. But I will be fine. Alice was right; he's just trying to scare me. But they're just words."

"Maybe." He walked over and sat down next to her. "But words can hurt. Sometimes more than a punch."

"I know. I just—" She broke off and wrung her hands.

"How do you rewire years of being told you're no more than a silly woman who knows nothing?"

"By reminding yourself that you've pulled yourself out of that situation and forged a new life." He brushed a lock of her hair off her shoulder and skimmed her cheek with his thumb. "Sofie, you're like one of those jewels you put in your jewelry; beautiful in its own right, but when surrounded by a solid foundation, you become a masterpiece. I think you're getting there, but you're still being built. Don't sell yourself short. It sounds like you've already come a long way."

Tears threatened again. Dammit, why did this man always make her cry? And in a good way? She nodded. "I know. And that's a lovely way to think of things. Thank you."

He leaned in and pressed a kiss to her forehead. Sofie's heart did a somersault. It didn't resume a normal pace until he pulled away and stood.

"I'm going to say goodnight. I have another early morning tomorrow."

"Okay. Thank you again for everything, Knox."

"You're welcome." He gave her a soft smile and moved toward the door. "Goodnight."

"Goodnight."

He closed the door, leaving her sitting there, wondering which angel God sent to Earth in the form of that man to help her find herself again.

Thirteen

The sound of a vehicle coming up the drive drew Knox out of the barn. He checked his watch, thinking it might be Alice, but it was too early yet for her to be here to work in her studio. As the car came into view, trepidation skated down Knox's spine. He didn't recognize the car. Hand reaching under the back of his coat, he felt the reassuring weight of the pistol he'd been carrying since they arrived home a week ago.

His long legs ate up the ground between the barn and the house, and he met the stranger as he exited his car.

"Can I help you?"

The man turned at the sound of Knox's voice and removed his sunglasses. Knox ran an assessing eye over the man. He was dressed in jeans and a wool coat like many ranchers, but there was an aura about him that felt off.

"Hi. I'm Nate Connors. I'm looking for Knox Duvall."

"You found him."

The man smiled. "I heard from a friend you're one of the best horse trainers outside of the racing industry."

Knox lifted a single brow. "So you decided to just drop in?"

"I was in the area. I live in Nevada. I figured I'd stop and see your operation for myself. If you have time, of course."

"Who's your friend?" Knox asked.

"Pardon?"

"Your friend who recommended me? Who is it?" Knox remembered the name of every person he'd ever sold a horse to or provided training services for. His smarts were good for something. "And keep in mind, I can verify your story with a single phone call to whomever you name."

The man looked down, then up through his lashes, a sheepish smile on his face. "Okay, so maybe I heard it more through the grapevine." He lifted his head. "But that doesn't mean I'm not still interested in your training services. I have several horses I bought from a breeder that I want to use for cutting, but they're untrained."

Knox stared at him a moment longer. He still didn't like the guy, but he wouldn't turn away a potential client over a feeling. He'd get more information and then decide. "I don't appreciate being lied to, Mr. Connors. If we're going to work together, you need to be straight with me."

"Of course, yes. I'm sorry. I figured a man of your talent might be more inclined to accept a new client if he's friends with a current one."

Did this guy think he was some kind of buffoon? "I accept based on my current workload. And right now, I don't have time to take on another animal, let alone several." Even if he did, he wasn't sure he wanted to work with this man. He was getting some serious creeper vibes from him.

The front door banged, and Knox turned to see Olive fly off the porch toward him.

"Mommy needs you!"

"What?" He caught the girl and lifted her into his arms. Alarm made his muscles tense. "What's wrong?"

"I don't know. She was talking on the phone, then she just kinda fell to the floor, crying."

Concern set his feet in motion. He glanced back at the stranger. "I'm sorry, Mr. Connors. You'll have to find yourself a horse trainer elsewhere."

"Do you need help?"

"No. I'm sure everything is fine. Good day." He took the steps in one leap, the man already forgotten as he pulled open the door to let himself inside. "Sofie?"

"She's in the living room." Olive pointed.

He followed Olive's direction and ran into the room. Sofie sat on the floor near the fireplace, staring off into space. Her cellphone laid in her lap and tear tracks stained her face. Knox set Olive on the couch, then crouched in front of her mother. "Sofie?" He cradled her face in one hand. "Hey. What's wrong? Is your mom okay?" he asked, thinking maybe something happened to Nori.

His touch brought her out of her daze. Her eyes met his, then she launched herself at him, wrapping her arms around his neck.

"Whoa. Hey, what's going on?" He put his arms around her and shifted so he was sitting, pulling her onto his lap. He glanced at Olive. "Do you know who she was talking to?"

The girl shook her head. "Is she okay, Mr. Knox?"

"I think so, honey. She's just upset. Why don't you go get a bottle of water from the fridge for her?" He hoped Olive leaving the room would loosen Sofie's tongue.

"Okay." The girl scrambled off the couch and left the room.

Knox leaned back so he could see Sofie's face. "Hey, it's just us now. Tell me what's going on, please."

Sofie sniffed and drew in a deep breath. "My lawyer called.

He heard from a friend at the courthouse that Lance is suing for full custody of Olive."

"Seriously? What judge in their right mind would give a convicted felon full custody over the child's mother—who's never been in any kind of trouble?"

"One in Lance's pocket."

"Okay, what exactly did your husband do for a living before he went to jail?"

"He was a salesman for a large pharmaceutical company."

Knox's eyes widened. "So he had deep pockets."

She nodded. "He still does. I got lucky, though. The judge who handled his trial was a hard-ass when it came to spousal abuse. He wasn't the one who granted his early release. I don't think he would have."

"Did your lawyer say what grounds he has for requesting full custody?"

"That I'm unfit. Jim got his hands on the documents. Lance says I'm unemployed and unable to provide for her."

"Isn't your ex unemployed too? And what about the violations of the protection order?"

"He got his job back, somehow. And it's my word against his that I saw him in town and that the video is too grainy to provide a hundred percent verification it was him on the ranch. His attorney is arguing that the notes could be from anyone. He never signed any of them. They're his handwriting, though, so I don't know how he's getting past that."

"If he has a sympathetic judge or has bribed one, it won't matter."

Olive ran back into the room with a bottle of water. "Here you go, Mommy."

Sofie took the water and unscrewed the cap. "Thank you, sweetie." She took a drink.

"Are you okay?" A furrow formed between her green eyes.

"Yes, I'm fine. I'm sorry if I scared you. Mommy just got

some unexpected news. I'm fine now. Why don't you go play upstairs?"

Her frown smoothed out some. "Okay." The girl leaned in and pressed a kiss to Sofie's cheek and hugged her tight, then ran out again. Her little feet pounded on the stairs as she ran up to her room.

Sofie sniffed. "I can't lose her, Knox. He won't take care of her. Not the way she deserves. He'll foist her off on a nanny or send her away to school. And if she messes up or says the wrong thing, he won't hesitate to hit her. I was the only thing that stood between her and his anger."

Knox tightened his arms around her. "We won't let any of that happen."

She swiped at the wetness on her face. "How? I may not be unemployed, but that doesn't mean I have the funds to fight him."

"You might not, but I doubt Silas is going to let Lance take her away from you."

"I can't ask him to do that. Do you know what a good family attorney costs?"

"Honey, you won't have to ask. He'll be on the phone calling his attorney as soon as the words are out of your mouth. If that guy can't handle it, he'll find someone who can."

She frowned, then groaned. "That will just add fuel to Lance's claims. Poor Sofie. She needs her new stepdad to help her fight her battles." She covered her face with her hands.

Knox pulled her hands away and fold them into his. "If you have a good attorney, he won't be able to. Silas would make sure of that."

"Even so, I'm living on Silas and Asa's land. I'm not technically on my own, even though my jewelry business would pay for a small apartment in addition to our other bills."

"Then tell the attorney that. You'll probably have to prove

it, but he shouldn't be able to take her away from you completely."

She growled and climbed off his lap. "I don't want him to have her at all." She ran a hand through her hair and paced away, then spun back to spear him with a look as he stood. "Does that make me a bad person? I don't want her to have anything to do with him. He doesn't really want to be a father. He just wants to spite me. I rebelled, and he's going to take it out on Olive."

"No." He took her face in his hands to hold her still. He could feel the tension running through her. "It doesn't make you a bad person. It makes you a good mother. You want to protect her, even if it's from a man who's supposed to love her no matter what."

Tears tracked down her cheeks, and she gripped his wrists. "I don't know what to do. What do I do?"

The broken whisper did him in. He hauled her into his chest and wrapped his arms around her. His heart thundered in his ears as he tried to keep his cool, when all he really wanted to do was find her ex and have a quick chat. "We're going to call Silas and your mom. Let him hire you a good custody lawyer. Then we'll do what the lawyer says." He pulled back to look at her again. "You're not alone, Sofie. You have your family. Me. We'll all be here to see you through this."

She hiccupped and nodded. "Thank you."

As he tucked her close again, he made a vow. Whatever she wanted of him—whatever she needed—he'd do it. This quiet woman, with her pretty smile and emerald green eyes that sparkled like jewels, had found a way into his heart, shouting that she was there to stay.

Fourteen

The scent of fresh coffee brought Knox awake. He stretched lazily, savoring the warmth of his bed. As the sleep fog cleared his brain, his eyes snapped open, and he sat up, looking at the clock. "Shit!" He shoved back the covers and scrambled out of bed. He slept through his alarm. Yanking on jeans and a thermal undershirt, he pulled on some thick wool socks, then grabbed a flannel from his closet and ran downstairs.

Sofie looked up from her plate and smiled. "Hey. I thought you were gone already."

"I should be." He hurried over to the counter and poured coffee into a silver travel mug.

"Do you want some breakfast?"

"I'll grab something later. I need to feed the animals, then get started on my training schedule."

"Well, here." She got up and went into the pantry. "At least take a protein bar. I've learned you'll stay out there until your work is done, even if you're starving."

A corner of his mouth tilted. She wasn't wrong. He accepted the chocolate fudge bar. "Thanks."

"You're welcome. Olive and I can feed the chickens if that helps."

"Yay!" Olive got out of her chair and came running over. "I want to feed the chickens!"

He grinned down at her, picking her up. "You do?" He tickled her tummy.

She giggled. "Yes."

"Okay." He placed a smacking kiss on her cheek and set her on the floor.

"I'm going to put my boots on!" She took off for the door.

"Are you sure you don't mind?" Knox turned back to Sofie.

She smiled. "No. We did it all the time on the Stone Creek."

"Well, if you're sure, I'd love the help. I never oversleep, but I sure did today." He was over an hour behind his normal schedule thanks to a restless night. Several restless nights, actually. Having Sofie in the house was keeping him awake. The more time he spent with her, the more he wanted to be around her. To just be near her. Knowing she was sleeping on the other side of the wall messed with his head. He wanted her in his bed, where he could hold her. His arms ached with the desire, but his brain said no. That they didn't know each other well enough for that. Hell, he hadn't even kissed her. Their interlude in Montana seemed like eons ago. If and when anything more happened between them, it had to come from her. He hadn't brought her to his home to put the moves on her.

"I guess you needed the extra sleep."

"I guess so. Anyway, I need to go. Thanks for the protein bar and for feeding the chickens."

"Yep. We'll see you later."

He nodded and headed for the mudroom, ruffling Olive's hair as he passed.

~

Olive kept up a steady stream of chatter as they walked to the chicken coop. The egg basket bumped her leg, tipping wildly as she scurried along beside her mother. Sofie was glad the basket was empty. She made a mental note not to let her carry it back to the house.

The chickens clucked as they saw Sofie and Olive coming, running to the gate to be let out for the day. Sofie opened the pen, shooing them back as they entered.

"They're hungry!" Olive giggled as the hens swarmed around them.

"Yep. It's past their breakfast time. Can you get the hose and fill up their water trough while I start scooping grain?"

"Sure can." The girl took off for the hose coiled up on the side of the coop. Several of the chickens followed her, but most stayed with Sofie.

"Shoo. Shoo. I can't feed you if I can't get in the bin." She nudged them out of her way to get inside the lean-to where Knox kept the chicken feed bin. She took a bucket off the hook on the wall, then unlatched the bin and started scooping. The chickens clucked louder. "Yeah, yeah, I'm hurrying."

With a full bucket, she waded through the birds to get to the coop. She stepped inside and poured the feed into the feeder trough, then jumped back with a laugh as they flocked to it.

"I'm all done, Mommy." Olive walked into the coop, her pants soaked.

"Did you jump in?"

The little girl giggled. "I got splashed."

"I see that. Let's collect the eggs and get you back to the house to change before you freeze."

Together, they moved through the nests and filled the basket.

"Did we get them all?" Sofie peered at the lower level of nests where Olive had been collecting eggs. She didn't see any more.

"I think so."

"Okay. Let me put another bucket of feed in the trough, then we can head back to the house. We'll get you changed, then clean these and put them away." She set the basket outside the coop, then refilled her bucket and filled the trough. Picking up the basket, she took Olive's hand to lead her back to the house.

As they crossed the yard, movement at the barn caught her attention. She turned her head to see Knox in the center of the corral, a silver horse on a long line running at a slow canter around him. The horse's breath puffed white in the chilly morning air, and the sun glowed behind them as it rose higher in the sky, adding a shimmer to the icy crystals in the fog.

Wow. It was like a scene from a movie, only it was very real.

Being in the same house with Knox, day and night, was rapidly eroding her self-control. Yesterday, she'd slipped out of her room to check on Olive before going to sleep, and he was coming up from the kitchen with a bottle of water. In just a t-shirt and pajama pants. The man was drool-worthy in his jeans, but in a snug white tee and thin gray lounge pants that left little to the imagination? She thought she'd have to scrape herself off the floor with a squeegee. It took all her strength to keep her knees locked, so she didn't melt at his feet. She'd offered him a tight smile and scurried past him to her daughter's room.

"Mommy, can we go watch Mr. Knox with the horses?"

Sofie turned her attention to Olive. "Sure. Let's get you into some dry clothes and clean the eggs first, though, okay?"

Olive nodded and ran up the steps into the house. Sofie helped her out of her winter clothes and her wet pants, then sent her to her room to get a dry pair. While she was gone, she started going through the basket of eggs, looking for cracked ones. They all looked good, and only a few had dirt on them. She dug under the sink for the fine-grit sandpaper Knox used to take small bits of dirt off the eggs and ran it over the spots, making sure not to damage the shells. She finished just as Olive came back into the room in dry pants.

"Can you get two egg cartons from the pantry, please?"

Olive changed direction. Sofie pulled a chair up to the counter so Olive could help.

"Here you go." The girl held up the cartons.

"Thank you." Sofie took the cartons and set them on the counter. "Hop up here and help."

She climbed the chair, and the two of them sorted the eggs by size into the cartons.

"There. Now we can go watch Knox."

Olive scrambled off her seat, pushing the chair back to the table, then ran into the mudroom to put her winter gear back on. Sofie followed her, and soon they were off again across the yard.

He saw them coming, smiling as they approached. "Hey. You come to watch?"

"Yep!" Olive ran up to the fence and climbed the first rail, peering through the slats.

Sofie helped her higher so she could sit on the top rail, then stood behind her so she didn't topple off. "Don't mind us. We just want to see what all the fuss is about."

His grin widened, and he turned back to the horse.

"What's its name?" Olive asked.

"This is Blanca."

"But she's not white." Sofie cocked her head, curious at the horse's name.

"I know. My dad started naming horses after mountain peaks in Colorado. I carried on the tradition. Not too many of them are feminine, so she gets to have a bit of an identity crisis."

Transfixed, Sofie watched as he worked the horse. He finished with the line and saddled the sleek animal, then mounted her to practice some quick turns. Olive clapped as she watched him make the horse do some fancy footwork. It was like a dance. Sofie was impressed.

He rode up to where they watched. "You want a ride, kiddo?"

Olive squealed. "Yes!"

He laughed and reached for her, settling her in front of him on the saddle. With a wink, he spun Blanca around and took off at a quick trot around the corral.

Sofie smiled as she watched them, but a pang of misgiving rang through her heart. She shouldn't encourage Olive and Knox's friendship; her daughter would only get hurt when they went back to the Stone Creek and she saw little of her new friend. But he was such a positive influence on her, and he seemed to enjoy his time with her as much as Olive did. When he had children, they were going to be the luckiest kids in the world.

Her thoughts strayed to her ex. It had been several days since the call from her lawyer about Lance's custody petition. She kept waiting to hear more, but so far nothing. It was maddening. She just wanted the other shoe to drop so she could respond.

Olive's laughter, ringing through the chilly air, drew her from her thoughts, and she smiled. Waiting wasn't all bad, though. Being on the Duvall ranch wasn't a hardship. She missed her mom, but spending time with Knox was nice.

He was a bit of a conundrum, though. She'd catch him staring at her, and she could swear sometimes he wanted to kiss her, but he never did more than touch her cheek or hold her hand for a moment.

But she so wanted him to. A couple times, she'd stopped herself from swaying into his touch, but it was getting harder all the time to keep her distance. She wasn't even sure she wanted to anymore. It wasn't the right time for her to get involved with anyone, though. Even with the kindest, most handsome man she'd ever met.

FIFTEEN

Sofie stared in dismay at the envelope in her hands. It arrived by special courier just a few minutes ago and bore the name of a law firm out of Chicago. Hands shaking, she flipped it over and reached for the flap, hesitating once more.

"Oh, this is ridiculous. Just open the damn thing, Sof." Growling, she tore it open and pulled out the papers. Even knowing they were coming, it was still a shock to see the petition for custody. She couldn't believe someone thought Lance would make a good full-time guardian for a four-year-old. She was just glad her attorney gave her a heads up so she could prepare.

After she'd composed herself from the call, she'd done as Knox said she should and called her mom and Silas. Knox had been right. She needed to rely on her family and not try to do everything by herself. Especially if going it alone meant she lost Olive.

He'd also been right that Silas wouldn't wait for her to ask if he could help her retain a custody lawyer. Nori had put them on speaker, and he'd been researching attorneys almost immediately. She now had one of the best in the business on her side. Since then, it had been a week of agonizing waiting as the paperwork cleared the judicial system in Chicago.

She flipped through the documents, reading the allegations Lance made against her, rolling her eyes and getting more incensed with every word.

Unstable, my ass!

He'd have fun proving that one. She was sure he'd get some of his friends to write affidavits claiming to have seen her ranting and raving, but she doubted those would hold a lot of weight. Her attorney said that for Olive to be removed from her care completely and placed in Lance's—a convicted felon's—they'd have to have physical proof she was a danger to Olive.

That was also the one thing she was lacking against Lance. She didn't regret putting herself between him and their daughter, but it meant there wasn't any documentation that he would hurt her the first time she misbehaved.

The back door opened and closed and Knox appeared in the kitchen where she sat at the dinette looking over the papers.

"I saw a car drive away. Everything all right?"

She held up the documents. "I've been served."

A frown formed on his handsome face, and he walked over to her to take them, glancing through them quickly. "Okay. It's not really anything we weren't expecting." He looked up. "What I want to know is how they found you."

Her eyes widened. He was right. Lance didn't know where she was. The only one who knew was her custody lawyer. She fished her phone out of her pocket. "I'm calling Adam and asking if he told Lance's attorney how to find me. Those papers came from Lance's lawyer's office, not mine." She dialed Adam Vancroft's number and put the phone on speaker.

"Vancroft."

"Adam, it's Sofie McAllister. I just got served with custody papers."

He sighed. "Yeah, they were just delivered to me, too."

"You don't understand. Lance doesn't know where I am. After the notes where he made veiled threats about taking Olive, we left and didn't tell anyone except family where we went. He shouldn't know where I am to be able to serve me these. Did you tell his attorney where to find me?"

"No. Have you noticed anyone lurking around or someone following you when you leave the ranch?"

This was why she liked this man. His no-nonsense tone and genuine concern helped her feel like things weren't spiraling out of control.

"No. There's been no one."

"Wait." Knox held up a hand. "There was a man. The day Jim Blackwell called to tell her he heard Lance was filing custody paperwork. Said his name was Nate Connors. He was looking for me to train some horses for him, but he seemed— off. He lied to me about how he heard of me. I didn't get a chance to dig deeper. Olive came out of the house to tell me Sofie needed help."

"You think he was fishing for information?" Adam asked.

"Maybe. We know Lance was at the Stone Creek while I was there. He could have taken pictures of us while we were out and about around town, then hired a private investigator to track everyone down once he realized Sofie and Olive were no longer on the ranch."

"And if that Connors fellow was a scout, or even the private investigator, he saw Olive, which is all the confirmation he'd need of where they are. Have you heard from him since?"

"No, but I told him I wasn't interested. He could be legit and took me at my word."

"I'll do some digging. He say where he was from?"

"Nevada."

"Okay, I'll see what I can turn up on him. Sofie, there's one thing in this petition that bothers me and could potentially be a problem."

She frowned and glanced up at Knox. His expression mirrored hers. "What?"

"It says that not only is your ex-husband gainfully employed, but that he's in a steady relationship with a woman named Carissa Mayweather."

Sofie gasped. She hadn't read that far. "That bitch!"

A beat of silence passed.

"Pardon?" Adam said.

"I know her. She lived down the hall from us."

"Sofie, did Lance ever spend time with her during your marriage without you present?" Adam asked.

"I'm not sure. Maybe? He'd go out and not tell me where he was going. Just that he'd be back later. He'd come home after I'd already gone to bed. But sometimes when I would do laundry, his clothes would smell like perfume that wasn't mine. She used to stop by and visit me, though. Bring me a brownie from a coffee shop she liked and chat for a bit. It always felt a little phony to me, like she was just trying to be nice, but didn't really care. She was more interested in Olive than me most of the time."

"Hmm. I'd just started looking into her when you called. She's a finance manager at a bank, no criminal history, widowed with no children. Does that sound right?"

Sofie's heart sank. She was perfect. "Yes."

"Why would a woman who seemingly has it all get involved with a man like Lance?" Knox asked. "I mean, living down the hall from them, she had to have known he was abusing Sofie."

"She did," Sofie added. "At least once he put me in the hospital, she knew. She came to visit me."

"I don't know why she would get involved with him, but there's a statement here from her saying they're engaged."

Sofie groaned. "Great."

"I have to say, his petition is good. I don't think he'll win full custody because of his recent criminal history, but he could get shared."

"What about the protection order? The judge in the criminal case ordered him not to have any contact with us and okayed my move out west. He's violated that. That video shows him on the ranch."

"It does, but it's also not the best quality. He wasn't close enough to the camera to get a good enough shot that anyone who doesn't know him would recognize. And I'm working on that, but it's part of this custody suit, too. He's asking for it to be dismissed."

Sofie groaned again. "This is a nightmare. How did it even get to this point?"

"Because your ex has connections. Deeper ones than I think you or Jim Blackwell realized."

Obviously. Sofie put her elbows on the table and rested her head in her hands.

"Would it help her case if she was in a stable relationship as well?" Knox asked.

Sofie turned to stare up at him with wide eyes.

"Of course. Are you?"

"What?" Sofie said, looking at the phone. "No."

"Yes." Knox spoke over her.

She looked up at him again. "Are you crazy?"

"No. Mr. Vancroft, let the judge in the case know that Sofie is also engaged."

"Knox!" She stood. He tried to speak, but she waved a hand and cut him off. "No. Adam, I'll call you back." She hung up and turned on Knox. "What the hell are you thinking?"

"That you can't compete with a man like your ex if he's stacked the deck against you. You need to stack it back."

"By pretending to be engaged? We've only known each other a few weeks!"

He shrugged. "So? People meet and get married in Vegas. Why can't we be similar? Love at first sight and all that."

"Because what judge—especially one already sympathetic to Lance—is going to believe we met and got engaged within a few weeks? The first thing they'll assume is that we had a one-night stand and I'm pregnant. Then, it'll only take them about five seconds in our presence for them to realize we're lying through our teeth about our relationship. We don't act like a couple because we aren't one."

"Really? Because I care about what happens to you, Sofie. You and Olive."

"I know that, and I love that you do, but there's nothing romantic about those feelings. People in relationships touch each other and kiss. We don't do that."

"That's not hard to fix."

Sofie sucked in a breath at the heat suddenly in his eyes. An answering one bloomed to life in her cheeks. She rolled her lips in, then licked her bottom lip and shook her head. "It would be a lie. And it could cost me everything."

"But what if it wasn't?"

"Wasn't a lie?"

He nodded, shuffling closer and taking her hands. "What if we get married?"

She knew she looked like a fish, her mouth working as she tried to form a response, but she couldn't help it. "You really have lost your mind."

"Hear me out. What if we"—he tipped his head back and forth—"stretch the truth a bit. We can tell the judge we fell for each other pretty much right away, but planned on a longer engagement. We wanted to spend more time getting to know each other, but still have that commitment an engagement offers. With the custody dispute, we stepped up our timeline to provide a more stable home for Olive."

Sofie stared at him, dumbfounded. "Why? Why would you want to do that for me? For us?" She narrowed her eyes. "What do you get out of this?"

He blew out a breath and let go of her hands to run them over his face. "Plain and simple?"

She nodded.

"I don't want you to leave."

He wanted her to stay? On his ranch? "Why?"

"I like having you here."

"You want to marry me because you like having me here?"

He sighed. "I don't do relationships. I've always been more comfortable by myself than around others. There's a reason the staff here is minimal. I don't trust many people, because not many people have given me a reason to trust them. When you get bullied like I did, you get choosy about your friends." He took her hands. "You—you trusted me on little more than my word—and Asa's—that I could help. In the process, you've shown me what it could be like to have someone who I could trust with everything. Having you and Olive here—I don't want to be alone anymore. I want you two here." He waved a hand. "That doesn't mean you need to stay for me. You asked what I'd get out of this arrangement. That's it."

She stared up at him and sighed. "So, what happens when the custody hearing is done? Do we divorce? Stay married? For real or as friends?"

Knox glanced away, thinking, then back at her. "I'm not sure. I think we play it by ear." He brought a hand up and touched the side of her face. "I like you. In a way I haven't liked a woman in a long time—maybe ever. I'd like to see where this goes, but if you're not ready for a relationship, I understand. I'll wait."

Sofie scarcely breathed. What he was offering—it was like a dream. "And what if I'm never ready?"

"Then I will always be here for you as a friend. But just know, the only reason I'm offering marriage at this point is to help Olive. Having you stay, anything that happens with us, it's all just a bonus."

She fought the urge to reach out and poke him to see if he was real. Knox was like one of those characters from a romance novel or a Hallmark Christmas movie. He was just too good to be true. But she'd seen evidence of his kindness from day one. If he had a malicious ulterior motive, he should change careers and become an actor, because she couldn't see it.

Did she dare take the chance and do what he proposed? What did that mean for the new life she wanted to build?

Would there be a life to build if Lance got what he wanted?

It was that last thought that had her reaching for the phone again.

"What are you doing?"

"Calling Adam back to tell him we're getting married."

Knox's hand on hers stopped her. "Are you sure?"

Sofie didn't hesitate. "Yes. You're right. I need to stack the deck back or I'm going to lose her. I don't like lying, but with you by my side, I know I stand a better chance at keeping that bastard away from my daughter. So, yes. I'm sure."

He let go. "Okay."

With a short nod, Sofie dialed.

Sixteen

Fresh snow crunched under Olive's little feet as she pushed a snowball through the yard to build the base for a snowman. Sofie stood off to the side, smiling at the determined look on her daughter's face. Her tongue peeked from between her lips and she grunted as she pushed the ever-growing ball around until she couldn't move it anymore.

"Do you want some help?"

"Uh-uh. I can do it." She shoved at the ball again, but it barely rocked. Maeve ran up and sniffed the girl, then took off again, snorting as she buried her nose in the snow. Jai barked at her, then the two took off, playing.

"Tell you what." Sofie crouched next to her. "How about you start on the middle section and I'll finish this one?"

"Okay." Olive smiled and began building another mound of snow.

Sofie pushed the ball, picking up more snow until she had a decent base. "Where should we put him?"

Olive glanced around and shrugged.

"How about right where he is?"

She nodded. "Is this good?" She pointed at the ball she'd rolled.

"Should be. Let's get it over here and see." Sofie rolled the ball over to hers. It looked like it would do. The problem was, she wasn't sure she could lift it on top of the other. "Um." She put her hands on her hips. "Hmm. Liv, we might have a problem."

Olive giggled. "Maybe we should ask Knox to lift it."

"He's working, honey." Knox was trying to get a full day of training sessions in before her mom and Silas arrived. She'd called them to tell them the news after she hung up with Adam Vancroft. Nori had been shocked, but hadn't tried to talk her out of it. Instead, she insisted on coming down for the wedding, even though it would be little more than a quick ceremony at the courthouse. Knox's dad said much the same thing and would arrive tomorrow.

Sofie glanced at her watch. They would be here soon.

"How do we make my snowman, then?"

The crunch of snow under a larger set of feet had them both turning before Sofie could answer. Knox smiled as they saw him crossing the yard.

"Need some help?"

Olive ran to him. "Knox! Mommy said you were working, but now you're not, so can you build my snowman?"

He laughed at her rapid-fire speech and picked her up as the dogs swarmed them. "Sure, sweetie." He looked at the two balls they'd rolled. "Where's his head?"

"We haven't gotten that far," Sofie said.

Olive squirmed in his arms, so he set her on her feet. She dropped to her knees and started another pile, giggling as Jai licked her face. She pushed him away. "Stop."

Knox snapped his fingers and the dog backed off, turning to run after Maeve again. He walked over to the smaller ball. "Is that where you want it to sit?" He pointed at the base.

"It's fine there, yes."

He wrapped his arms around the middle ball and lifted it, walking over to the base. "Guide me down, Sof."

She helped him position the ball, then stood back with him to make sure it was straight. "It looks good."

He nodded and turned to Olive. "You got the head made, Liv?"

"Almost." She rolled the smaller ball through the snow a few more feet.

"I think that's good." Knox walked over and picked it up. "Let's see." She followed him as he put the head on the snowman. "What do you think?"

"I like it. Now it needs arms. And a nose and eyes."

"Why don't you run into the house and get a carrot?" Sofie said. "Knox and I will find arms and eyes."

"Okay." Olive took off for the house. The dogs changed direction to follow her.

Knox grinned. "We're going to have a wet kitchen floor."

Sofie giggled. And probably a hallway and a living room, too, if Olive let the dogs in with her. "It'll dry. Let's find this guy some accessories." She headed for the stand of pine trees while Knox turned to the driveway in search of stones. Branches littered the ground, but she wasn't sure any of them were the right length for snowman arms. She might have better luck with the big oak behind the house.

Icy, wet snow hit the back of her neck and slid down inside her coat. Sofie gasped and spun around. Knox grinned at her from twenty feet away.

"That's cold!"

He laughed, waving another snowball.

She shrieked and ducked as it flew past her head. Laughing, she scooped up a handful of snow, packing it tight while she moved. He lobbed another one at her, missing again. She threw hers, and it glanced off his arm.

"We're supposed to be finishing a snowman." She packed another snowball.

"I found my parts." He skirted closer and threw more snow. It hit her in the chest, splattering her face with tiny crystals.

"Well, I haven't." Sofie ducked behind a pine tree and plunged her hands into the snow, forming ball after ball while she had cover.

"Sofie."

Knox's singsong voice was closer than she'd like. She needed more ammunition.

"You can't stay back there forever."

Laughing quietly, she quickly made several more snowballs, adding them to her stack. She could hear him moving. When he came around the tree, she'd be ready.

His steps reached the edge of the tree line and paused. She picked up a snowball and cocked her arm. He jumped out and she let it fly, smacking him square in the chest.

Their laughter rang through the air as he scooped more snow and she kept up a constant barrage until he ran forward and tackled her into the fresh powder.

He grabbed a handful of snow and stuffed it down the front of her coat.

Sofie shrieked as it hit her chest. She took a handful of her own and put it down the back of his collar. He yelped, still laughing, and wrapped his arms around her so she couldn't do it again.

"No fair," she gasped between bouts of laughter. She squirmed, trying to get her arms free. He rolled, using his weight to hold her down, letting go of her, only to trap her hands over her head in one of his. "You suck."

His eyes met hers and their laughter died as awareness dawned. The cold inside her shirt and at her back faded as the heat from his body overpowered it.

One gloved finger touched her cheek. His eyes searched hers. Sofie knew what he'd find. The same desire she saw in his. A desire she was tired of fighting. She lifted her head and kissed him.

Explosions of light and heat went off behind her eyelids; the shock waves spread down her body in every increasing ripples. He let go of her hands to hold her head, angling it to get better access. Sofie clutched the front of his coat, holding him to her as they kissed. It was exquisite and so much more than she ever thought it would be.

"Mommy!"

Olive's voice in the yard broke them apart. They stared at each other for an intense moment before Knox got up and offered her a hand.

"We're back here," he yelled to the girl.

Sofie took his hand and brushed the snow off her backside, doing her best to calm her quaking muscles as Jai and Maeve found them. Olive ran around the trees a few moments later.

"I got the carrot." She held up the vegetable.

"Good." Sofie cleared her throat and stepped past Knox, her eyes straying to his for a brief moment. It was enough for her to see the heat banked there. A flush stained her cheeks again, and she focused on Olive. "Let's go put it on him while Knox finds some arms."

"Hey, that was your job."

She glanced back with a sweet smile, struggling to keep it on her face as she took in his stance. He had his fists propped on his narrow hips. In their scuffle, he'd lost his hat, and his blonde hair lay tousled over his forehead. "Not anymore."

He chuckled and ran his fingers through his blonde locks. "I guess I deserve that."

"You did distract me."

Heat licked his gaze, and Sofie regretted her choice of

words. Their interlude had awakened something that she had a feeling would refuse to be caged.

"Go give that snowman a nose. I'll catch up."

She nodded and laid a hand on Olive's shoulder. "Come on. Let's go give your snowman a face."

~

Knox took a deep breath of the crisp air as Sofie disappeared with Olive and the dogs. He hadn't meant for that kiss to happen. He'd been in a playful mood, buoyed by the first big snowfall they'd had since Sofie and Olive moved in, and he couldn't resist tossing a snowball. He hadn't counted on the fierce fight Sofie put up. Tackling her was the only way he'd seen to stop her from unleashing the small arsenal she created while hiding behind the pines.

He shook his head and crouched to look beneath the pine boughs for a twig suitable for a snowman arm. Once his body registered hers under it, he'd been lost. He'd been half a beat from kissing her when she sealed her mouth to his and turned his world on its axis. Keeping his hands off his bride wasn't going to be an easy task.

Finding what he needed, he wandered back into the middle of the yard. The growl of an engine split the air as he handed the branches to Olive, lifting her so she could stick them in the side of her snowman.

A truck rolled up the drive, and he recognized Nori and Silas through the windshield.

"Grandma!"

Olive squirmed in his arms, but he held onto her. "Let's wait for them to come to a stop." The dogs barked and took off for the vehicle. Knox's sharp whistle brought them to a halt. He called them back.

The girl's wiggling stopped, but she still bounced with

excitement. She'd been looking forward to Nori and Silas's visit since Sofie told her they were coming.

He still couldn't believe how well the girl took their news about getting married. They'd sat down with her that evening and told her they'd decided to get married. She'd been excited about getting to stay here and continuing her riding lessons. They'd left out the reason why they were getting married, instead telling her they'd decided they wanted to be a family. Sofie and Knox figured they would cross the bridge about what Lance was up to if they needed to. Worrying Olive that her dad was going to take her away wouldn't do anything for the girl. Even at four, she understood her father was not a good man. She never asked about him or wondered when she would see him. Knox got the feeling she didn't think about him much. Sofie said he was an absent father, only showing up when it would make him look good.

Sourness turned Knox's stomach. Lance McAllister was an idiot. He'd ruined the best thing to ever happen to him and didn't even care. But his loss was Knox's gain. He aimed to make Sofie and Olive blissfully happy. He hadn't lied when he said he didn't want them to leave.

The truck came to a halt in front of the house, and Silas cut the engine. Knox set Olive on her feet and watched her high-step through the snow to get to her grandmother. He released the dogs from their heel and they tore off through the yard after her.

"Grandma!"

"Hi, button!" Nori climbed out of the truck and scooped the child into her arms, dodging wagging tails and wet noses. "Oh, I've missed you." She squeezed the girl, then pulled back to kiss her cheek. "Have you been good for Mommy?"

Olive nodded. "Yep."

"Good."

"Where's my hug?" Silas stepped around the front of the truck.

Nori handed the girl to him, and she wrapped her little body around his large frame.

"Hi, Grandpa."

Knox and Sofie reached the older couple. Nori enveloped Sofie in a hug while Knox held out a hand to Silas.

"Sir, good to see you."

Silas put Olive down and smacked Knox's hand away, yanking him into a hug. "Cut the sir crap." He slapped Knox on the back, then let him go. Knox smiled.

Nori released Sofie and turned to him, holding out her arms. He hugged her.

"You better treat my baby right," she whispered in his ear.

He squeezed her tighter. "I will." He pulled back to look at her, hoping she could see his sincerity.

She patted his cheek, giving him a smile, then stepped back.

"Did you have a good trip?" Sofie asked.

Silas nodded. "Can't complain. The weather was decent. We just missed the snowstorm that came through here."

"You should have seen it, Grandpa. I couldn't see the barn!"

"I bet. I see you're hard at work on a snowman, though."

"Come see it!" She took his hand and tugged him toward the snowman they'd built.

"That's a nice snowman, Olive. But where are his eyes?" Silas tilted his head as he looked at it.

"Oh, right." Knox dug into his coat pocket and took out the two stones he'd picked up from the driveway. He handed them to Olive.

Silas picked her up, and she pushed them into the snowman's head.

"There, now he's perfect," Nori said. She looked at her granddaughter. "What's his name?"

"Um." Olive tapped her chin. "Percival."

The adults laughed.

"Where did you hear that name?" Sofie asked.

"It was on my cartoon this morning."

Knox caught Sofie's eye and shrugged, smiling, then looked at Olive. "Percival it is."

"Let's go inside." Silas gave Olive a bounce in his arms, and she giggled. "I bet you could use some hot chocolate."

"Yummy!"

They traipsed through the snow to the door. Silas set Olive on the back porch, then looked at Knox. "Help me with the luggage?"

Knox nodded, the first set of nerves suddenly fluttering in his stomach. He had a feeling Silas wanted more than help with the luggage.

They didn't get very far before he discovered he was right.

"So, you and Sofie, huh?"

"Yes, sir."

Silas narrowed his eyes. "What did I say about that sir, crap? How long have I known you? Just because you're marrying my stepdaughter, doesn't mean you need to treat me differently."

"Right. Sorry." Silas was right. They'd been friends long before Sofie entered either of their lives. Knox opened the back passenger door and took out a suitcase.

"I only want to know one thing." Silas took the suitcase from him. "What happens when this business with Lance is behind you?"

Knox took out the smaller overnight bag and Nori's purse and closed the door. "I don't know. That's up to Sofie."

Silas frowned. "What do you mean?"

"Exactly what I said. As far as I'm concerned, she never has to leave. But that's up to her. I want her to stay. I want both of them to stay."

"Why?"

Knox knew what he was aiming at, but he couldn't say the words to Silas before he said them to Sofie. And he wasn't ready to do that yet, even if they rattled around in his head and his heart louder than any drum. She wasn't ready to hear them, and he still had a hard time believing they were true. He might have said they should use the love at first sight excuse as the reason why they got engaged so soon after they met, but that didn't mean he believed in such a thing. But it was hard to deny what Sofie made him feel.

"I admire her. She's unlike any woman I've ever met. You know me. I don't like people much. But I want to be around her. She and Olive make my world brighter. I look forward to coming in from the barn every night in a way I never have before."

"Hmm." Silas eyed him a moment, then gave a short nod. "Okay." He hefted the suitcase and started for the house.

"Okay?" Knox turned to look at him, staying beside the truck. That was it?

Silas looked back and nodded. "Yep. Come on. We've got hot chocolate to drink."

SEVENTEEN

The creak of the leather saddle beneath him and the wind whistling past his ears did little to soothe Knox's nerves as he waited for his dad to arrive. He shouldn't be anxious, but he was. His father's approval meant a lot, and Knox wanted him to like Sofie. And for Sofie to like his dad. They were both important to him, and he wanted them to get along.

Jai's bark made him look back. Sunlight glinted off glass as an SUV passed through the trees and into the yard. Knox turned Blanca around and spurred her into a trot to meet the car. His dad saw him and waved, steering the vehicle toward the barn. He parked and shut off the engine.

Knox grinned as his father stepped out. "Hey, Dad."

Greg Duvall smiled up at his son. "You going to come down here and give your old man a hug?"

Smile widening, Knox dismounted. Nerves aside, it was great to see him. He'd missed his dad.

Greg stepped up and enveloped him, thumping him on the back. "It's good to see you." He stepped back and patted Knox's shoulder. "I'm glad I caught you out here. I have something for you before we go inside."

"Oh?"

"Yeah." Greg opened the passenger door and reached into the overnight bag on the seat. "So, I know we haven't talked about this, but I want you to have your mother's engagement ring to give to Sofie."

Knox frowned. "Dad—"

Greg waved a hand. "Have you bought her one?"

"Well, no. There hasn't been time, but—"

"No buts. The woman needs a ring." He held out a ring box. "Take it."

Knox stared at the box. He didn't understand. "Dad, why would you want me to give that to Sofie? You know the situation and why I'm marrying her."

"I do. I also know you. I've waited your entire life for you to find the woman who would pull you out of your head and get you to see that being by yourself isn't always the best thing for you. You wouldn't offer her space in your life, let alone your name, if she wasn't special. A woman like that deserves your mama's ring." He motioned for him to take the box.

Knox hesitated, thinking about what he said. Sofie was special. She made him want to share things. Not just his time, but his feelings. He never shared his feelings with a woman. Didn't want them trampled on when he couldn't give her what she needed. But Sofie didn't make him feel that way. For some inexplicable reason, he trusted her.

It was that trust that made him reach out and take the ring.

Greg smiled. "Good boy."

Knox rolled his eyes.

Greg chuckled and slapped Knox on the back. "Seriously, though, I can't wait to meet this woman. She has to be something to get you to open up."

Staring at the ring box, Knox nodded. "Yeah, she is. So is her daughter." He tipped his head toward the house. "Let me put Blanca away and I'll introduce you. Leave your luggage. We'll get it later."

Greg followed him into the barn and helped him get the horse settled, then they made their way across the yard to the house. Knox mounted the back porch steps and let them inside. Little feet—and big paws—scrabbled over the floor of the dining room.

Knox grinned and looked at his dad. "Brace yourself." Both dogs barreled into the kitchen, headed for the mudroom. Olive followed, her dark hair flying out behind her. He let out a sharp whistle. Jai and Maeve skidded to a stop and sat, butts wiggling with their tails.

Olive kept coming, running at him. "You're back!"

He caught her, scooping her into his arms. She patted his face, then looked at his dad.

Greg smiled. "Hi, there. You must be Olive."

She smiled back. "Hi. You're Knox's daddy?"

He nodded. "I am. It's nice to meet you."

The dogs' heads turned before Olive could reply, as Sofie entered the kitchen. She paused in the doorway, tangling a hand in her long, dark blue sweater as she offered Greg a soft smile.

"Hello."

Greg glanced at Knox, raising a brow and one corner of his mouth before stepping into the kitchen. He extended a hand. "Hello. I'm Greg. It's very nice to meet you, Sofie."

She shook his hand, relaxing some. "You too. Did you have a nice trip up?"

He nodded. "Can't complain. Though I don't miss the snow."

"We made a snowman," Olive said.

"I saw that on my way in. It's a very nice snowman."

More commotion in the dining room drew their attention. Nori and Silas walked in.

"Silas," Greg turned to the older couple.

Silas grinned. "It's been a long time." He shook Greg's hand. "How've you been?"

"Good, real good. I see you have too." He looked at Nori. "You must be Noreen."

Nori smiled. "Nori, please." She shook his hand.

"You're as pretty as your daughter. I see where she and your granddaughter get it." He smiled and looked at Silas. "You're a lucky man, though I never thought I'd see the day you'd settle down."

Silas wrapped an arm around his wife. "When it's right, you just know."

Greg glanced at Knox. "That's the truth, right, son?"

Knox pressed his lips together, inhaling a breath before nodding. "Dad, why don't we take this into the living room? You'd probably like to sit."

"I've been sitting for hours. First on a plane, then in that rental car. What I'd like is to get to know my new daughter-in-law and granddaughter."

"I can show you my room," Olive said. She wiggled in Knox's arms, so he set her down. "Come on." She took Greg's hand.

"I bet you have some nice toys up there. Let me take my coat and boots off."

The little girl waited while he did that, then tugged him from the room. He grinned as he let her lead him away. Jai and Maeve ran after them.

Knox couldn't stop the smile that spread over his face as he removed his own coat and boots. It was nice to give his dad something he'd wanted for many years. They'd all thought it would be Alice who would give him grandkids.

He stepped into the kitchen after hanging up his coat and walked over to Sofie. "That didn't take long."

Her mouth tipped up, a cute frown forming on her face. "What didn't?"

"For her to wrap him around her little finger."

Silas laughed, having overheard. "He never stood a chance."

Knox grinned. "No, he didn't. I'll be right back. I need to run upstairs for a minute." The ring box in his pocket burned his skin. His dad's words about knowing when something was right echoed through his head as he looked at Sofie. He hadn't been sure about giving her his mother's ring at first, but now that was all he wanted to do.

But not yet. Not with so many witnesses. That was a moment he wanted them to share alone.

With a gentle squeeze to her arm, he left the room, heading upstairs. As he hit the landing, he could hear Olive's little voice, then his dad's low chuckle. Knox smiled and stopped in the doorway.

Olive saw him and smiled. "Do you want to play too?"

"Maybe in a little while. I need to do something first."

"Oh, okay." She turned back to her dolls.

Greg handed her the blonde doll he held. "I'll be right back, sweetie." He rose and followed Knox from the room. "She's certainly something."

A smile split Knox's face. "Yep."

"Does she react to all new people that way?"

He shrugged. "She has so far, but everyone she's been introduced to lately, Sofie or I trust."

Greg's expression turned serious. "It's amazing she's as happy as she is after what she's been through."

"Sofie sheltered her from a lot of it." Knox turned into his bedroom and headed for the closet to stow the ring in his safe. "She remembers her dad yelling a lot and hitting her mom, but he never laid a finger on her. Sofie wouldn't let him."

"Good on her."

"Yeah. I wish she'd left sooner, but I'm not sorry it brought them here."

"Me, either."

Knox looked at him in surprise.

"It's put a smile on your face I've never seen."

A corner of Knox's mouth lifted. "Yeah, well, she's brought a lot of firsts with her." No matter how things played out in the next few months, he knew his life would never be the same. He didn't want it to be.

Greg gripped Knox's shoulder and smiled. "Good. Now, if you'll excuse me, I have a playdate to get back to."

Eighteen

Sofie stared at herself in the mirror, smoothing her hands down the light gray dress Nori brought with her from Montana. It was her wedding day. Nerves caused her hands to shake and made her thankful for antiperspirants.

The door snicked open, and Sofie glanced behind herself in the mirror to see her mom walk in.

"I think you look lovelier today than at that lavish affair Lance insisted upon." Nori smiled and closed the door.

Sofie focused on herself again and frowned. "There's no less pressure, though. It's just different." When she married Lance, he'd demanded perfection, both in her appearance and decorum, but also in the way the day's events unfolded. In hindsight, she should have backed out, but she'd been young and naïve and fancied herself in love. Her mother's words that Lance was only out to control her had fallen on deaf ears. She wished she'd listened. But she was also glad she didn't. She wouldn't have Olive, and that little girl was her world.

Nori wrapped her arms around Sofie and laid her head on her shoulder. Sofie tipped her head to rest it against the top of her mom's.

"Thank you."

Nori's eyes caught hers in the mirror. "For what?"

"For not giving up on me when I told you that I loved Lance and to butt out." A tear trickled out of her eye. "I know now you were just trying to protect me. I love you."

Nori's gaze turned watery. "It's what mothers do. I will always be here for you; through the good and the bad. And for the record, I think today is part of the good."

Sofie inhaled a shaky breath and straightened. "I hope so."

"Can I ask you something?"

"Sure."

"Do you love Knox?"

Sofie rolled her lips in and glanced away. That was a good question. She felt something for the man, but she was afraid she was confusing love with gratitude. "I'm not sure. Does it matter?"

"Of course it matters. I know you're getting married regardless, but later, when all of this nonsense with Lance is behind you, it will matter a lot."

"I can't think about that right now." If she did, she'd end up in a watery heap on the floor. Right now, she had enough emotional fortitude to focus on keeping Lance away from Olive. What she felt for Knox—that had to stay locked up a little while longer. She needed her wits about her to thwart the representative coming in two days to assess their new little family unit. Sofie was just grateful her attorney managed to get a local, unbiased social worker appointed to the case. Lance's attorney had wanted to send someone out here from Chicago.

The door opened again, and Olive ran inside, stopping when she saw her mother. "Wow, you look pretty, Mommy."

Sofie smiled and swiped the tear off her face. She crouched and held out her arms to give Olive a hug. "Thank you, sweetie."

"Grandpa said to tell you they're ready." Olive leaned back to look at her.

"Okay." Sofie let her go and stood. She blew out a breath. "I guess it's time to get this show on the road."

Nori stared at her for a moment, then turned to Olive. "Honey, run back downstairs and tell Grandpa we're on our way."

Olive nodded and left as quickly as she came. Sofie took another deep breath and stepped toward the door, but Nori's hand on her arm stopped her. She frowned at her mom.

"I want to say one thing and then we can go."

"Okay." Sofie's frown deepened.

"Give him a chance. He's a good man, and I think you could be happy here."

Her expression cleared, and she nodded. "I think so too."

Nori smiled, and she held up her arm. "Come on. Your groom is waiting."

Sofie chuckled and took her arm. They left the room and headed downstairs to the living room where Knox and their family waited with a judge Brady Archer's brother Sebastian knew. Knox had mentioned the situation to Brady, who called Seb, who then called in a favor. Sofie was glad. The idea of going to the courthouse to get married felt so impersonal.

They'd opted for no music, since their only guests were family. Nori and Silas. Olive. Knox's sister, Alice, and his dad, Greg. So, when Sofie stepped around the corner into the living room, she heard Knox's sharp intake of breath. Sofie knew how he felt. She felt like someone had punched her in the gut and stolen all her air. He looked magnificent in his light gray suit and tie. That longish blonde hair flowed to one side in a sleek wave. Since they'd been in Colorado, he hadn't shaved, but for the occasion, he'd trimmed his reddish gold beard. He looked like he'd just stepped off the cover of a GQ magazine.

I'm going to be married to him. Sofie's lady parts woke up and did a little dance. She forced her gaze off him and onto Olive in an effort to calm herself. There would be no wedding night for them, no matter how much she wanted a repeat and more of that kiss in the snow two days ago.

Nori led her through the room to Knox's side in front of the fireplace. Judge Lisa Kennedy stood with her back to the fireplace, smiling as Sofie approached.

With a squeeze of her hand, Nori let go and took her place next to Silas, who held Olive.

"Are we ready?" Judge Kennedy asked.

Sofie nodded, glancing at Knox, who had his eyes locked on her.

"Yes." His deep voice was sure.

"Take each other's hands."

Knox reached for her hands. It was then she felt the fine tremor running through him, belying his outwardly confident appearance. Some of her nerves disappeared, knowing she wasn't the only one who was apprehensive about the commitment they would soon make.

"Normally, I would do my, 'dearly beloved, we're gathered here today' speech, but seeing as there are only five guests, we're going to skip it and jump right in, if that's all right?"

Knox and Sofie nodded.

Sofie forced her heart to slow. She didn't know about Knox, but she didn't want to stand here waiting any longer than necessary.

The judge smiled. "Okay. Knox, repeat after me. I, Knox Alexander Duvall, take thee Sofia Grace Brannon McAllister to be my wife."

Knox's deep voice repeated the words. In his eyes, Sofie could see he meant every word. This man would be her fiercest protector and most tender friend through all their ups and downs. Emotion swelled in her chest, and she took a steady breath. She was still scared they were rushing into something as a knee-jerk reaction, but a little less so now. Hearing him pledge himself to her—and mean it—calmed her fears. She wasn't sure how she got so lucky, but she thanked God for sending her this man.

It was Sofie's turn to repeat her vows. She tried to inject the same feeling of sureness as Knox, hearing only a slight wobble in her voice, but that was more from overwhelming gratefulness than anything else. As she pledged herself to Knox, she vowed to herself to be a wife he could be proud of. One who loved and valued herself and put that into their relationship. She vowed not to be the wife who only lived to serve her husband as she'd done with Lance. Sofie knew now if she had valued herself, she'd have left Lance long before he nearly killed her.

The judge asked Silas for the wedding rings. He laid the simple gold bands in her Bible.

"These rings represent the bond between a husband and wife. They might take some dings and lose a little of their luster, but when cared for, they'll last unbroken the rest of your days. Knox, please take Sofie's ring and place it on her finger."

He picked up the band and slid the cool metal onto her hand, then repeated the judge's words. Sofie did the same, then blew out a slow breath, only to suck one in again at her next words.

"By the power vested in me by the state of Colorado, I pronounce you husband and wife. You may kiss your bride."

Butterflies erupted in Sofie's belly. Knox's fingers tightened around hers, and he drew her into his body, wrapping an arm around her waist. She brought a hand up to settle against his jaw as she stared at him. He held her gaze a moment longer, then closed his eyes and dipped his head. Sweet pleasure erupted along Sofie's nerve-endings as their lips touched. The touch was fleeting, but the feeling lingered as they parted. She opened her eyes to see his icy blue ones watching her with an emotion she couldn't decipher.

Clapping drew her attention, and they turned to look at the others.

"I present to you, Mr. and Mrs. Knox Duvall."

Silas let out a loud whistle at the judge's proclamation. Greg let out a whoop, while Olive, Alice, and Nori all clapped louder. Sofie giggled at their antics. It might have been last minute and only had five attendees, but she much preferred this wedding to her first.

∾

Knox leaned against the doorjamb of Olive's room as Sofie finished reading the girl a bedtime story. Olive's eyelids drooped until she could barely keep them open. Sofie finished the book and laid it on the nightstand. She tucked the covers around the girl and smoothed her dark hair back, kissing her forehead.

"Goodnight, sweetie."

"Night, Mommy." She started to snuggle into her blankets, then sat up and held out her arms to Knox. "Hug?"

He stepped into the room and moved to her bedside, dropping down to fold the small girl into his arms. His heart swelled with love for the little sprite. This love was uncomplicated, and he embraced it. Whatever happened with Sofie, he would always be there for Olive. "Goodnight, Olive. We'll see you in the morning."

She yawned and sagged. "Okay." He laid her back on the bed and adjusted her blankets.

Standing, he patted her covered arm, then motioned Sofie out of the room. She twitched the blanket into a better position and followed him into the hall.

"Come here." He took her hand. "I want to show you something."

With a curious frown, she let him lead her down the hall to his bedroom.

"What are we doing?"

He glanced back with a smile. "Trust me?"

She nodded. "Of course."

He pulled her into the room and pushed her down onto the trunk at the foot of his bed. "Wait here." When she nodded again, he let go of her hand and went into his closet, retrieving the ring box from his safe, then returned to her side to sit down next to her. He held up the small box. "I wanted to give this to you today before the wedding, but, well, I wanted to do it when we were alone." The wait had been a bit agonizing, but this was something only for them. He wanted Sofie to know what she meant to him without having to spell it out and make her uncomfortable with words neither of them were ready to share.

So, he waited. Until Alice went home, and his dad, then Nori and Silas retired to their rooms, and Olive went to bed. Now he had her undivided attention.

Her eyes widened. "Knox—"

He waved a hand. "Let me explain before you say anything."

She rolled her lips in and nodded.

"This was my mother's. Dad brought it with him and offered it to me to give to you." He flipped the lid open and showed her what was inside. Nestled on the creamy satin was a round cut diamond engagement ring surrounded by smaller diamonds.

Sofie gasped and covered her mouth. Her eyes flew to his.

"I want you to have it."

"Knox, no, I can't."

"You can." He took her left hand and held it, his thumb

toying with the wedding ring on her finger. "For one thing, you need an engagement ring. We don't have time to go buy one, and I know you can resize this one if it doesn't fit. Second, I don't plan on ever marrying again whether you and I stay married or not. And third, I can't think of any woman my mom would see as more deserving of it than you." He glanced down at their hands, toying with her wedding band again before looking up. "She would have loved you. And Olive. Mostly for who you are, but also because you make me smile."

Sofie touched his face with her free hand, holding his gaze. "You are the sweetest, kindest man I've ever met. Everyone— your sister, Daisy, Asa, even Silas—have all told me you're this surly touch-me-not, but I don't see it."

"Because I'm not with you. You're different."

She shook her head. "I don't know why, but I'm glad you think so."

A small smile tugged a corner of his mouth. "So, will you wear this ring?"

She drew in a shaky breath and nodded. "Yes. I'd be honored."

His smile bloomed and a weight lifted from his shoulders. He took the ring from its box and slid it onto her hand. "There. And it's a perfect fit." The ring sat on her finger like it was made for her.

She smiled. "Thank you." She leaned in and pressed a kiss to his cheek.

Knox closed his eyes, inhaling her scent. His blood pressure spiked, so he pictured shoveling out horse stalls, trying to get control of himself before he grabbed her and kissed her senseless. Their kisses the other day and this afternoon had cracked opened the floodgates. Desire pressed against them, threatening to burst free.

He opened his eyes to see her hovering close. Her gaze darted to his mouth. The gate cracked a little wider. "Sofie.

Don't look at me like that. I'm hanging on by a thread here."

"Me too," she whispered.

It was the tortured note to her voice that did him in. It was too much like what he felt. He framed her face in his hands and pressed his mouth to hers with a groan.

Her sharp intake of breath parted her lips, and he took full advantage, sweeping inside to taste her. The flavor of the coffee she drank earlier lingered, along with the chocolate from the wedding cake Alice surprised them with. He gathered her into his larger frame, enjoying the feel of her in his arms.

She shifted, turning into him, and he pulled her onto his lap, thrusting a hand into her dark hair to hold her in place. Her hand tunneled under his collar to grip the muscles on the top of his shoulder. He gripped her hip, his thumb sneaking under the hem of her sweater to touch the bare skin on her waist. Her thigh bumped the ridge behind his fly. It took all of Knox's self-control to pull back and not press for more, but he knew pushing forward would harm their relationship more than help it. He wasn't in this for a quick roll in the sheets. If and when they ended up in bed, it would be because they decided to make this work.

He gentled the kiss and lifted his head. She glanced up at him through her lashes.

"We should go to bed." His cheeks colored. "Separately. I meant separately."

She giggled, dispelling the tension. "Yeah." Her eyes wandered around the room, and she frowned. "What are we going to do about our sleeping arrangements, anyway? We haven't talked about it."

Knox shrugged. "I assumed we'd leave them the same."

"I'm not sure we should."

His eyes widened a fraction. "Sofie, I'm not sure that's such a good idea. We might be married in the eyes of God and the law, but we both know it's too soon for us to go down that road."

Her face flushed, and she cleared her throat. "I know. What I meant was we should sleep in the same room. Maybe one of us on an air mattress." She frowned. "No, that wouldn't work. We'd have to blow it up and deflate it every day." She looked at the bed. "I suppose we could share the bed. It's plenty big."

Knox's frown intensified. "What are you talking about? Why would we change things up?"

"Because of the interviews and home visits we have to do for the custody dispute. More than likely, the social worker will want a tour of the house. It would be easy enough to make it look like we're living in the same room, but the one thing we can't count on is Olive. She could let it slip that we don't sleep together."

Understanding dawned, and his expression cleared. "Gotcha. Yeah, okay. Um, do you want to stay in here tonight, and we can move all your clothes into my closet and dresser tomorrow? I can sleep on the floor."

"I'm not kicking you out of your bed." She stood. "We're both adults. We can share."

His muscles tensed, and his pants grew tight again. He blinked up at her, then stood. Her eyes widened and her nostrils flared as he invaded her space. "But will we sleep?"

She swallowed hard. "Eventually."

Knox bit back a moan and closed his eyes, fighting the urge to kiss her again. He took a deep breath and shoved the desire hardening his muscles and other parts of his anatomy back into the box deep in his brain, then opened his eyes. "I'm going to take a shower."

"Okay. I will too. By myself, I mean."

He nodded. She continued to stand there, staring at him. He cocked an eyebrow. "Sofie?"

"Hmm?"

"Were you going to go shower?"

"Yes."

He tilted his head and glanced past her at the door.

"Oh, right. This isn't my room." She spun on her heel. "Sorry."

He watched her go, his eyes lingering on her legs and butt as she hurried away. When she disappeared through the door, he let loose the groan stuck in his throat and rubbed his hands over his face. If he got even an hour of sleep tonight, it would be a miracle. With a sigh, he went to his dresser and grabbed some clean underwear and a t-shirt. As an afterthought, he took out a pair of athletic shorts. He normally slept in his boxer-briefs or nothing, but that wasn't an option for the foreseeable future.

Heading into the en suite, he ran through his nightly routine. Once he was clean and his teeth brushed, he donned his clothes and exited the bathroom. Sofie hadn't returned yet, so he turned off the light and climbed into bed, hoping the darkness would help with the awkwardness that was sure to hit once she came to bed.

The floorboard outside his bedroom door creaked minutes later, then he heard the whisper of her feet on the hardwood floor as she crossed the room. The bed dipped as she got in. Knox stared at the wall, his back to her, and pretended to be asleep. He could feel the heat from her body under the blankets. Awareness crept in, making his muscles tense. He squeezed his eyes closed and willed himself to relax. Dawn couldn't come soon enough.

Nineteen

Stifling a yawn brought on by the lack of sleep the last two nights, Sofie glanced at the clock, then out the window at the barn. Knox needed to hurry and get back here with Olive. The social worker would be here any moment.

No sooner did she have that thought than she heard a car coming up the drive.

"Dammit. What's taking so long?" She growled and spun away from the window to find her shoes. After stuffing her feet in a pair of tennis shoes, she hurried to the front door to greet the woman coming up the steps.

Sofie stood just out of view of the window in the door-frame and smoothed her sweaty palms down her jeans. The woman knocked, and she took a deep breath before stepping forward to answer the door.

The fortyish woman with light brown hair smiled as Sofie pulled the door open.

"Hello. I'm Brianna Tarlson with Boone County Social Services."

Sofie smiled and held out a hand. "Sofie McAllister—

sorry, Duvall. Still getting used to that." She shook the woman's hand. "Come in, please."

Ms. Tarlson stepped inside, her eyes roving over the entryway.

"Can I take your coat?"

"Oh, yes." The woman shrugged out of the deep green peacoat and handed it to Sofie, who hung it in the hall closet. "Where's your husband? I thought this was a meeting with both of you."

"It is. He took Olive out to the barn for a riding lesson. They must have lost track of time."

"Well, then, how about you give me a tour while we wait?"

"Sure. Um, this is the living room." She pointed to their right. "Through the door over there is a short hallway that leads to an office and a half-bath." She gestured to a door at the rear of the living room, then turned around, pointing to her left. "The dining room is through there and the kitchen beyond that. All the bedrooms are upstairs." She motioned to the staircase in front of them.

"May I see your kitchen, then the bedrooms?" She wrinkled her nose and smiled. "I know it seems like I'm being nosy, but it's all just procedure. We all want what's best for the child."

Sofie bit her tongue. If that were truly the case, Lance wouldn't have gotten this far. "Of course. Follow me." She headed into the dining room to the kitchen. Ms. Tarlson stepped into the room and glanced around.

"This is very nice. You must like cooking in here."

"I do, actually." The kitchen had an amazing stove. "Knox cooks, too."

"Really? Is he any good?"

Sofie smiled. "Yes. He's been living alone for a long time and doesn't have a housekeeper. He learned to cook so he didn't have to live on frozen dinners."

"So you share dinner duties?"

"Somewhat. I've been making most of the meals, but he's cooked a couple times since we moved in. The first week or so, he was playing catch-up from being away. By that point, we just sort of fell into a routine where I made dinner."

"Yes, you came back with him from your cousin's wedding in Montana, correct?"

Sofie nodded.

"I'm going to be very forthright with you, Mrs. Duvall."

"Sofie, please."

The woman nodded, giving her a smile. "Call me Bree. I'll be honest, when I read this case file, it was like a comedy of errors. I'm interested to see the actual dynamics between you, your daughter, and your new husband. Tell me, why so fast?"

"Why did we get engaged so fast?"

"And married, yes."

"Things between us just clicked. Olive took an instant liking to him. He was friendly and courteous to her, but not in a fake way like some adults are when kids try to talk to them."

Bree smiled. "I know what you mean."

"He was a natural with her. And watching him interact with her and take a genuine interest in what she had to say, it was hard not to like him." A soft smile spread over Sofie's face. "He's so kind and gentle. It's what makes him so good with horses. I'm sure if you ask around town, people will tell you he's standoffish, but it's just because he's shy. He's very smart and was bullied as a teenager because of it, and it's made him wary of getting too close to people. Once you get to know him, there isn't a better soul on the planet."

"He got close to you, though. And fast."

Sofie shrugged. "I don't know what to tell you. We just fit."

Bree stared at her a moment, a thoughtful look on her face, then she nodded. "Okay. Take me upstairs now."

"Sure." Sofie turned and headed from the room, blowing out a breath. She hoped she'd just cleared the first hurdle.

They made their way upstairs, and she showed Bree around before leading her back to the living room. The house was still quiet.

"You know, I'm not sure what the holdup is. He knew what time you were coming. Maybe I should go check."

"I'll come along. I'd like to see the barn." She grinned. "I'm a bit of a horse nut, and there isn't a better horse trainer around than Knox Duvall."

Sofie smiled, opening the closet to get Bree's coat. She handed it to the woman. "Are you from here?"

Bree nodded and followed her through the dining room to the kitchen. "Born and raised. I've met Knox a couple of times, but always just in passing. I love horses, but I'm a townie. I don't get much chance to ride. The extent of my experience is the horseback riding excursions my husband takes me on when we go on vacation."

"I'd never been on a horse before I moved to Colorado except for some pony rides as a kid. I still don't ride much, but it's more a lack of time and the weather than anything else." She stepped into the mudroom and took her coat off the peg, shrugging into it, then opened the back door.

"If I lived out here, I'd make time, weather be damned."

The two women trudged across the yard through the snow to the barn. Sofie wished she'd put on her boots. At least Bree had on dress boots. Her feet were probably still cold, but at least there wasn't snow inside her shoes. Sofie could feel the wetness seeping through her socks.

They reached the barn, and she pulled open the door, letting them inside. She led Bree down the aisle to the arena at the far end. She could hear Olive's laughter before they ever reached the doorway.

"She sounds like she's having fun."

Sofie nodded. "If she's on a horse, I can guarantee she is." She passed through the door and stopped at the fence, watching with wide eyes as Knox stood in the middle of the arena, while Sofie rode at a trot around him.

"Pull him into a walk," Knox instructed.

Olive pulled up on the reins and the horse slowed. She looked up with a grin and spotted her mother.

"Mommy! Did you see?"

Knox spun around, his eyes going wide as he took in the woman next to Sofie.

Sofie held his gaze for a moment, then smiled at Olive. "I did. You did great."

The girl rode the horse over to the fence, Knox walking at her side.

"I'm so sorry. I lost track of time. We were working on rein control and she was doing great."

"I can see that."

He blew out a breath and looked at the social worker. "Hi. Knox Duvall." He held out a hand.

The woman smiled. "Brianna Tarlson. Bree, please."

"Let me get this horse taken care of, and we can chat. It won't take long."

Bree nodded.

He glanced up at Olive. "Lesson's over, sweetie. That woman Mommy and I told you about is here."

Olive peered around her horse's head. "Hi! I'm Olive. What's your name?"

Bree grinned. "Bree. It's nice to meet you, Olive."

"You too." In one fluid motion, Olive leaned forward, then spun and slithered over the side of the horse, her little feet sending up puffs of dirt as she landed on the arena floor.

Sofie stared at her, open-mouthed. When did she learn that move?

Knox grinned at her. "We've been practicing."

"Obviously."

He took the horse's reins and turned for the gate leading into the barn. Olive hurried to his side.

"Do you mind if we walk with you, Mr. Duvall?" Bree asked.

He glanced back. "Not at all. We can talk while I work. And it's Knox."

Sofie motioned Bree to follow her around the fence to the door they came through, meeting Knox and Olive as they came through the gate.

"So, what's this horse's name?"

"Harvard," Olive said.

Bree cocked an eyebrow. "Like the college?"

Knox chuckled. "No. Like the mountain peak."

"Oh."

"All the horses are named after Colorado peaks," Sofie explained.

"Oh, that's interesting."

The loud whinny of a horse filled the barn, followed by a man's shout and a loud bang. Thirty feet ahead, Sofie saw the wall shake, then a stall door fly open. Before any of them could react, the horse turned and bolted toward them. Sofie's heart stopped as she realized Olive was directly in the horse's path.

"Olive!"

Knox jumped in front of them, grabbing the girl. The horse clipped his shoulder as it ran past, knocking him into a stall. He slammed his head on the wall and dropped to the floor.

"Oh my God! Knox!" Sofie ran to him, landing on her knees by his side.

He moaned and tried to sit up, but his arm gave out and he hit the floor, eyes closed. Olive sat up under his other arm. "Knox?" She patted his cheek. "Wake up."

Sofie pulled her away, checking her over quickly. "Are you all right, honey?"

Olive nodded. "I'm okay. Knox is hurt, Mommy!"

"I know, sweetie. Can you stand with Ms. Tarlson while I help him?" She nudged her daughter toward the social worker.

"Come here, Olive." Bree reached out and pulled the girl to her.

Sofie turned her attention to Knox. He was trying to sit up again. Blood flowed from a wound on his head near his hairline. "Knox. Hey. Look at me." She helped him sit up, then cradled his face. His eyes were unfocused.

"Boss?" A man stumbled down the aisle, holding his side.

Sofie glanced at him. It was one of the hands. "Tanner, are you okay?"

"I'll be all right. Damn horse went nuts on me while I was brushing him down." He crouched next to her. "Looks like Knox took the brunt of things."

"He saved Olive."

Tanner's eyes widened.

"Call for help. I think he has a concussion. At the very least, he's going to need some stitches."

Banging sounded from the arena along with more loud whinnies.

"And catch that horse."

Tanner stood. "Yes, ma'am."

"I'll call for help," Bree said. "You go get the horse before he hurts himself or anyone else." She withdrew her phone from her pocket while holding Olive close and dialed.

Knox moaned and pushed himself into a better position, leaning back against the wall. "Damn."

Sofie turned to him. His eyes were clearing. "You took quite the hit. Do you know what day it is?"

"Um." He pinched the bridge of his nose, closing his eyes. "Monday."

That was good; he was right. "Do you remember what happened?"

"Yeah. Capitol busted out of his stall and ran me over." He froze, then sat forward with a wince. "Olive. Is she okay?" His eyes landed on the girl. "Are you okay, baby?"

The girl nodded, her eyes watery.

"Thank God." He sagged. "There's a first aid kit in the office." He lifted an arm to point behind her.

Sofie got up and ran to retrieve it, finding it on the wall just inside the door. She pulled it open as she returned to his side, finding some thick gauze pads.

"An ambulance is on its way," Bree said, crouching down next to Sofie to help.

He waved a hand. "I'm fine. Call them back and tell them not to come."

Sofie frowned and ripped open two of the gauze packets. "You're bleeding quite nicely. You need stitches."

"Which doesn't require an ambulance. You can drive me to the emergency room. Hell, Dad can stitch me up. He's done it before."

"He went to Billings with Mom and Silas, remember?" Their parents, knowing they had their custodial interview today, went shopping in Billings together.

"Right." He blinked hard. "Damn, my head hurts."

Sofie pressed the gauze to the wound on his head. He hissed.

"Sorry." She pulled the gauze away to get a better look at the gash. It definitely needed stitches. With his confusion, she had a feeling they might want to CT his head too. And he was right. They didn't need to wait for an ambulance. She glanced at Bree. "Could you call them back and tell them I'm just going to drive him? It'll be faster and less of a hassle for all of us."

The woman nodded. "Of course." She turned to her phone.

Sofie found a roll of gauze in the kit and two fresh gauze pads. While Bree called emergency services back, she wrapped his head to staunch the flow of blood and used a wipe to clean some of it off his face.

"There. That should hold you until we get to the hospital." She stood and looked at the social worker. "I'm sorry our interview got interrupted."

Bree rose, holding Olive. "Nonsense. For one thing, it was an accident. And for another, I think I've seen all I need to see."

Sofie frowned. "You did?"

She nodded. "Yes. It's obvious the two of you care deeply for each other, and that Knox is a wonderful stepfather to Olive. When we entered the barn, it was evident Olive was comfortable with him. And he had little regard for himself when that horse escaped. He dove at her without a thought. Then, even dazed, his first concern was her well-being. I'll be writing up my report to send to the judge in Chicago as soon as I get back to my office. As far as I'm concerned, the two of you are fantastic parents, and Olive is one very lucky little girl."

Surprise made Sofie's eyes round. "But what about the allegations my ex-husband made? That I'm unfit."

Bree's face pulled, and she rolled her eyes, turning to the child in her arms. "Olive? Can you answer a couple of questions for me?"

The girl nodded.

"Do you get regular meals? Breakfast, lunch, and dinner?"
"Yes."
"Are your clothes clean?"
"No."
Bree frowned. "No?"

Olive shook her head. "I got dirt all over me."

The woman laughed. "You are very right. Let me rephrase that. When you get dressed in the morning, do you put on fresh, clean clothes?"

Olive nodded.

"When you're sick, does your mommy take care of you and take you to the doctor if you need to go?"

"Yes." Olive's face soured. "They give me yucky medicine, and I don't like it."

"None of us do, but it makes us feel better, doesn't it?"

"I guess."

"Do you feel safe with your mommy and Knox?"

"Yes. I like living here. Knox is nice. He helps me learn stuff, and he makes Mommy smile."

Bree gave a quick nod. "Good." She looked at Sofie. "You pass. Now get your husband to the hospital."

A bright smile lit Sofie's face, despite the situation. "Okay, then. Can Olive stay with you while I go get the car? I'm not sure he can walk back to the house."

"It's just a bump, Sofie. I'm okay."

She scoffed. "And if you collapse because you're dizzy on the way to the garage, I'll never be able to drag you the rest of the way."

He leaned his head against the wall. "Fair point." He pointed to the door. "Go."

Sofie looked at Bree.

She nodded. "We'll be fine. You go ahead."

"Thank you." Sofie sprinted out of the barn for the house. The snow slowed her down, but she didn't have to go that far. She hurried up the steps and through the back door. Inside, she snatched her purse from the counter, then grabbed a set of keys from the hook and went into the garage, climbing into Knox's truck. After adjusting the seat, she opened the garage door and backed out, bumping up the drive to the barn.

As she pulled up, the man-door opened and Knox emerged with Bree and Olive. Sofie got out of the truck and opened the passenger door for him while Bree buckled Olive into her car seat.

"Do you want me to lock up?" Bree asked. "I need to get my purse from inside."

"Oh." Sofie glanced at the house. "You can, yes. There's a house key on this set."

"Okay, I will." She stepped back and shut the door. "I hope everything checks out okay. Let me know if there's anything I can do."

Emotion clogged Sofie's throat. "Your report is plenty. Thank you."

Bree smiled. "Not a problem. I wish all the families I interviewed were like yours." She tipped her head to the truck. "Go get his head patched up."

Sofie smiled. "Thank you." She ran around the front of the vehicle and hopped inside. After fastening her seatbelt, she put the truck in drive and pulled away.

∿

Head pounding, Knox crawled into bed. It had been awhile since he had his bell rung like that. Thankfully, all his tests checked out fine. He had a concussion, and it took five stitches to close his head wound, but he escaped anything more serious. Now he just wanted to rest.

The sound of Sofie's bare feet shuffling over the floor had him opening his eyes. She was dressed for bed.

"Olive go to sleep all right?" The girl hardly left his side once they got home. They'd curled up on the couch with the dogs, and she watched a movie while Sofie made dinner and Knox rested his eyes.

"Yeah." She got in next to him. "I had to read her two stories. She wanted to sleep with us."

He closed his eyes again. "You could have let her."

Sofie giggled. "You've never slept with her. She kicks like a mule."

He smiled, not looking at her. "That probably wouldn't be the best thing for me tonight."

"It's never good on any night. I've taken some serious shots to the kidney in the past. She was like that even before she was born. At least now I can get away from her."

An image of Sofie pregnant with his child entered his mind. Something visceral shifted inside him. He hoped one day they could make that a reality.

"Do you want more children?" he asked.

"If the timing is right, sure."

He opened his eyes and turned his head to look at her. "Let me know when you feel like that's the case."

Her eyes grew round. Pink tinged her cheeks.

Knox reached over and touched her face with one finger. "You're so beautiful. If I felt better, I'd kiss you goodnight."

She frowned. "Do you need some more pain medicine?"

A smile tipped his lips. "No. Theoretically, I could still kiss you, but it wouldn't be the way I really want to, which would just leave me aching and frustrated. I'm already frustrated, so I'd rather not make it worse."

Her gaze roved over his face. "I'm sorry."

"For what?"

She touched the bandage on his forehead. "That you got hurt."

"I'd do it all over again. I'm just glad she didn't get a scratch on her."

"Me too. And I never thanked you for saving her."

"You don't need to thank me. I will always protect her. Even if you and I divorce and we go our separate ways, a phone call is all it will take for me to be there whenever she needs me."

Tears welled in Sofie's eyes.

"Hey." He wiped away one that fell with his thumb. "Why the tears?"

"I don't know what I did to deserve you. Or why you want to be anywhere near me and my toxic relationship with my ex."

"Simple explanation—because something about you speaks to me. You're a rare jewel, Sofie. One that you can search for years to find, and once you finally get your hands on it, you don't ever want to let it go. You want to protect it and keep it safe. That's all I want to do with you. And with Olive." He smiled. "She's the best stepdaughter any man could ask for. Even with what you've been through with her father, you've done amazing with her." He swiped more tears from her face, then despite what he said about kissing her, he leaned in to press his mouth to hers in a soft caress.

With a quiet groan, he pulled back. "Come here." He tugged her into his chest and tucked her against his side. "Let's get some rest." Her small hand rested on his abdomen as she got comfortable. Knox sighed in contentment and laid his hand over hers. His finger brushed the cool metal of her wedding rings.

He still found it hard to believe she was his wife. That he was married. He'd given up hope of ever meeting a woman who would put up with him. He wasn't hard to live with; he just had a tendency to be aloof. But he wasn't that way with her. Or with Olive. They brought out the best in him. Whatever happened in the next few weeks, he would be forever thankful to Sofie for showing him this side of himself.

TWENTY

"Alice, that pie is a work of art." Sofie's eyes widened as her sister-in-law removed the cover from the apple pie she brought for Thanksgiving. She'd seen pictures of sculpted pies online, but never in person. Alice's was magnificent. The crust looked like a blooming apple blossom.

"Thanks." Alice smiled. "It wasn't hard."

Sofie snorted. "For you. I can move metal, but sculpting like that?" She shook her head. "More power to you."

Alice giggled and set the pie on the counter with the other goodies.

Greg stepped up to peer over her shoulder. "What did you bring, kiddo?"

"Apple pie." Alice glanced up at her dad with a smile.

"Your mom's recipe?"

Alice nodded.

"You made two, right? Because I'll eat all that myself."

She rolled her eyes. "You sound like Knox. But yes, I did, actually. I knew the two of you would devour a whole one."

Sofie's eyes widened. "Knox and Greg will eat a whole pie together?"

"Every year," Alice said. "It's the only time they do it."

"Good to know."

"Nori said the turkey needs carved." Knox entered the kitchen, pushing up the sleeves on his long-sleeved henley.

Sofie bit her lip and looked away from the muscles flexing in his arms and bulging beneath the waffled fabric. Her eyes met Alice's, and the other woman grinned. Sofie's cheeks heated. She shouldn't be embarrassed about ogling Knox. They were married, after all. But they all knew it was in name only. She and Knox might have talked about where their relationship was going, but they weren't there yet.

Clearing her throat, Sofie picked up a carving knife and meat fork, holding them out to her husband. "Here. The bird's on the washer in the mudroom to keep Jai's nose out of it." She pointed to the doorway at the back of the kitchen and the baby gate blocking it. Jai sat on the floor next to it, tongue lolling from the side of his mouth as he stared into the mudroom.

Knox laughed. "You could have let him outside. It's warm enough."

"It's also muddy. You know he'll roll around if he's left out there too long." She narrowed her eyes at the dog. "Why can't you behave like Maeve?" The other dog was in the living room, letting Olive dress her up in Nori's scarves. Jai ignored her.

"He does behave. So long as we're watching." Knox grinned.

"Exactly."

He laughed again, then sent Jai into the living room, so they could finish prepping the food. Greg stepped over the gate to get the turkey, then set it on the counter. Knox held out the carving utensils.

"No." Greg shook his head. "I think since your wife cooked it, you should be the one to carve it."

Knox looked back at Sofie. A soft blush stole over her cheeks. She was still getting used to that word. *Wife*. She'd been a wife before, but it didn't take her long to wish she wasn't. With Knox, she found herself hoping she always would be.

He smiled at her, then stepped in front of the turkey. "Okay, bird. Let's see what you've got."

~

Laughter rang around the table as they sat in the dining room, eating. Sofie was already stuffed and hadn't even had dessert. She leaned back and rested a hand on her belly. Alice sat back next to her.

"I'm stuffed."

"Agreed," Alice said.

"I still want some of your pie, though. I'm afraid I won't get any if I don't go now." She glanced at Knox, who'd already devoured one piece. So had Greg.

Alice waved a hand. "I hid the other one."

A laugh bubbled from Sofie's lips. "That was probably smart."

"For sure." Alice giggled. She glanced around the table. "Your mom is really nice. I didn't get to spend much time with her while we were at the Stone Creek. She was always running around, doing some task. It's been fun getting to know her."

Sofie smiled as she looked at her mom across the table. Nori lounged in her chair, talking to Silas. "Yeah, she's great. I don't know what I would have done this past year without her."

"You moved in with her in Chicago, right?"

Sofie nodded. "I should have done it sooner. Should have listened to her."

Alice shrugged. "Maybe. But everything happens for a

reason. Daisy's spat with her brothers led her to Montana and Asa, which led Nori to Silas, and you to Knox. You wouldn't be here if you didn't move in with her, would you?"

Sofie tipped her head. "I guess not. I also wouldn't be contemplating opening my own store, either."

Alice's face lit up. "You mentioned that before. I'm still interested in contributing."

"I'd love that. Your pottery would sell well." Alice's pieces were stunning. She didn't know why the woman didn't do more with it.

"If you're serious, I should probably start now, making a few extra pieces every week, or it'll be slim pickings."

"You could, yes. I don't know when I'll actually open, though, if I do decide to go ahead with it. It depends on what happens with Lance." And with Knox. She might end up staying in Colorado and opening the store in Silver Gap.

Her eyes went to her mother again. She wasn't sure how she felt about being so far away from her only family. Her mom had been her lifeline for a long time. Even though she no longer needed the extra support, they remained close.

Knox's laugh turned her head. His attention was on his dad. The two men had delved into conversation while carving the turkey and it continued once they sat down. Having Greg here showed Sofie why Knox was so good with Olive; he had a wonderful role model. Her husband had a deep, abiding respect for Greg. Which, having gotten to know the older man in the last few days, Sofie knew was born from a lifetime of love and acceptance. It was obvious from the way Greg spoke to his son that he respected Knox's intelligence and accepted his need to live life his own way. Knox already gave Olive the same love and acceptance. She knew he'd do the same to any child of his own.

The image of a tiny baby with his icy blue eyes crossed her mind. A fierce desire to meet that child struck Sofie in the gut.

She slammed the brakes on that line of thinking. She had to get through the custody battle for Olive first, before she could even entertain thoughts like those. Before she made any decisions about her future at all.

She sighed as she looked around the table. Regardless of how things turned out, right now, she felt like she belonged here. In this family. A family that included her mom *and* Knox. She just didn't know how she could make that an everyday reality.

TWENTY-ONE

The ring of her cellphone brought Sofie's head up from her task. She pushed her magnifying glasses up and set down the necklace she was working on for a client back in Chicago. Picking up the phone, a glance at the caller ID revealed her attorney's name. Her pulse kicked up several notches, and she slid her thumb over the screen to answer. "Hello?"

"Sofie, hi. It's Adam Vancroft. I have some news for you."

"Oh?" It had been ten days since Brianna Tarlson submitted her report to the judge in Chicago. Ten excruciating days during which Sofie had prayed she wouldn't have to pack a bag to take her daughter back to Chicago for a visit with her father.

"Do you remember how I said I was looking into Lance's fiancée?"

"Yes."

"Well, I haven't been idle while we waited for the social worker here to file her report on your ex and Ms. Mayweather. I dug deeper into her personal and professional life."

"Okay." Her heart rate ratcheted even higher. "What did you find out?"

"A whole host of things. Like, she's addicted to cocaine, and Lance is her dealer."

"What?" The starch left Sofie's body, and she sagged on her stool. Only the table in front of her kept her from falling to the floor. That was news to her. She'd never seen Lance do drugs.

"I hired a private investigator—a very, very good one—and we have photographic and video evidence of Lance supplying his fiancée with the drug, then of her using it. It's my belief that he's blackmailing her into playing the part of his fiancée to help himself look good for the court. Also, my P.I. followed Lance to work and witnessed him supplying drugs to several of his co-workers, including his boss. I've turned all the evidence over to the police department. A warrant is being drafted for his arrest as we speak."

Sofie tried to make her lungs work, but all the air in them was frozen. "What—what does that mean for the custody suit?"

"My team has filed to have the suit dismissed in light of the new charges against Mr. McAllister. I also filed a motion to have the judge removed from the case. My P.I. discovered that he plays golf with Lance's boss."

"Um, who decides if the judge is removed?"

"The evidence is presented to him first. If he refuses to recuse himself, it goes to a judicial review board. Charges are pending against your ex-husband's boss for drugs as well, so I have a feeling Judge Barnett will want to distance himself from everyone involved."

Sofie stared at the half-finished piece of jewelry in front of her, her mind swirling. "Adam—I don't know what to say."

"You don't have to say anything. It's cases like these that got me into this line of work. I promise you, I will do everything in my power to have him prosecuted to the full extent of the law. He will not see the outside of a jail cell for a very long time. Hopefully, not until after Olive turns eighteen and you no longer have to worry about him demanding a role in her life. At that point, it will be up to her to decide."

Tears flowed over her eyelids and down her face. "Thank you."

"You're very welcome, Sofie. I will call you with updates as I get them. Go enjoy that daughter of yours."

"I will."

He said goodbye and hung up. Sofie stared at the phone, numb. It was over. Olive was safe. They could go back to living their lives. Go back to Montana, if that's what they wanted.

Her eyes caught on the rings on her finger. But going back to the Stone Creek meant leaving Knox. The thought of that made her want to cry—and not in a good way. Things were good between them. Thanksgiving had been wonderful. She felt like she belonged. But would that all end now that there was no need for them to stay married? They'd talked a bit about making their marriage work, but what did that look like? Did she stay here and they worked on it while they lived together? Did she move out of his bedroom and back into the guest room she started in? Did she go back to Montana and they dated long distance? Adam's news hadn't made her life any less complicated. It just changed the complications.

Sofie sighed and pushed away from the table. Whatever the case, this wasn't news she could keep from Knox. He was as vested in Olive's future as she was, and she would never keep something like this from him to avoid a difficult conversation about their relationship.

Hurrying out of the spare room Knox set up for her to craft her jewelry in, Sofie ducked into Olive's room where the girl played with her dolls in the giant dollhouse Knox made for her while he'd been unable to ride this past week.

"Hey, sweetie. We need to go out to the barn. I need to talk to Knox."

"Can I ride Harvard?"

"Maybe later. You can pet him, though, okay?"

"Okay." The girl put down her doll and stood, following her mother from the room.

After donning their winter gear, they traipsed across the frozen yard to the barn. All the snow had melted, then the water froze, so now the dead grass crunched under their feet and tiny, icy puddles sat in the dips in the yard.

Sofie pulled open the man-door on the horse barn and let them inside. She unwound her scarf from her neck and tucked her gloves into her pockets, glancing in stalls as they walked further into the building, looking for Knox. They found him in the arena, working with Capitol, the horse that nearly trampled him and Olive.

He saw them approach the fence and reined the horse in, riding up to them. "Hey. What are you guys doing out here?"

"Can I talk to you for a minute?"

He frowned, taking in the seriousness on her face, then nodded. "Sure." He dismounted and tied Capitol to the rail.

"I told Olive she could pet Harvard while we talked."

"Let's get her a stool to stand on. I don't want her inside the stall alone."

Knox ducked through rail, and they followed him back into the barn. He found a stepladder in the supply room and set it up in front of Harvard's stall, then lifted the girl onto it.

"We'll be just down the hall, okay? You stay right here." Sofie touched Olive's arm.

"Okay, Mommy." Olive reached up to pet Harvard's muzzle as the horse lifted his head over the bottom stall door to blow air over her face, making her giggle.

Sofie smiled, then turned to Knox, motioning for him to follow her down the aisle out of the girl's earshot.

"Is everything okay?" He took her hand as they stopped about ten yards from Harvard's stall.

She took a steadying breath and offered him a shaky smile. "I heard from Adam Vancroft."

Knox's posture stiffened. "And?"

"And he hired a private investigator who turned up some very interesting things about Lance and Carissa. Apparently, he's started dealing drugs and Carissa's one of his clients. Along with several people at his work, including his boss. Adam turned all the evidence the P.I. gathered over to the district attorney's office. They're issuing a warrant for his arrest."

His eyes widened with every word. "Are you serious? What about the custody case?"

"He filed a motion to dismiss it. And to get it moved to a different courtroom. The P.I. also discovered the judge is friends with Lance's boss." A smile bloomed on her face. Regardless of what it meant for them, Olive was safe from Lance. "It's over."

Knox let out a whoop and wrapped his hands around her waist, lifting her in the air and twirling her around. Sofie clutched his shoulders and laughed. He drew her into his body and pressed a kiss to her lips. She curled her hands into his shirt and kissed him back. Heat suffused her from head to toe.

He broke away, clearing his throat, desire glittering in his eyes for a moment longer before he smiled, dispelling it. "We need to celebrate."

She unfurled her hands, but didn't push out of his arms. "Okay. How?"

He glanced up at the rafters as he thought. "How about I take you all to the Heartwood for dinner? We'll let Olive stuff herself with chicken tenders and an ice cream sundae from the dessert menu."

Sofie laughed, joy filling her. "That sounds nice."

He leaned in and kissed her again. Pulling back, he stroked her cheek, smiling. "Come on. Let's go celebrate."

~

Noise swelled as Knox tugged open the door to The Heartwood Grill. He stood back and let Sofie and Olive enter, then stepped in behind them. The hostess greeted them and led them to a table near the windows. She took their drink orders, then left. Knox glanced around the room and did his best to ignore the crowd. He didn't like people looking at him, even though he knew none of them were whispering about the freak who read weird books for fun.

"This place is amazing."

Sofie's soft voice drew him out of his head, and he smiled at her. "Yeah. Tara's an amazing photographer." His friend Brady's sister owned the restaurant. In a previous life, she was a photojournalist and brought her love of photography into the artwork in her restaurant.

"If she can cook half as well as she can take pictures, I'm going to love the food."

"Oh, she can."

"Knox. I thought that was you."

A voice intruded on their conversation. He turned to see Macy walking up to them, a broad smile on her face.

He smiled back. "Hey. What are you doing out here? Isn't it a little early for you to be home yet?" Macy's café, Peppy Brewster, didn't close until six o'clock. It was only a little after five.

"My assistant manager is covering for me. One of the kids Lee and Jenny fosters has a birthday today. We're having a small party. I came to pick up the pulled pork Tara made for it. She had a bit of a kitchen emergency, so I told her I'd stop on my way home, so they could eat without waiting on her."

He frowned. "Is everything okay?" Nothing seemed amiss in the busy restaurant.

"Yeah. One of her refrigerators blew a cooling element. She had to come up with a new plan last minute for the special tonight." Macy's gaze moved to Sofie and Olive. "Family dinner?"

"Yes. We got some good news, so we're celebrating," Knox said.

"Mommy said I can have ice cream!" Olive interrupted before he could say more.

Macy grinned. "She did? Wow. You make sure you eat a good dinner, though, first. So you don't get a tummy ache."

Olive nodded, her expression serious. "I'm gonna have chicken tenders."

"Good choice. Tara makes great chicken tenders." Her eyes moved to Sofie, the smile on her face encompassing the other woman. "It's good to see you again. Sorry I didn't make it out to offer my help when bonehead here took a header into the wall. I've been so busy lately. Brady said you all were good, though."

Sofie let out a soft giggle. "Yeah, it only kept him down a couple of days. I thought I would have to put a padlock on the tack room, though. He went a little nuts not being able to ride."

Knox frowned at her. "I did not."

She rolled her eyes. "I saw you staring longingly at the tack room door more than once. And you didn't wait even an hour after the doctor cleared you to ride. We got home and you took off for the barn and were on Blanca in minutes."

He felt his cheeks heat. "I had a lot of work to catch up on."

"On a fully trained horse?"

He shrugged. She was right, but he wasn't about to admit that out loud.

Macy laughed. "She's good for you."

He agreed with that too.

"I should get going. It was nice to see you. We need to all get together and play cards or something."

Knox nodded. "You guys tell us when. Your schedule is a little fuller than ours."

"I will." She waggled her fingers at them. "See you guys later." Spinning on her heel, her long legs ate up the ground as she walked away.

He watched her go for a moment, then turned back to Sofie and Olive. As his gaze traveled over the restaurant, he paused on a man near the fireplace. His muscles stiffened, and he squinted, trying to get a better look.

The man looked up and saw Knox staring at him. Recognition punched him in the gut. It was Nate Connors, the man who stopped at the ranch to inquire about horse training. Knox stood.

"Knox?"

He glanced at Sofie. "Stay here. Don't leave the booth."

"What—"

He walked away before she could ask more questions, weaving through the tables toward the fireplace. The man had disappeared. "Dammit." The noisy restaurant swallowed his harsh whisper. He glanced around, not seeing the man, then headed toward the exit. The guy didn't just vanish into thin air.

Steps quickening, he burst through the doors, but saw no one. He ran through the aisles of parked cars, looking through windshields, but all the cars were empty.

"Where the hell did he go?" Eyes roving the drive and the

open fields beyond the restaurant toward the ranch buildings, he walked back inside.

Sofie frowned at him as he sat down. She cast a glance at Olive, who was lost in her coloring, then back at him. "What the hell was that all about?"

"Did Vancroft mention anything about the guy who stopped to ask about horse training? Wasn't he going to look into him?"

Understanding dawned on her face. "You saw him?"

He nodded.

"Adam didn't say anything. I can call him."

"When we get home, yes. He shouldn't still be in the area if he was just passing through. If he has business that brought him back here again, I want to know what it is. There's something off about that guy."

A young woman in the restaurant's uniform and a waist apron appeared beside their table to take their orders. Knox glanced over the menu quickly while Sofie ordered for herself and Olive, then asked for a steak and baked potato. The euphoria he felt earlier was gone. Something wasn't right.

TWENTY-TWO

Sofie tucked the blanket around Olive's shoulders and leaned in to kiss the girl's forehead. It had taken forever for her to wind down tonight thanks to the ice cream at dinner. But she was finally asleep. Sighing, she stood and walked out of the room, going downstairs to find Knox. They'd texted Adam Vancroft when they got home, asking if they could call later. Later had arrived.

She found him in his office. He had his laptop open and stared at something on the screen, but glanced up when she entered.

"That took awhile." He closed the lid on the computer.

"Yeah." Sofie sank into the chair opposite his desk. "No more ice cream sundaes that late in the day."

He smiled. "She deserved it. We all did."

"Yes, well, I will definitely reserve it for very special occasions. Hyper Olive is tiring. You ready to call Adam?"

His smile faded. "Yeah." He picked up his phone and called the lawyer.

Adam picked up on the second ring. "Vancroft."

"Adam, it's Knox and Sofie."

"You said in your text you had something you needed to talk to me about?"

"Yes. Did you dig up anything on Nate Connors?" Knox asked. "The man who came to me to ask if I'd train his horses?"

"Actually, no. I couldn't find a man by that name in Nevada who owned the kind of spread you indicated he had."

Knox cursed. "I was afraid of that. I saw him again tonight. We went to dinner, and he was at the restaurant."

"You're sure?" Adam's tone changed.

"Yes. He disappeared before I could catch up to him."

Adam blew out a breath. "Damn. I was hoping he was just somewhere the police didn't know about, but now I'm not so sure."

Sofie glanced at Knox and was met with a frown similar to her own. She looked at the phone. "What are you talking about? Hoping who was somewhere else?"

"Lance. The police haven't picked him up yet. I was going to call you in the morning if they didn't find him. Now I'm wondering if he's returned to Colorado and if your horse friend is working with him."

Sofie eye's widened as Knox cursed again.

"You said you saw this guy at a restaurant?"

"Yes," Knox said. "Why?"

"Does the place have surveillance cameras? If we can pull an image, I might be able to track him down and find out who he really is."

Knox sat forward. "Okay. I'll call Tara and have her get a screen grab from her system. Keep us updated on Lance's whereabouts."

"I will. You keep your eyes open out there. We know he's well-connected. Someone could have tipped him off and he skipped town. He doesn't have anything to lose by coming out there."

"We'll stay alert. Thanks for the info." Knox's thumb hovered over the button to end the call.

"Yep. Get me that image. Talk to you soon."

Knox ended the call and set the phone down. Sofie stared at him, eyes wide. The magnitude of what Adam told them hit her, and she stood up and walked to the window, a hand covering her mouth.

"Sofie." Knox came up behind her and put his hands on her shoulders.

She swallowed hard. Why couldn't it be over? She just wanted her baby to be safe.

Turning her in his arms, Knox tucked her face into his chest. "Hey. It's okay. He won't get to her. I won't let him."

Sofie buried her nose in his shirt and took a deep breath, letting his scent ground her.

He tipped her head up to look into her eyes. "We need to talk."

She frowned and sniffed. "About what?"

"Getting you and Olive out of town."

She straightened. "And go where? I don't have any place left to go. You were it."

He took a breath and glanced away for a moment. "I have a friend from college—"

She pushed out of his arms. "No. I'm not running anymore. He's pushed me out of two homes. I'm done. This ends here." Thoughts swarmed Sofie's mind, but one stood out above all others. She was done running. From Lance. From herself. From life. She wanted to live. To love, and to be loved. She was slowly losing her mind living in Knox's house, sleeping in his bed, but not being his wife in every way.

He nodded, oblivious to her inner debate. "Okay, so we take a stand. If he shows up, we deal with it. You and Olive just need to be careful moving about outside the house until we know if he's coming here for sure, or whether he fled some-where to escape prosecution."

"That's my plan, but I had more in mind than simply watching my back when I said I'm done running." She grasped his face. "I meant I'm home. Here. With you."

His eyes grew round, and he covered her hands with his. "Sofie?"

"You said you wanted to see where this could go when the custody dispute was over. That you didn't want me to leave." She shook her head. "I know it's not over yet, but I don't want to leave either."

Those icy blue eyes held hers. "Are you sure? Your mom—"

"Will understand." Her mouth tipped. "She moved halfway across the country for love. I only moved two states away."

One blonde eyebrow winged upward. "Love?"

Butterflies started in her stomach, but she couldn't hold on to the words any longer. "Love, Knox. I love you."

A bright smile lit his face. "I love you too. I have almost from the moment I met you." He moved his hands to hold her head, then leaned in to kiss her.

Sofie rose on her toes to press closer, moaning softly as he pushed past her lips to taste her. She let go of his face to run her hands into his hair, gripping the silky strands. He groaned and dropped his hands to circle her waist and lift her against him. All the desire they'd held on a leash for so long pushed free.

With a growl, he tore his mouth away from hers. Arousal turned his eyes a steely blue. He traced her cheekbone with his thumb. "I want to take you upstairs and make you my wife in every sense of the word." He swallowed hard. "But even though you say you love me, we still haven't known each other long."

She laid a finger over his lips. "I know all I need to know. You're kind and gentle. Honorable and steadfast. You're my friend and my husband. I want to know you. All of you." She replaced her finger with her mouth.

He kissed her back, then broke off the kiss to swing her up into his arms and carry her from the room. Sofie giggled as he ran up the stairs two at a time to their room.

"In a rush?"

"Only to spend the rest of my life with you."

She giggled again. "That was corny, but sweet."

He grinned and kicked the door closed as he crossed the threshold. "You bring out the poet in me." His mouth crashed onto hers as he laid her on the bed.

Sofie held on as he plundered her mouth, sending her arousal to a fevered pitch. Suddenly, they both wore too many clothes for her liking. She squirmed against him, trying to get her hands between them so she could unbutton his shirt. The closeness of their bodies hindered her efforts, but she managed to find his waist. She pulled his shirt free of his pants and thrust her hands beneath the fabric. Silky smooth skin over rock-hard steel met her fingertips as she traced the muscles of his back.

He gasped and sat up. "I'm going to have to tie you up, so this lasts longer than a few minutes."

She offered him a frisky smile. "Promises, promises."

Growling, he dipped his head and nipped at her neck, laving the pulse point and making her eyes roll up into her head. Moisture flooded her core and she squirmed for a new reason.

Knox pulled back, a devilish smile on his handsome face. "I intend to make you writhe six ways from Sunday before I put either of us out of our misery."

"Again with the promises."

His hands skimmed up the outside of her thighs and over

her hipbones to delve under her shirt. His rough hands slid over the soft skin of her abdomen, sending shards of heat through her. Sofie's nipples tightened and her inner muscles clenched. Her breath caught in her throat as he went higher, blowing out on a puff as he closed his fingers over her breasts. She dug her nails into his thighs on either side of her hips and prayed for mercy.

"I want to see you. Taste you." Knox withdrew his hands and pulled her sweater up in one swift move.

Sofie raised her arms and let him pull it over her head, then reached behind her back to open the clasp on her bra. His pupils dilated, and he froze as he took in her bare torso.

The pause didn't last long. Once he looked his fill, he laid her back and latched onto her breast, suckling at it while he tugged at the tip of the other one. Every pull, every lick and nip, sent shafts of need through Sofie's body until she felt like jelly. She tried to touch him and return the favor, but he wouldn't let her do more than stroke a hand over his fully clothed form.

When she thought she'd go mad from his mouth alone, he sat back and reached for the button on her jeans. Sofie covered it with her hand. "Uh-uh. Lose the shirt."

He arched a brow and stared at her. She narrowed her eyes and laid an arm over her bare breasts.

"Oh, you fight dirty." He quickly undid the buttons on his shirt and shrugged the fabric off his shoulders. "Happy?"

"Very." She sat up and grabbed the back of his neck, pressing her mouth to his, moaning as his hand covered her breast again. He used the other to unbutton her pants and drag the zipper down. She moaned as his fingers delved beneath her underwear to slide through her drenched folds.

"I want to take this slow, but you're making it damn hard." Knox rested his forehead against hers, his breath coming in short pants.

A jerky nod was her answer as he continued to stroke her heated flesh. When he withdrew his fingers, she whimpered.

"Shh. I need better access." Moving again, he scooted down her legs to pull off her jeans and panties.

A moment of shyness hit Sofie. No man had seen her naked since Lance, and he'd always told her she wasn't anything special. But the look on Knox's face bolstered her confidence. Slack-jawed, his icy blue eyes held a look of reverence as he stared at her. After a moment, he shook that off and a sexy determination filled his gaze. He dropped down on his hands to hover above her.

"I'm going to lick every inch of you, then do it again."

Before she could utter a word, he kissed her, his tongue tangling with hers briefly before he set off to blaze a hot trail down her body, doing exactly what he promised. He paid particular attention to her breasts and navel on his way south. By the time he reached her core, she was ready to come apart.

He wedged his shoulders between her knees, exposing her to his gaze. Sofie tensed. Lance never went down on her. The one time he did, she didn't enjoy it. He'd been much too rough, which she knew now was probably to discourage her from wanting it in the future.

Knox leaned in, his warm breath puffing against her sensitive flesh, pushing out thoughts of her ex. When he drew his tongue along the seam of her womanhood, all coherent thought fled. Her hips lifted, and she whimpered with need.

"Feel good?" She felt him smile against her.

A strangled groan was her only reply. He chuckled and licked her again, then sucked the bud of nerves at the top of her mound into his mouth, raking it with his teeth. She let out an airy howl as her world shattered around her.

Knox didn't give her a chance to recover. He pulled away only to replace his mouth with his hand, pushing two fingers into her channel and stroking her inner walls as his thumb swirled through her folds.

Sofie's eyes crossed as they rolled back into her head from the pleasure he created. It had never been like this. Even in the early days with Lance, when things were good. She didn't know it could feel this amazing.

Her climax broke again, sending her to what felt like a new plane of existence. One where only pleasure existed and she was nothing more than stardust, twinkling in the glow of the sun.

A heavy but comforting weight settled over her.

"Sofie?" Knox's low voice sounded in her ear.

"Hmm?" She wanted to open her eyes, but couldn't make her eyelids cooperate.

"You ready for round three?"

He rocked his hips, and she felt his erection at her entrance. Moisture pooled again and her body registered the hard planes and angles pressed against it. She shifted, rubbing the tips of her breasts through the smattering of dark blonde hair on his chest. She bit her lip as her mind came down out of the clouds, then nodded. "Yes. I want you inside me."

With a moan, he probed her entrance. "Open your eyes."

She looked at him.

He held her gaze as he pushed deeper, stealing the air from her lungs. The sound of their soft pants and quiet sighs filled the bedroom as he brought them both into the clouds with slow strokes.

When Sofie broke again, it was like a waterfall crashing down from a thousand-foot drop, sluicing over her in waves and dragging her under. She rode the swirling waters until she popped up for air. Knox rested on top of her, his chest heaving as he rode out his own wave of bliss.

She made one arm move and brought a hand up to stroke through his blonde locks. Her heart swelled with love for this beautiful man and his equally beautiful soul. She didn't know what she did to deserve him, but she was thankful for him. He'd shown her what love was supposed to be. And he was her friend. Her best friend.

A smile quirked her lips. She had her very own romance book hero. Sofie couldn't stop the giggle that slid free at that thought.

He lifted his head to look at her. "What's so funny?"

"Nothing. I was just thinking I feel like I'm living in a romance novel. Woman, down and out on her luck, trying to put her life back together, befriends a handsome rancher, who whisks her away from her violent ex-husband to his idyllic ranch. There, she and her little girl fall in love with the blonde Adonis and live happily ever after."

He smiled and shifted, so the bulk of his weight was no longer directly on her. "It feels a bit like a fairytale to me too. Handsome loner rescues the beautiful damsel in distress, and they fall in love." He shook his head. "When I met you, all I wanted was to get to know you. I'd hoped that by the time I left Asa's after the wedding, we would be at a point where you'd let me call you from time to time. I can't say I'm sorry that your ex-husband's plans messed with mine. We wouldn't be where we are now, and I don't just mean naked in bed." He stroked her face, staring into her eyes. "I love you, Sofie Duvall. Never doubt that."

Those pesky tears came back. She blinked them away and nodded. "I know you do. I love you too."

He pulled himself up to press a soft but potent kiss to her lips, then tucked her into his side. A yawn stole over Sofie's face as the euphoria and adrenaline from their lovemaking waned. Her eyelids drooped, and she gave in to the sleep tugging at the edges of her mind, content.

TWENTY-THREE

Sofie hummed as she chopped vegetables for dinner. She'd decided to make vegetable soup and fresh bread. The day was a frigid one and the warm soup would be a nice counter to the temps outside. She knew Knox would appreciate the hot food after being in the barn all day. The building and the arena were temperature controlled, but it was still chilly enough he had to wear a coat and gloves while he worked.

Her phone trilled from its spot on the counter, and she glanced at it. Adam Vancroft's name flashed over the screen. Heart rate kicking up, she set her knife down, then wiped her hands on a towel and answered it.

"Hello?"

"Hi Sofie, it's Adam. I have some news. The police caught Carissa Mayweather. Faced with all the charges against her, she offered up some information on Lance. It seems we were right; he was blackmailing her into being his fiancée. It's also how he got his job back. His boss is still being tightlipped, but Ms. Mayweather didn't have any problem sharing what she knew about their relationship."

"Okay. Do they have any idea where he went?"

"From what we've learned, I hate to say it, but I think he's coming after Olive before disappearing for good. Ms. Mayweather indicated he'd been stashing money from his drug trade in preparation for running. He knew gaining full custody of your daughter would be a long-shot, but he only needed to get partial custody, then disappear when it was his turn with her."

Sofie's knees softened, and she sat down at the dinette before she ended up on the floor.

"Have you alerted the local authorities?"

"Um, yes. When we got the image from the restaurant cameras, we informed the local sheriff. He's a family friend of Knox's and the restaurant owner's older brother."

"Good. Relay what I just told you and keep an eye out. My P.I. hasn't been able to track down Mr. Connors."

"Okay, thank you for the information."

There was a brief pause. "Sofie... I know this is a shock, but try not to fret too much? With the local authorities there involved, there are eyes watching for him. They'll catch him."

She let out an inelegant snort. "In town, maybe. We live in the sticks. There's nothing out here but us. I'll make sure all the ranch hands know to watch for strangers and anything unusual, though. Thank you again for the warning."

"You're welcome. Please call me if you need anything else."

"I will. You've been a fantastic help. You've saved my daughter."

"No, you did that by bringing the right people into your life. Smart choices are what win cases. I'll talk to you soon."

A weak smile crossed Sofie's face. "Okay. Bye." He echoed her salutation, and she hung up.

Lance is coming here.

The thought hit her like a truck, sending air sawing in and out of her lungs. Her phone clattered onto the granite countertop, and she gripped the edge, making her knuckles turn white.

Breathe, Sofie!

She sucked in a deep breath as her subconscious screamed in her head. This wasn't anything she didn't already suspect.

Some of her panic cleared, and she peeled her fingers from the counter to pick up her phone again. She needed to talk to Knox.

Finding his name on her contact list, she called him, praying he had the ringer on and could answer.

It rang in her ear several times, each one sending her anxiety higher. "Pick up the phone, honey. Pick up, pick up, pick up." She repeated her mantra as she listened to the trill.

"Hey, hon."

Thank God! "Adam called. We have a problem."

Knox cursed, then sighed. "What happened?"

"Lance for sure skipped town. The police caught Carissa. She said his plan is to come here and kidnap Olive, then go into hiding."

"Damn. Okay. You two stay inside. I'll call Seb and let him know what's going on. I'll let the hands know too. I know you're worried, but I promise I'll keep her safe, Sofie."

Emotion choked her. "I know," she whispered. And she did. He loved Olive as much as she did. He would do everything he could to protect her. It was part of why she loved him.

"Keep your phone on you. Even in the bathroom. Call me if anything weird happens."

"I will. Be careful. I don't know what he'll do to get to her. You're in his way, so he might try to take you out." The thought was nearly crippling. She prayed Lance wouldn't hurt him. She couldn't lose Knox any more than she could lose Olive.

"I'll be careful. I love you."

"Love you too." The phone clicked in her ear as he hung up. She put it down and propped her elbows on the counter, resting her head in her hands. Tears formed in her eyes, but she refused to let them fall. Sniffling, she straightened and dashed the moisture from her eyes. The only thing crying did was give her a headache. She needed a plan. And weapons.

Mind spinning, she catalogued what she had in the kitchen and moved the knife block closer to the door into the dining room. The scissors were in the drawer near the mudroom. She wanted things evenly spaced, so she never had far to go to grab something to defend herself and Olive.

Sofie left the kitchen and repeated the process in every room of the house, looking for anything sharp or heavy and making subtle adjustments. The only room she didn't touch was Olive's, because the girl was in there playing. She would go through it later.

It briefly crossed her mind to put together a bag and just take off with Olive right now. But she couldn't. Not only did she mean it when she told Knox she wasn't running anymore, she couldn't leave him. No, if she left, he was coming with her.

Satisfied she could at least attempt to fight off Lance or any lackey he sent no matter what room they were in, she peeked in on Olive.

"Everybody saddle up. We need to round up the cows before it snows." Olive's voice was pitched low. "Make sure to bring the cookies," she said, voice pitched a little higher. "Yes, we can't forget the cookies." Her voice dropped again.

Sofie smothered a giggle. Olive glanced over.

"Hi, Mommy."

"Hi, sweetie. What are you playing?"

"Roundup."

"And they need cookies?"

"Everybody needs cookies."

Sofie walked into the room and picked Olive up from amongst her toys. "I agree. How about we get some?"

"Yay! Can I have milk, too?"

"Of course." Smiling, she left Olive's room and headed downstairs. The back door opened as they returned to the kitchen, admitting Knox.

"Knox! You're just in time. Mommy said we could have cookies!"

He used the bootjack to remove his boots, then crossed the threshold from the mudroom. "Before dinner?"

Sofie shrugged. "Why not?"

He walked over and dropped a kiss on her lips, then turned to Olive. "What kind of cookies are we having?"

The little girl shrugged, and she held up her hands. "She just said cookies."

Sofie chuckled. "Chocolate chip."

"Oh, those are the best kind." Knox held up a hand to the side of his mouth and stage whispered to Olive.

Olive giggled.

With a smile, Sofie set Olive down, then took the milk from the fridge and poured three glasses. She brought over the container of cookies she baked yesterday, and they sat down at the dinette to munch on their snack. When she finished, Olive asked to go play again, leaving Knox and Sofie alone.

Knox walked up and trapped her against the counter as she put Olive's glass in the sink. "I see you moved the knife block."

She huffed. Of course he would notice. The man missed nothing. He wasn't like some geniuses where they were oblivious to their surroundings. No, he noticed everything. "I wanted to be prepared. In case he makes it inside. I want to be able to defend us."

"Do you know how to shoot a gun?"

Nerves made her palms itch. "No." Her parents didn't own any. Lance did, but he'd kept them from her.

"We need to fix that." He took her hand and pulled her toward the dining room, yelling for Olive as he entered the foyer.

"What? Right now?"

"No time like the present. You need to learn, anyway. We have some large predators, so you should know how to use a shotgun at the very least."

The soft thud of Olive's feet on the stairs heralded her arrival.

"Go put your boots and coat on. I'm going to give you and your mom a lesson on guns."

The girl's eyes widened, and she stared at him.

"It's for your safety. It occurred to me you don't know how to handle one. I just want you to be safe, okay?"

Olive nodded.

"Good. Go do as I asked, please."

She ran past them to the kitchen.

"Go put your stuff on. I'm going to run up and get a couple of my guns from the safe."

Sofie nodded, her eyes still rounder than normal. He noticed and leaned in to press a kiss to her mouth.

"Relax. This is why we're practicing. So you're comfortable using them. They're not scary once you know what you're doing."

She drew in a shaky breath to steady herself. He was right. She was sure she'd feel much better about them once she had more knowledge.

"Dig some bottles and cans from the recycling, too."

"Okay." Sofie followed Olive into the mudroom while Knox ran upstairs to the gun safe in the closet. By the time he returned, they were ready to go outside, and she had a grocery sack full of things to shoot.

He handed her a shotgun and rifle to hold and laid a small duffle on the washer while he put his boots and coat on.

"Everyone ready?"

Sofie and Olive nodded, and he led them outside, making sure the dogs stayed inside. At the barn, he loaded two bales of straw onto the back of a utility vehicle, then they climbed inside and bumped over the frozen ground, past the stand of pine trees near the house. While he stacked the bales and set targets on top, Sofie and Olive huddled on the UTV seat to keep warm. She hoped she could pull the trigger. Her hands were already feeling the frigid temps. She tugged Olive's hat down further on her head and checked that her scarf was tucked securely around her neck. It was cold.

"Okay. Let's do this and go back inside where it's warm. I didn't think this through." A corner of his mouth lifted. "Olive, come here."

The girl scrabbled off Sofie's lap to stand next to Knox. He crouched to show her the pistol he held. "First things first. You are never to touch any of the guns we own, or anyone else's without permission from an adult, understand?"

Olive nodded.

"Not even if you're curious or one of your friends wants to see them. They're off-limits unless your mother or I give you express permission."

"Okay."

"Good. Now, I'm going to show you how they work, so you can understand how to keep yourself and everyone else safe if you do handle one."

She nodded again. Sofie paid attention, even though he spoke to Olive. She didn't want him to have to repeat himself.

"First, never point it at anyone you don't intend to shoot and keep your finger off the trigger until you're ready to fire. Even if you're aiming at someone, don't put your finger on the trigger until you're ready to shoot. It keeps you from accidentally discharging the weapon." He pushed a button and the bottom slid out of the gun.

Sofie leaned in as he showed them the different parts of the weapon and how to make sure it was unloaded and safe.

"Bottom line," he said as he stood. "Always treat a gun like it's loaded, even when you know it's not." He popped the magazine free again and loaded three bullets into it, then put it back in the gun. "Sofie, come here. Olive, sit in the UTV."

She took a deep breath and stood next to him. He moved slightly behind her and handed her the gun once Olive was safely in the vehicle. He folded her hands around the weapon and helped her take the correct stance. She kept her finger along the slide like he said and aimed the weapon at the cans on the straw bales.

"Look down the sights at one of the cans and fire. It'll kick a bit, but I started you with a small caliber, so it won't be too bad."

Sofie nodded. She inhaled another deep breath and tipped her head, putting an empty green bean can in the sights, then touched the trigger and squeezed. The can pinged and flew off the bale.

"Whoa." She lowered her arms and glanced at Knox, a smile forming on her face. "I hit it!"

Eyes wide, he smiled back. "You sure did. Damn. I'm impressed. Okay, try again. You've got two shots left."

Sofie smiled and turned back to the cans, raising her arms. She repeated what she did with the first shot and knocked two more cans off.

"You're a natural. Let's try a bigger caliber and see how you do." He loaded a different handgun and gave it to her.

Sofie braced herself for a bigger kick and pulled the trigger. The shot went wide as the gun bucked in her grip. She readjusted for the kickback and shot a bottle and another can.

"Well, I guess I won't have to worry about you missing if you need to use a gun."

She sucked her lip in, a frown forming as she thought about what that meant. If she ever pointed a gun at someone, she needed to be prepared for that person to die. Because he was right. She wouldn't miss.

They spent another fifteen minutes going over the rifle and the shotgun. Sofie didn't like the shotgun. It kicked like a mule and she was sure to have a bruise on her shoulder later. The rifle wasn't bad, though. She wished the weather was warmer. She wouldn't mind setting up some targets further away and practicing.

"Okay, I think that's enough for now. Do you feel somewhat comfortable with the weapons?" Knox stowed the pistols in the duffel and put it in the UTV with the rifle and shotgun.

"Yes." Sofie got in the vehicle and pulled Olive onto her lap. "You were right. I just needed to understand them."

He gave a short nod and got in the driver's seat. "I hope you never need to use one." He started the UTV and drove them back to the house.

Once inside, Sofie went back to making dinner, feeling a little better about Lance being in the wind and possibly on his way here now that they'd put everyone on notice and had organized some semblance of defense. She would still stick close to home with Olive for the foreseeable future, but she didn't feel quite so unprepared. Part of her hoped he showed up and tried something. She wasn't the mouse he married anymore. She wouldn't hesitate to protect her daughter.

Twenty-Four

K nox blinked slowly as something drew him from sleep. He paused, listening. Then, hearing nothing, rolled over. Sighing as he got comfortable again, the orange glow coming through the window registered. His eyes popped open, and he sat up.

"What the hell?" He got out of bed and crossed to the window to look out. "Fuck!" He ran back to the bed. "Sofie! Baby, wake up. The barn's on fire."

She stirred, rubbing her eyes. "What? Did you say the barn's on fire?"

"Yes. Call the fire department and get dressed." He was already hopping into a pair of jeans. Finding a shirt and socks, he ran from the room. Jai followed him, and he saw Maeve poke her head out of Olive's room. Hurrying downstairs to the mudroom, he sat on the bench and tugged on his socks and boots, then shrugged into his shirt and coat. The dogs pushed past him as he opened the door, taking off into the yard. Knox let them go and ran toward the burning barn.

As he neared, the horses' screams sounded over the roar of

the flames. He saw Tanner and his other live-in ranch hand, Buck, running for the barn.

"Get the doors open and let out as many as you can," he yelled. "We'll worry about rounding them up later." The men hopped the fence at the corral and ran for the back doors as Knox went through the man-door.

Smoke and heat enveloped him as he entered. Coughing and eyes stinging, he ran for the main door, lifting the bar holding it shut and pushed them open. The dogs stood outside, barking furiously. He drew his shirt over his face as he turned and ran down the aisle, letting the horses out as he moved deeper into the structure. From what he could tell, only part of the barn was on fire. It looked like it was coming from their hay stores, but if they didn't contain it, it would spread to the rest of the building. His first priority, though, was releasing the horses.

Hooves clattered on the concrete floor and loud whinnies competed with the roar of the flames as he, Tanner, and Buck opened stall after stall. The roof creaked as the fire reached the rafters, weakening it.

"We need to get out of here before the roof caves in," Buck said.

"Go." Knox pushed him toward the door and gestured for Tanner to follow. "I'll get the last two."

The men took off. Knox ran in the opposite direction to let Capitol and Blanca out of their stalls. Blanca took off for the door as soon as he opened her stall, but Capitol was panicking. Through the smoke, Knox could see the blood trickling down the horse's leg as he pounded on the stall door and screamed in terror. The wood on the bottom door was splintered from his actions. He was amazed the horse hadn't broken the latch and let himself out.

Flipping open the bar, Knox pulled the door open and flattened himself against the wall to get out of the terrified animal's path. Capitol let out another loud whinny and ran out of the barn.

Coughing hard enough to rattle his ribs, Knox followed him out into the cold night air.

"Boss!"

He looked left to see Tanner and Buck. "Did we get them all?" he managed between coughs.

"I think so," Tanner said. "How did it catch fire?"

Knox shook his head. "Don't know. You two see anything strange?"

They shook their heads.

"No. We were asleep. I heard banging and looked out to see the fire," Buck said.

"Okay. Let's start rounding up the horses. Tanner, get the ones that ran into the corral to the back section of it. Buck, help me catch the ones running free."

He and Buck ran for the outbuilding adjacent to the barn, where they kept extra supplies and the ATVs. They were going to need the speed to catch some of the horses.

They loaded rope onto the ATVs and rolled up the door. As they pulled out of the building, the first trucks bearing help drove up to the house. He started his ATV and headed for the one he recognized as Brady's. Jai and Maeve ran up, circling them, then ran back into the dark.

"Declan's on the truck responding to the call. He called us. What do you need?" Brady ran around the front of the truck to meet him as Knox came to a stop. Macy looked down from the passenger seat.

"I've got horses running free. And Tanner's in the corral, trying to herd the ones that ran out the back of the barn into the rear of the corral."

"I'll go help him."

"What do you need me to do?" Macy asked.

"Sofie's inside. Maybe keep her company for now?"

Two more trucks pulled up and the rest of the Archer men, minus Declan, spilled out. Knox gave them each instructions, and they split up. By the time the first firetruck pulled into the yard, they'd taken a head count of his horses and caught two of the eight running free.

Knox tried not to watch as the firefighters attacked the fire. He'd gotten a good enough look before the firetrucks arrived to know the building was a total loss. Once he caught the last of his horses, he needed to find places to house them all. He knew Brady would take some, but the Archers didn't have room for all his horses.

Shaking off the fatigue that came with the thought of his to-do list, he concentrated on catching the rest of his herd. The other stuff would come in time.

$\sim$

Worrying her lower lip, Sofie stared out the kitchen window at the fire as it consumed the barn. She could see Knox and the ranch hands, as well as Brady and the other Archer men, riding around, gathering up the loose horses. "I can't believe this." She glanced at Macy, who'd come with Brady. A thought occurred to her. "What are the chances this is accidental?"

Macy frowned. "What do you mean?"

"I know Knox told Brady about the things going on with my ex. Did Brady mention any of it to you?"

"Well, yeah. You think your ex-husband had something to do with the barn fire?"

"Maybe."

"But why?" She glanced at the window. "What would he gain by torching a horse barn?"

Sofie's eyes widened and swung toward the ceiling. "Olive."

"Huh?"

"It got Knox and the dogs out of the house. It got me downstairs. No one's paying attention to Olive's room." Fear sent goosebumps racing over her skin.

The women shared a look, then took off running for the stairs. Sofie felt the cool night air as soon as she hit the second story landing. "No. Olive!" She ran down the hall and threw Olive's door open. The lavender curtains floated in the breeze coming through the window. The bed was empty.

"Oh no," Macy whispered.

Sofie walked forward and picked up the purple unicorn sitting on the floor. Rage flooded her veins. When she found Lance, he had better hope there were witnesses around. She stalked to the window and peered out. Imprints from a ladder were visible in the frosty grass. So were two sets of footprints, both large, coming toward the house. But there was only one set going away from the structure.

She popped her head back and turned to Macy. "He's still in the house."

"What?"

Sofie pointed outside. "There's only one set of prints leading away, but there are two leading to the house. He's still here."

Macy spun and took two running steps to the closet and yanked the doors open. Nothing but clothes and shoes met them.

"We need to search the rest of the house." Macy turned back to her.

"We need weapons first. Come on." She scurried toward the door, leaving the unicorn on the bed, and ran down the hall to the master bedroom. A thud behind her made her spin.

"Hello, dear."

The blood drained from Sofie's face as she saw Lance standing in the hallway. He held the ball bat she'd stashed under Olive's bed, and Macy lay at his feet, blood trickling from the wound on her head.

"Where's Olive?" His arms were empty save the bat.

He opened the linen closet. Olive sat on the floor, her hands and feet bound and her mouth gagged. "I was just coming to find you when you ran upstairs. I have to say, I didn't think you'd put two and two together quite so fast."

"Yeah, well, we were expecting you to show up at some point."

He grimaced. "That attorney of yours is better than I imagined. It seems I underestimated your resources. I have to admit, I'm surprised by what you were willing to do to fight me for custody. Getting married? Moving way out here? It's like you're afraid of me." He smiled an evil smile. "Are you afraid?"

Her spine stiffened. "No."

His expression turned speculative as he regarded her. "No, I don't believe you are. You used to be. You still should be." His smile died, and he removed a revolver from beneath his coat. "Come here."

Sofie stayed where she was.

Anger bloomed on his face. He pointed the gun at Olive. "I said, come here."

Her eyes darted to her daughter. Tears swam in the girl's round green eyes as she stared back.

"Okay." Sofie held her hands out. "Don't hurt her. I'll do whatever you want."

He laughed. "You always did. Having a kid was the best thing we ever did. It kept you in line."

"Until you nearly killed me." She walked closer.

"Yes, I admit, I went a little far. Then. Now, it doesn't matter."

Before Sofie could react, he brought the gun up and

slammed it into the side of her head. She dropped to the floor next to Macy, dazed and her ears ringing.

"I should kill you for what you did. No one leaves me unless I say. You're mine! But I think a better punishment for you is knowing you couldn't keep your daughter away from me. For the rest of your life, you're going to wonder where she is. If she's still alive. What kind of life she's living." He yanked Olive from the closet. "It's what you deserve."

Sofie tried to get up, but her vision swam and her stomach rebelled. She dropped back to the floor, rolling onto her back.

"Say goodbye to Mommy, honey."

"No!" Sofie reached a hand up, her voice barely a whisper. "Olive. Please."

Olive's muffled screams faded as Lance carried her down the stairs. Adrenaline pushed some of the dizziness away, and Sofie was able to get to her hands and knees before blackness enveloped her.

TWENTY-FIVE

Sooty and exhausted, Knox and Brady let themselves into the house. There were still two horses missing—Capitol and Lincoln—and the firefighters were still mopping up hotspots, but for now, things were calm. They both needed some water, and Knox wanted to give Sofie an update.

He pushed the back door open and continued into the kitchen, not caring if he was traipsing mud all over. He'd clean it up later.

"Sofie?" He frowned as silence greeted him. Even if she and Macy were in the living room, he should hear them coming this way as they came to find out what was going on with the fire.

He glanced at Brady, who frowned.

"Where are they?" Brady asked.

"I don't know. Maybe they fell asleep." Knox walked out of the kitchen and headed for the living room. As he passed the stairs, a moan caught his attention. His head whipped around to look up at the second floor. "Did you hear that?"

"Yeah." Brady bounded up the stairs, Knox on his heels. "Jesus! Macy!"

"Dear God, Sofie?"

Both men landed on their knees next to their wives. Knox took Sofie's face in his hands and tapped her cheek. "Sofie, baby, wake up."

She moaned.

Macy groaned as Brady lifted her. Knox glanced over to see blood matting her hair and dripping off the side of her face as he picked her up. He turned back to Sofie.

"Honey, look at me."

Sofie moaned again, and her eyelids fluttered. Some of the confusion in her gaze cleared as she saw his face. "Olive?"

Dread punched Knox in the gut. He looked to Olive's room. The door stood open, and he could feel the cold air now. "Shit! Sof, did Lance do this? Did he take her?"

A sob ripped free from her chest. "Yes."

Knox and Brady shared a look.

"Let's get them some help, then start looking for Olive." Knox gathered Sofie into his arms.

Brady stood holding Macy and fled down the stairs. Knox followed. They ran to the firetrucks, yelling for help as they got close.

Declan, Macy's brother and the fire lieutenant on scene, turned at the sound of the shouts. His eyes went wide, and he ran toward them. "What happened?"

"Sofie's ex got into the house during the confusion. He knocked them out and took Olive."

"Jesus." He glanced around, frowning at the cold ground. "Put them in the back of the truck for now." He lifted his mic. "Stickley, Murphy, get back to the truck. We have two with head injuries." He paused as his men radioed an affirmative, then hurried around the side to get a medical bag and climb into the cab with the women. "Do you know what happened?"

Knox shook his head and scooted back to give Declan room. The man shone a light in his sister's eyes, then Sofie's.

"Both have good pupillary reactions, though Macy's are a bit sluggish." He held Sofie's head in his hands and probed at her wound. "Any idea how long you were unconscious?"

She moaned. "What time is it?"

Brady glanced at his watch and told her.

"It's been about thirty minutes." Tears welled in her eyes. "He's got Olive."

Knox ground his molars and took her hand. "I'm going to find her. I don't care what it takes."

With a weak nod, Sofie laid her head against the seat and closed her eyes.

Commotion outside heralded the arrival of Declan's men. Knox and Brady jumped out of the truck to give them some space.

"Where's Seb?" Knox asked, scanning the yard.

Brady's gaze followed his, then he pointed. "Over there."

Knox took off with his friend on his heels.

Seb looked up and cursed when he saw their faces. "What happened?"

"Lance took Olive. Macy and Sofie both have head injuries. They're in the firetruck with Declan. We need to find my daughter." The first note of desperation entered Knox's voice. He took a shaky breath and clenched his fists, willing his emotions back into their box.

At his statement, Seb's face hardened and he went into cop mode. The next few minutes were a blur as Seb organized a search and called in additional units to patrol the roads in the area. Knox tried not to go crazy standing around while others started looking for Lance and Olive.

Finally, he couldn't take it anymore. "Seb, give me something to do. I can't just stand around, waiting."

"Go with Sofie to the hospital."

"What?" He frowned. "No. I need to be out looking for Olive."

"They've got a decent head start, Knox. You need to let me mount a coordinated search. My deputies know what they're doing. The best thing you can do is stay with Sofie and offer her support. We've got their description. I even sent it to my colleagues at the FBI. My old partner said he'd put it on the wire. Lance won't get far with her."

Knox growled and thrust his hands into his hair. The rational part of his mind knew Seb was right, but not the emotional part. That part wanted to tear off into the night, find Lance, and rip his head off.

Brady put a hand on Knox's shoulder. "Seb will find her."

He blew out a breath. "I know." He looked at Seb. "The moment you know anything—"

"You'll be the first call I make."

With a curt nod, Knox turned, jogging to the firetruck, knowing Sofie needed him.

TWENTY-SIX

Muffled voices came through the closed door of Sofie's hospital room, but she ignored them as she stared out the window. The bleak sky matched her mood. It had been twelve hours since she woke up in the hallway. Twelve hours and still no word on Olive.

The door opened, and she turned her head, expecting to see the nurse or Knox. But it was neither.

"Only for you would I step foot back inside a hospital." Daisy smiled as she breezed through the door, Asa behind her.

Sofie's eyes widened, and she sat up, wincing as the movement made her head pound. "What are you two doing here?"

"Seriously? My favorite little cousin gets kidnapped and you have to ask that question?" Daisy walked over and perched in the chair next to the bed. She took Sofie's hand. "How are you doing?"

"I'm fine."

Daisy arched an eyebrow.

"I am. I'm pissed."

"Good. It'll keep you sharp." Asa pulled up a chair next to his wife. "What can we do to help?"

Sofie frowned and looked out the window again. "Nothing unless you have a magic ball that tells us where Lance is holed up."

"Do the police have any leads?" Daisy asked.

"Very few. They know he hasn't boarded any form of public transportation. Seb blasted their pictures out to all regional airports, train and bus stations within ninety minutes of the kidnapping. His crime scene team found tire impressions and matched them to large SUV tires, but they're not specific to any particular model. And Declan found accelerants on the barn, so we know the fire was deliberately set."

"What about the guy he's supposedly working with?" Asa asked.

"You know about him?" Surprise colored Sofie's voice.

He nodded. "Knox mentioned him when he called last night. What do we know about him?"

"Still no name, but Seb turned his image over to his FBI friends, so hopefully that changes soon. Knox called the attorney Silas hired for us and asked him to have the P.I. look into any friends Lance has out this way. The cogs are turning, but nothing's happening." Her voice broke. She took a shaky breath.

Daisy squeezed her hand. "They'll find her."

Sofie nodded. She had to believe that or she'd break down into a sobbing, blubbering heap. "Did my mom come with you?"

"Yes," Daisy said. "But she and Silas rented their own car. They wanted to stop at the police station first and get the latest information. I think she just wanted to see for herself that they were doing everything possible to track them down."

"Trust me, if I weren't stuck in this bed, that's where I'd be too."

"How long do you have to stay here?"

"Probably just until morning. Macy too. She woke up not

long after we got here. They want to monitor us for a little while. That and make sure we stay down." She rolled her eyes.

"Well, they're right. It won't do Olive any good if you collapse looking for her."

"But at least I'm doing something. The waiting is driving me insane."

The door opened again and Knox came in. He smiled when he saw Asa and Daisy, holding out a hand to his friend. "Thanks for coming."

"Of course. Sofie was just filling us in on what's happened."

"About that—" His eyes cut to Sofie. "I just heard from Seb. His FBI colleagues found something on the man who showed up at the ranch."

Sofie held her breath.

"His real name is Nathan Fielding. He's a security consultant for the rich and shady."

Asa frowned. "Fielding, you said?"

Knox tipped his head and stared at his friend. "Yes. Why?"

"There was an—incident—a few years back with one of the producers on the movie I was filming. Allegations he was dabbling in the drug trade. The rumors were all over the set that an intern went to the police when he asked for more than money in exchange for her drugs. I asked my manager, Marty, about it, and he said the executive producer took care of it. Later, one of the other actors mentioned he hired a man named Fielding to handle it. I never saw the producer or the intern on set again."

Knox took his phone from his pocket. "What was the producer's name? The one who hired him."

Asa gave him the name as he dialed.

"Who are you calling?" Sofie asked.

"Seb."

The line connected and Knox relayed the information, then hung up.

"What do you hope to get by knowing the producer's name?" Daisy asked.

Knox shrugged. "Maybe he has some idea how to contact the man. He's done it once. Maybe he knows someone the guy knows, who knows where he might lay low."

The urge to go look for Olive made Sofie's entire body itch. She needed out of this bed. Latching on to the tape over her IV, she yanked it out of her arm, pressing her fingers over the spot to stem the bleeding.

"Sofie, what are you doing?" Knox came around to the other side of the bed as she swung her legs over the side and stood. He caught her as she swayed. "Baby, get back in bed."

"No. I want to go look for Olive."

"Honey, we don't even know where to start. Seb's handling it."

"Is he?" Her shrill voice bounced off the walls. "Why hasn't he found her? Why didn't you keep her safe like you promised?" A sob pushed past her lips. "Why didn't I?"

He swung her into his arms and sat on the bed, rocking her gently as he kissed her hair. Sofie heard the door close quietly and knew Daisy and Asa left to give them some privacy. She didn't care if they stayed. She was beyond caring who saw her break down. All she wanted was her baby back.

"We'll find her, Sofie. If I have to search every inch of the Earth, I will find our daughter and bring her home."

Sofie's sobs turned to broken hiccups at his words. She knew he felt the same agony she did. In a month's time, he'd become more of a father to Olive than Lance ever was, and he loved the girl as his own. He needed Sofie to be strong for him as much as she needed him to be strong for her.

Sniffling and wiping her face, she looked up at him. "Where do we start?"

"With trusting Seb to do his job. But we will be there when they find her. I promise you that."

~

Sofie jolted awake as her phone rang. She'd been discharged a few hours ago and fell asleep on the couch while Knox went outside to check on the livestock. The Archers took most of the horses, splitting them between the Broken Bow and the stables at Thomas Archer's new vet clinic. The last few went to Thomas's wife's family farm. They still had the chickens, though, and the goats and cattle.

She rubbed her eyes and picked up the cell from the end table, frowning as she didn't recognize the number. Sliding her thumb over the screen, she answered it. "Hello?"

"Mommy?"

Sofie's heart leaped into her throat. "Olive?"

"That's your confirmation the kid's alive." Lance's voice replaced Olive's.

"Lance? Why are you calling me? I thought you wanted me to suffer by wondering where she was and how she was doing?"

He sighed. "I did, but she's been nothing but an inconsolable brat, whining that she wants her mother. So, I've decided to indulge her. I know you're alone. I watched your mom and her husband leave earlier, and my associate has eyes on your husband and cousins. Go out your back door and start walking toward the road. If you even hint to your husband that you're going somewhere, Nate will put a bullet through his brain, understand?"

"Yes." Sofie stood. The dogs, who'd been sleeping at her feet, rose. Jai cocked his head.

"I mean it, Sofie. Not a word. Leave your phone in the

house, put your shoes and coat on, and leave now. If you're not outside in thirty seconds, Knox dies." He hung up.

She flew toward the kitchen, both dogs following. Dizziness threatened to send her to the floor, but the adrenaline surge she had going kept it manageable. She opened her notepad app as she moved and did her best to type out a note on her phone, hoping Knox would have the forethought to look through it when he found her missing. It was brief and likely a bit incoherent, but she didn't have any time to spare.

Message written, she left the phone on the counter and hurried into the mudroom to shove her feet into her snow boots and throw on her coat. Jai and Maeve swarmed around her. She pushed them away. "You two have to stay. And be quiet." She gave each dog a pat, telling them to sit, then opened the back door, glancing around for Knox or any of the hands before she slipped outside.

As she rounded the house and headed for the road, she did her best to leave a trail. She never said she would make their escape easy for Lance. She crossed the yard and disappeared into the trees without incident, following the driveway to the road. When she broke through the tree line, a short honk of a horn drew her to her left. She looked over to see a man with a rifle standing in the open doorway of a Bronco.

"Get in."

She hurried toward him and opened the passenger door, sliding onto the seat.

"Hold out your hands."

Sofie looked at him to see him pick up a roll of duct tape from the center console. Mouth tight, she did as he asked. "Where's my daughter?"

"Patience." He wrapped several layers of tape around her wrists, then tossed the roll in the backseat and started the truck.

Sofie frowned, but said nothing. Instead, she sank deeper

into her seat and willed her head to stop spinning, praying her lunch stayed down.

~

Warmth blasted Knox in the face as he walked inside with Asa and Daisy after checking on all the livestock. It hadn't really needed to be done—his ranch hands were on top of things—but he needed to be doing something to keep the restlessness in his mind at bay. Jai and Maeve greeted them, and he gave them both a scratch on their scruffy heads.

"It's quiet in here," Daisy said as they left their winter clothing in the mudroom and crossed into the kitchen. "Sofie must be sleeping."

"She said she was going to try to nap," Asa said.

"I'm going to check on her." Knox headed for the door out of the kitchen.

"I'll start some coffee to warm us up." Daisy moved to the counter and the coffeepot.

Knox waved in acknowledgement and left the room, wandering through the house to the living room, where they left Sofie an hour earlier. A blanket laid on the couch, but the room was empty.

With a frown, he retraced his steps to the stairs. Maybe she decided to lie down in bed. He would chew her out if he found her up there. He asked her before he left if she wanted to sleep in their bed, not wanting her to attempt the stairs on her own yet.

His sock-covered feet whispered over the hardwood floors as he walked down the hallway to the master bedroom. He nudged the open door wider and peeked inside, only to frown as he saw the empty bed.

"Sofie?" Frowning harder, he stepped inside, looking in

the en suite, but not finding her. He went back into the hallway and hurried to Olive's room, but it, too, was empty.

Worry edged its way in. Where was she?

"Sofie!" He ran downstairs, yelling her name.

Asa stepped out of the dining room. "What's wrong?"

"I can't find Sofie."

"Did you try calling her yet?"

"No." Knox took out his phone and dialed his wife's number. Her ringtone trilled from the kitchen. He shared a look with Asa, and they ran into the room.

Daisy held the phone. She looked up from the screen with a frown.

"Dammit." He crossed the kitchen to the mudroom, cursing again as he glanced around the small room. He ducked back into the kitchen. "Her coat and boots are gone."

"What?" Daisy looked at the phone in her hand again. "Why would she leave the house? And without her phone?"

Knox could only think of one reason. "Let me see that."

She handed him the phone, and he typed in Sofie's passcode. The screen opened to the notepad app. His frown intensified. "Goddamn son-of-a-bitch!" He closed the notepad and went to her recent calls.

"What?" Asa said. "What is it?"

"Lance called her. And not that long ago." He lifted his phone. "I need to call Seb."

Daisy lifted Sofie's phone from his fingers as he dialed the sheriff. "Dear God. Asa, listen to this. Lance called. Wants me. Nate watching."

Knox lifted his phone, his jaw clenching as she read Sofie's short message.

"Hey, Knox." The line connected and Seb's voice came over it. "I don't have anything new."

"I do. Lance just called Sofie's phone. She's gone. We were outside, and she snuck out."

"What? Christ. How long ago?"

"Ten minutes, if the timestamp on his call is anything to go by."

"I'll reroute deputies to the area. Give me the number he called on. I'll put a trace on it."

Knox looked at Daisy. "Read me Lance's number." She rattled it off, and he repeated it to Seb. "I'm not waiting around this time. She could still be on the property."

"Agreed. But watch yourself. He's got a partner."

"I will." Knox hung up and looked at his friends. "I'm going to search for her."

"I'm coming with you." Asa followed him as he headed for the mudroom and his boots.

"I'll start calling people to organize a search." Daisy already had her phone out.

Knox nodded, stuffing his feet into his shoes. "Start with the Nyderts. The number is in Sofie's phone. They're the closest. She hasn't been gone long, and we're so spread out up here that they haven't passed another driveway yet, no matter which direction they went. Call the Archers next. Make sure they all know not to be spotted. Following Sofie is our best chance of finding Olive."

"On it."

Knox finished dressing and barreled out the door, Asa close behind. He paused at the base of the stairs to look around for any sign of where she went. Footprints to the right drew his attention.

"There." He pointed, cursing. "How did we miss these when we came inside?" He took off at a jog, following them.

"We weren't expecting her to be gone, Knox. Don't beat yourself up."

Knox's jaw worked. He knew Asa was right, but he was more observant than this. He should have noticed.

The footprints curved around the house, then went

straight into the trees. Once past the tree line, her trail was harder to follow, but they managed to keep on it all the way to the road, where it went left and followed the shoulder for a short distance, then ended.

"Dammit!" He looked up and down the road, hoping for anything that would tell them which way they went.

"Knox, look." Asa pointed at the ground near where Sofie's trail ended.

He stepped over and saw another set of tracks, bigger than Sofie's. "They must be from Lance's partner. She said he was watching. He probably followed her through the woods and had a car waiting."

"Or Lance was waiting for them both."

"Either way, she's gone, and we don't have a clue as to where."

"No, but this might be the break needed to find Olive. If Sofie's with her, she can work on a way to get them out, or to call for help. Olive wouldn't know how to do that. We find Sofie, we find them both now."

Knox scrubbed his hands over his face. While he was glad they were together, it didn't change the fact that his family was missing and he felt just as helpless as before.

Twenty-Seven

Trees flew by in a blur as Nate drove. She was surprised to see they were driving closer to town instead of away from it. He'd told her to stay down, but she kept her head high enough to see where they went. She wanted to be able to find help quickly once she escaped with her daughter.

And escape she would. She wasn't sure how yet, but she would find a way to get them out of his clutches.

Just past the Archer's ranch, he turned onto a road that led into national forest land. Sofie sat up, wondering just where they were going. There was nothing but wilderness up this way.

They wove through the trees until they came to a cluster of campsites. At one there was an RV. Sofie's heart rate sped up, and she sat higher in her seat.

Nate pulled up next to the RV and shut off the car. "Time to go see your hubby."

Sofie glared at him. He gave a low laugh and got out, coming around to open her door. She climbed out and walked ahead of him to the RV, eager to see her daughter. As they got closer, she could hear Olive's quiet cries coming from inside.

"Olive!" Sofie hurried up the steps, pulling open the screen door with her bound hands. The inner door opened to reveal Lance's trim form. She took in his haggard appearance, happy to see how disheveled he looked. Served him right.

Despite that, though, he grinned at her. "Hello, my dear."

She put her bound hands in the middle of his chest and shoved him out of her way. "Move."

"Mommy!" Olive ran forward, but Lance snagged Sofie's arm and pulled her back before the girl could reach her.

Sofie whipped her head up to glare at him with hard eyes. "You brought me here to calm her. Let go."

He held her gaze for a moment. Sofie saw the indecision in his eyes before he released her. She dropped to her knees and Olive launched herself at her mother.

Tears spilled down Sofie's cheeks. "Oh, my baby. It's okay." She stroked her bound hands down Olive's dark hair, then pulled back to look into her face. "Are you all right?"

Olive hiccupped and nodded. "I'm scared."

"I know, baby, but we're going to get out of here."

"That's enough of that. Go sit down." Lance nudged Sofie in the back with his foot.

She glared at him again, but lifted Olive into her arms and stood, walking over to the bench along the wall to sit. "You've got me. Now what?"

"Now, we wait here for a little while until the heat on the search for you cools a little, then we hightail it for parts unknown. Canada's nice, I hear."

Sofie did her best to keep her expression neutral, even though her heart beat a staccato in her chest. If he took them over the border, there was no guarantee he couldn't get them on a plane and to some foreign nation where they were never heard from again. She doubted the travel alert extended past American borders. She was curious, though, how he would get them into Canada. Probably sneak them over the border in the wilderness somewhere. She could only guess what would wait for them on the other side. Lance knew people everywhere because of his job.

Lance looked at Nate, who'd followed Sofie inside. "Go make sure they don't find us."

Nate nodded and left.

Sofie held Olive close as the door closed, leaving them alone with Lance. He turned to them and smiled.

"Well, if this isn't like old times."

Rolling her eyes, Sofie turned her head to look out the window.

"Don't ignore me, Sofia."

She turned her glare on him again. "Or you'll what? Beat me until I'm nearly dead? I survived once. I'll survive again. Why don't you go do whatever it is you do, and we'll just sit here and pretend we don't exist? That's really all you ever wanted, right?"

He growled, then a sardonic smile tilted his mouth. "You've changed."

"Yeah, well, I had a good reason."

His smile turned bitter. "That new husband of yours?" He shook his head. "I should have had Nate kill him. Maybe I still will."

Olive started to cry again. Sofie's anger surged. Gently, she set Olive on the seat and stood. "I changed because Olive deserved better than a mother who let herself get beaten on a regular basis. And if you touch Knox, I will kill you myself. Don't forget, I protect the ones I love." She knew she was taking a chance, declaring her love for another man to Lance, but she was counting on him not knowing how to deal with her when she wasn't afraid of him.

The backhanded slap came out of nowhere. Sofie grunted and covered her face.

"Sit down and shut up." He pushed her onto the bench.

She glared up at him, still not afraid.

His jaw worked, and he turned, storming outside.

A smile bloomed on Sofie's face. Stupid man. She couldn't believe he left her alone in here.

"Are you okay, Mommy?"

"I'm fine, sweetie. Let's see what we can find to help us get out of here, okay?"

Olive nodded.

"Can you stand there by the door and keep an eye out for your dad? Let me know when he's coming back."

The girl stood in front of the door and peered through the blinds. Sofie headed for the small kitchen area. She doubted Lance would leave any actual weapons where she could find them. He seemed to intend for them to live in this RV for the time being. But that didn't mean there weren't other things she could use to defend them. She opened the drawers, finding plastic utensils and cooking tools. The little butter knives were sharp enough for her to tear through the tape on her wrists, but she'd need Olive's help. The girl might be able to peel it off without it. She pocketed one and moved on.

She opened the upper cabinets, finding boxed and canned foods. She debated grabbing a few of the cans to throw, but it would only distract him. She needed something that would give them time to get away.

Dropping to her haunches, she rested a hand on the cabinet face as her head spun. *Damn concussion.* Taking a deep breath, she opened the lower cabinets. "Jackpot." She reached in and removed a cast-iron skillet. He must have rented this RV. She didn't think Lance even knew what a cast-iron skillet was.

"Olive, help me take this tape off." She walked over to the girl, keeping one eye on the exterior of the RV. Lance stood about thirty feet away, a phone to his ear. "If you can't peel it off, I found a plastic knife."

The girl found the end of the tape and pulled. It came up, then twisted and stuck. Sofie lifted her hands and grabbed the end with her teeth and yanked. She spun her wrists and freed them.

Just in time, too. She saw Lance coming back.

"Olive, listen to me. We're getting out of here. Stay close and if I tell you to run, you do it. No questions, okay?"

"Okay, Mommy." Olive gave a solemn nod.

Sofie tucked the girl between the front seats, then crouched behind the door just as Lance walked up the steps. She waited, muscles tensed.

The door opened, and he walked in.

In one quick motion, Sofie stood and brought the skillet up, smacking him in the head with it. He stumbled forward, and she swung again. Dizziness made her swing a little wild, but she still hit him on the back of his skull. He dropped like a sack of potatoes, landing in a heap on the floor.

Sofie let the skillet fall. She picked up Olive's coat, then took the girl's hand. "Let's go." Peering through the doorway, she looked for Nate, knowing he could derail their escape. She glanced at Olive. "Be as quiet as you can, okay?"

Olive nodded. Sofie helped her into her coat, then lowered her to the ground. Moving quickly, they hurried away from the RV and deeper into the forest. If she could get them back to the road, they could follow it to help.

～

Eyes darting from side to side, Knox drove down the winding road near the Broken Bow, hoping for a glimpse of the car Lee Archer reported just after Daisy called them to tell them Sofie was missing. His phone rang, and he glanced at the infotainment screen to see Seb's name. Heart skipping, he glanced at Asa, then pushed the button on his steering wheel to answer.

"I got something!" Seb's voice boomed through the truck before Knox could utter a word.

"What?" He braked, pulling over.

"The cell Lance used to call Sofie just pinged. He's on the national forest land between the Broken Bow and town."

Knox glanced in his mirrors, then pulled a U-turn. He'd just passed the road that led to there. "We just passed the turnoff."

"I'm sending deputies your way. Watch yourself."

"We will. Thanks." Knox ended the call and pressed harder on the accelerator.

Asa took a rifle from the back seat and checked it. "What's the plan?"

"Find my family."

"Is there any other way in or out of the forest?"

"A few." His mouth pulled in a frown. "They could be anywhere, though. There are several remote campgrounds and a ton of service roads that lead deeper into the woods. We just have to start searching." He reached the road and hung a hard right, slowing so they could get a better look through the trees and to make their presence less noticeable.

He drove up the road, seeing nothing. With every passing minute, his tension escalated until he felt like he could crush his steering wheel to powder. He loosened his fingers, wiggling them to get the blood flowing again. "Anything?"

"No."

Knox cursed and continued to drive.

The windshield spider-webbed as a bullet slammed into it.

"Whoa!" He slammed on the brakes, ducking as another bullet hit the glass. He threw the truck in park. Staying low, he grabbed his pistol from the back and looped a rifle over his shoulders.

"We can't stay here." Asa tucked a handgun into his jeans.

He peered over the dash for whoever was shooting at them, then reached for his door handle.

Knox agreed. They were sitting ducks. He nodded. "On three." He grasped the handle. "One... two... three!" Both men dove out of the vehicle, firing ahead of them as they ran for cover. Knox angled himself behind a tree, flinching as a piece of bark winged past his head when a bullet hit the tree.

He looked past his truck at Asa. "See anything?"

Asa shook his head. Knox motioned for him to fire while he took a long look. The other man brought his rifle up and fired a shot while Knox looked around the tree. A muzzle flashed thirty yards away, and a bullet hit the tree Asa hid behind. Another slammed into Knox's tree.

Knox cocked his rifle. His muscles tensed as he prepared to step out from behind the tree to get a clean shot.

A feminine shout stopped him. A man grunted. Knox spun around to peer past the tree trunk. He saw a flash of khaki between two trees in the distance. As he stared, he could make out a man struggling with a woman. She had her legs and arms wrapped around his back.

His heart stopped, then jumped into his throat. "Sofie."

"Olive, run!" Sofie shouted.

Knox's gaze jumped to a bright purple streak dashing through the trees toward them. The air froze in his lungs. He forced a breath in. "Olive, over here!"

The girl didn't hesitate. Her little legs changed direction, and she made a beeline for him. Knox kept one eye on her and the other on Sofie. He lifted his rifle, but couldn't get a clean shot. As he watched, the man he recognized as Nate backed up into a tree, slamming Sofie into it. Stunned, she let go and slid from his back. Nate turned, pointing his rifle at her.

Knox pulled the trigger. The other man jerked. His rifle discharged, the round hitting the ground to Sofie's left. He spun as his knees gave way and he hit the dirt, a hole through the back of his head.

Looping his rifle over his shoulder, Knox ran forward, scooping Olive into his arms, but not stopping as he ran to Sofie. "Sofie!" He landed on his knees beside her, pulling her into his arms with Olive.

"Knox?" Her trembling hand touched his face.

A tear spilled over his eyelid. "Yeah." He kissed her. "You're safe. Where's Lance?"

She pointed up the road. "RV. I knocked him out with a frying pan. Guess I didn't need the gun lesson after all. At least, not for this." She blew out a breath and leaned into him, clutching his sleeve.

He chuckled and tucked her face into his neck, inhaling her scent, then looked at Olive, who clung to him. "It's over, sweetie. It's all over." He pressed a kiss to her cheek.

Asa ran up. "Are they okay?"

Knox nodded, not letting them go. "They're fine." He blew out a shaky breath and hugged them tighter.

~

Sofie watched from her position in Brady's truck as Seb escorted Lance's stretcher to the waiting ambulance. Her ex-husband had his eyes closed as he leaned his head back, pain etched on his face. She felt a perverse sense of satisfaction that she was the one to cause it. The bastard deserved everything he got. Including the very long prison sentence coming his way.

Olive shifted in her lap as she slept. Sofie hugged the girl closer. It would be awhile yet before she put the girl down.

The driver's door opened and Knox got in. She smiled at him. "Hi."

He smiled back. "Hey. You ready to go home?"

A quizzical frown dipped her brows. "What do you mean? Don't we need to stay for a bit yet?"

He shook his head. "I gave my statement to Seb. Did you?" She nodded.

"Okay, then. A tow company's coming to get my truck. Brady said I could use his. He'll catch a ride home with one of his brothers, then come get the car tomorrow."

A bright smile stole over her face. "Let's go home, then."

With a smile to match hers, he nodded to Olive. "We better buckle her up."

Sofie's mouth pulled, but he was right. She couldn't ride home on her lap.

"I'll go get her car seat from my truck." He got out and disappeared, returning a few moments later with the seat. After securing it in the back, he lifted the sleeping child from Sofie's lap and buckled her into it. Olive stirred long enough for them to get her situated, then promptly fell asleep again. The ordeal with her father wore her out. Sofie hoped when she woke up in the morning, she'd be, if not her old self, close to it.

Knox climbed back into the driver's seat and started the truck. He weaved through the emergency vehicles and headed for home. Headlights behind them made her frown.

"Who's following us?"

He glanced in the rearview mirror. "Your mom and Silas. Asa and Daisy are with them."

"Oh." She'd forgotten all about them. After she gave Seb her statement, she'd climbed in Brady's truck and let her brain shut down, just enjoying the feel of her baby in her arms.

The miles ticked by as they made their way back to the ranch. Knox turned into the drive and headed for the house, pulling up to the back door. Silas came to a stop next to them.

Sofie opened her door and slid to the ground. Her knees buckled, and she made a grab for the door to stay upright.

"Whoa, there." Knox ran around the hood and lifted her into his arms, then turned toward the house.

"Olive—" Sofie looked back.

"We'll take care of her," Nori said. She waved her daughter away. "Let Knox take care of you."

Knox offered her a nod. "Thanks." He caught Sofie's gaze. "She'll be okay. Your mom is right. Let me take care of you."

Sofie sighed and looped her arms around his neck. "Okay."

He pressed a quick kiss to her lips, then let them inside. Not bothering to remove his shoes or coat, he carried her through the kitchen and dining room and up the stairs to their room, heading straight into the en suite bathroom.

She frowned softly as he set her on her feet next to the tub. "What are you doing?"

"Taking care of you. We're going to soak in this tub together, then go to bed."

A blush stained her cheeks. "Knox—"

He laid a finger over her lips. "We're bathing, then sleeping. I just want to hold you. I know your body isn't capable of anything else at the moment. We have the rest of our lives for the other stuff."

Despite her exhausted and injured state, her body heated at the thought of that other stuff. She bit her lip and nodded, knowing if they tried, she'd probably just fall asleep on him.

He leaned over and turned on the faucet in the tub, adjusting the temperature, then straightened. His hands went to her jacket, and he unzipped it, pushing it off her shoulders. He tackled her sweater next, drawing it over her head. Her bra followed, then he drew her leggings and underwear down her legs. Sofie held onto his shoulders as he crouched to remove her pants and shoes.

As he straightened, he ran his hands up her legs, skimming her curves. Goosebumps erupted over her body. She might be beat up and ready to sink into oblivion for the next ten hours, but she wasn't immune to the effect he had on her. Once her body healed, she intended to show him exactly how he made her feel.

Peeling off his clothes, he stepped into the tub and held out a hand to her, helping her in with him. Water sloshed over the edge as they settled in. Sofie turned off the tap, then relaxed into Knox's chest. His hand covered her stomach, cocooning her in warmth. She let out a deep sigh.

His low chuckle rumbled through her back. "You're going to fall asleep in here, aren't you?"

"Wasn't that the plan?" Her eyelids grew heavy.

"Possibly. I wanted to talk first."

She pushed against the fatigue. "About what?"

"Our next moves."

She angled her head to look at him. "What do you mean?"

He pressed his lips together, glancing away before meeting her gaze. "Us. This house. My business."

She frowned, not understanding what he was getting at.

"I've been thinking. With the barn gone, my business is kind of on hold. The horses belonging to others that were here for training are going back to their owners, which leaves me with just my animals for now. What if we moved?"

She sat up to look at him better. "Move? Where?"

"Montana."

Her eyes went wide. "You want to move to Montana? What about your ranch?"

He shrugged. "It's just land. And not really ancestral. Dad bought it when I was young. Thomas and Rayna have been looking for a bigger spread so she can expand her produce business. Other than Alice, there's nothing really tying me here. All your family is in Pine Ridge."

Sofie stared at him, unable to comprehend what she was hearing. "You want to move—for me?"

He nodded and brushed her dark hair away from her

shoulder, his hand tracing her collarbone. "I think you—and Olive—need to be near Nori right now. With all the tumult of the last few months, I think you need the normalcy."

"Okay, but moving? Where would we move to? I can't imagine it would be easy to find a spread like what you have here."

"I don't need that much, to be honest. A barn and some pasture land. A decent arena. All that can be built. So long as we have a house to start with, I can board my animals with Asa. The proceeds from this place will pay for anything I need to start fresh."

Her heart soared. Other than Knox and Olive, her mother was the most important person in her life. She'd moved out west to stay near her. She wasn't going to lie and say it wasn't hard to be so far away from her.

He raised a brow. "What do you say? Will you start fresh with me? We'll build a life that's ours."

She regarded him a moment longer before a bright smile spread over her face. She squealed and wrapped him in a hug. Water splashed onto the floor, but she paid it little heed.

He laughed. "Is that a yes?"

Her face hovered inches from his. "That's a yes."

EPILOGUE

"Is that everything?" Knox glanced at his wife.

She nodded. "We just need to get our suitcases."

"Okay." He shut the trailer door. Sighing, he walked over to loop an arm around her waist and turned to stare at the house. "I'm going to miss this place."

She rested her head on his shoulder. "Me too."

Knox's eyes roved over the property, from the house to the bare ground where his horse barn used to be. It had been home almost his entire life, but he was ready for a new chapter. Other than Alice, he didn't have any ties to the area anymore, and there was a good chance she was going to follow them to Pine Ridge if the conversations he heard between her and Sofie about that gift shop were any indication. But Sofie had ties to Montana. With his business on hold until he rebuilt his barn, it seemed like a good time to make a change and bring all of his family together.

"Thank you." Sofie's quiet voice pulled him out of his thoughts.

He glanced down at her. "For what?"

"For giving all this up and starting over. I know it wasn't an easy decision."

Knox pressed a kiss to the top of her head. "That's where you're wrong. It was the easiest decision I've ever made. Except perhaps marrying you. I've seen the bond between you and your mom. The bond she has with Olive. I was in a position to rebuild elsewhere. I can train a horse from anywhere. Why not Montana?"

She smiled up at him. "I love you."

He dropped a kiss on her lips. "I love you too."

"I'm glad we're moving now. In a few months, I'd be miserable trying to do all this."

He frowned. "What do you mean?"

"I mean, I'll be as big as a house." Her smile grew.

His mouth went slack and his eyes widened. "Wait. You're —" He couldn't finish his sentence. The words wouldn't come.

She nodded, a bright, cheery laugh breaking free. "You're going to be a daddy again. And you get to start at the beginning this time." He'd been a wonderful father to Olive, but she was eager to see him with a newborn. She imagined, like everything he did, he'd figure it out quickly and be the best he could be.

He picked her up with a whoop and spun her around, then lowered her to her feet, holding her close. "A baby." His smile could light the sun. "Thank you. For taking a chance on a loner like me."

She ran her fingers through his silky hair. "Nah, you're not a loner. You just needed the right people."

"You. You and Olive are my people." His mouth crashed onto hers.

Sofie wrapped her arms around his neck and kissed him back. Yes, they were.

~

Keep reading for a sneak peek of *Shark*, book 3 in the *Pine Ridge* series.

Thank you for reading Loner! I hope you enjoyed it.

Want to read an EXCLUSIVE and FREE book? Sign up for my mailing list. You can find the sign-up form on my website, ashleyaquinn.com. My list also receives sneak peeks of my latest work and access to exclusive giveaways. Also, please consider leaving a rating or review on Amazon and or Goodreads. It would be greatly appreciated!

Thanks again for reading!
   - Ashley

~

Keep reading for a sneak peek at Book 3, Shark in the Pine Ridge Series.

SHARK

PINE RIDGE
BOOK 3

ONE

Music blasted through Sara Katsaros's bluetooth speaker, filling the kitchen. She hummed along as she prepped meatloaf for tomorrow. Once she was done with these, she planned to make more pie crust and freeze it, so she had it for later this week.

Banging sounded over the music. Sara paused, wrist deep in meatloaf mixture. She glanced at her hands, then to the back door. "Dammit." She shook her hands, trying to remove some of the meat and egg coating her fingers.

Sighing, she grabbed a handful of paper towels, wiping them the best she could as whoever was on the other side banged on the metal door again.

"I'm coming, I'm coming," she grumbled. Tossing the towels in the trash, she grabbed a few more, so she didn't have to touch the handle with her yucky fingers.

The door rattled again as she reached it. With a huff, she unlocked it and twisted the knob, throwing it open. "What? Oh. Marci. Hi. What are you doing here?" She frowned as she saw her friend, Marci Red Feather standing on the other side, glaring at her. "Is something wrong?"

"Damn straight, something's wrong. Did you forget what tonight is?"

A frown marred Sara's brow for a split second before she groaned and looked skyward. "I'm sorry. I totally forgot." She and Marci were supposed to be at the Stone Creek for a girls' night so Daisy could tell them all about her honeymoon.

"You sure did, sunshine. Which is the reason Daisy and I are your only friends. We're the only ones who love you enough to put up with your one-track mind."

Sara blew her bangs off her face as she sighed. She wasn't wrong there. If they hadn't moved away, her old friends eventually just stopped calling because she didn't have time for them. Marci was the only one who really stuck by her. And now there was Daisy, who just abjectly refused to be ignored. She was grateful for them both. They kept her from sinking too deep into her restaurant.

"It's also why I'm here, fetching you, instead of stuffing my face with cookies and laughing at Daisy's recount of her ride in a golf cart through the jungle. Go put away whatever it is you're making and get your stuff."

"But I—" She motioned toward the kitchen, glancing back.

"No buts, Sarafina. I haven't had an evening away from Sloan in months. I want cookies, wine, and lots of laughs with my two best friends. Your workaholic tendencies are not going to get in the way of that."

Sara giggled, relenting. She motioned Marci inside. "Fine. But when I act like a zombie early next week because I had to get up super early to make pie crust because I didn't get it made tonight, remember it's your fault." She cast a smile over her shoulder as they walked deeper into the kitchen.

Marci snickered. "Duly noted." Her smile fell away as she took in the mess. "Oh, boy." She heaved a sigh and shrugged out of her coat, hanging it over a wire shelf. "You finish portioning that out. I'll start cleaning up."

"You don't have to help me." Sara moved to the bowl of meatloaf mixture and thrust her hands back in.

Marci snorted. "Yes, I do. Or we'll be here all night. Cookies, wine and BFFs, remember?"

Sara laughed. "Yeah. Okay, thanks."

She quickly added the rest of the ingredients to the bowl and kneaded everything together. Before she started, she'd greased several roasting pans, so she portioned the meatloaf into them, then covered them with plastic wrap. As she carried the last one into the cooler, Marci put the final load of dishes through the dishwasher. Sara grabbed her disinfectant and wiped down the table.

"Is that it?" Marci glanced around.

"Yep."

"Awesome, let's go. Do you want to ride with me or follow?"

"I'll follow you. I have to be back here in the morning, so even if I sleep there, I need to have a way back at an ungodly hour."

Marci chuckled. "Okay."

Sara grabbed her coat and purse from the office, and they left. In her car, Sara cranked the heat and turned on her butt warmer, having forgot—again—to use the remote start and warm up her car. She'd blame it on the rush job, but she forgot when she wasn't rushed.

Pulling out of the parking lot, she followed Marci out of town and up the winding mountain road to the Stone Creek. Half an hour later, they drove through the gates and up to the house, parking in the long driveway.

Lights blazed in the lower level of the house. As she and Marci neared the front door, Sara could hear music and laughter coming from inside. Marci opened the door, and the music swelled. Sharing an amused look, they followed the sound into the living room. Asa belted out the melody to the song playing through the speakers while he waltzed around the room. Daisy stood on his feet, laughing hysterically as he held her close and whirled.

He spotted them on a turn through the room, and paused, grinning widely. "Hey."

Daisy stepped off his feet, stumbling slightly, her balance still off from the injuries she sustained in her car accident. Asa steadied her, then picked up her cane from where it rested on the couch and handed it to her.

"It's about time you got here." Daisy walked over to the stereo and turned the volume down.

"Yeah, well, *someone* was elbow deep in ground beef when I found her." Marci hooked a thumb at Sara.

"I forgot. I'm sorry." Sara held her hands up near her shoulders. "But I'm ready to hear about this golf cart adventure."

Asa laughed. "And on that note, I'll see you later, sweetness." He gave Daisy a quick kiss, waved to them, then left the room.

"Is he going to hang out with your husband?" Sara looked at Marci.

She nodded. "Sloan should be asleep, so I think they're going to watch a basketball game on TV or something." Her husband, Chet, was home with their nine-month-old son.

"Where's your mom and Silas?" Sara asked.

"Billings. They wanted to give us some space so we could adjust to being in the house as a married couple." Daisy grinned. "I'm glad, because it means we get to practice being quiet."

Sara laughed. "How's that going?"

"The practice part is great. The being quiet part, not so much. We might have to add some soundproofing." Her mouth pulled, and she shrugged. "Anyway," she tamped her cane on the hard floor. "Who's ready for some cookies?"

"Me." Sara raised a hand and spun on her heel, heading for the kitchen. Just because she forgot about their plans didn't mean she wasn't ready now for chocolate. Especially since no one made chocolate chip cookies like Daisy.

They all dove into the plate on the counter. Marci grabbed a bottle of wine from the rack on the wall and poured them each a glass.

"So, tell us about this golf cart." Marci wiped a chocolate smear from the corner of her lip. "Chet wouldn't tell me anything. Just that I should ask you."

Daisy rolled her eyes. "No matter what anyone says, it was not my fault."

Sara paused, lips around her cookie. She bit off the chunk and stuffed it into her cheek so she could talk. "Oh, this should be epic."

"Agreed. Spill." Marci picked up her wineglass and took a sip.

Daisy giggled. "Okay. So, we decided to take a tour through the area the resort had that was kind of like an animal preserve. It has this nice concrete road going through it, which was perfect because walking long distances still sucks. Anyway, we took one of the golf carts—Asa was driving—and we stopped because there was a troop of monkeys making a ruckus in the trees, and we wanted to get a better look. We got out and I left my cane on the seat—I had Asa there, we weren't walking more than a few feet, I was fine."

"What happened?" Sara leaned forward and picked up a second cookie.

"We were staring up at the trees, watching them leap from limb to limb, when we heard a clatter behind us. We turned around, and one of them had jumped into the golf cart and had my cane."

"Oh, geez." Marci sipped her wine. "What did you do?"

"I elbowed Asa and told him to do something, so he crept forward, talking to this monkey all soft-like. It cocked its head and did that monkey chatter thing Macaques do. Then it banged the damn thing on the frame, which startled it, but only for a moment. The next thing I knew, it smacked everything it could, using it like a bloody drumstick."

"Oh, no," Marci said.

"Yeah. Because that drew the attention of all his buddies. They swarmed us, all of them wanting to know what he had. One of the bigger ones ran up and just took it from him and hopped into the road. That set them all off and it was a free-for-all. They took off back into the trees." She held up her cane and looked at it. "Asa had to buy me a new cane."

Sara arched an eyebrow and grinned. "Is that why it's glittery pink now? I thought you just painted your old one."

Daisy grinned. "I did paint it, but it's not the old one. We found a man on the street who was making figurines out of wood. Asa asked him to make me a cane. He whittled this out in a few hours, but he didn't have any varnish, so we found a place to buy paint, and they had pink glitter spray paint."

Sara and Marci laughed.

"I told Asa I'm going to put this thing in our closet once I can get around without it, then bring it out once I'm old and gray and need to use it again. I'll be the coolest grandma on the block." She laughed, joining in with her friends.

Taking a drink of her wine, Sara felt herself finally start to relax. Marci was right. She worked too damn much. She shouldn't forget her friends, and it shouldn't take her almost an hour to just start to unwind.

But she didn't know any other way to live. She didn't have a family to speak of around here anymore. Her parents were states away, and she was an only child. Until recently, Marci was her only real friend—all the others moving away for better jobs, or just falling out of touch as Sara threw herself into her business.

And men were few and far between. It wasn't like there were many prospects in Pine Ridge. She knew all the ones her age and had for years. Which meant she knew all their secrets and bad habits.

She could do better, though. Be a better friend. She might not get what Marci and Daisy had with Chet and Asa, but she could still live a full life. She did live a full life. And she was content with what she had.

Really?

She lifted her wineglass again to disguise the frown that formed as her conscience had its say. She smacked it in the face and shoved it back in its box. It could stay there. She *was* happy. She didn't need a man or a family. They were just icing on her already delicious cake.

But you like frosting...

She rolled her eyes at her thoughts and picked up a third cookie.

Two

Car horns and shouts assaulted James O'Malley's ears as he stepped out the front door of his apartment building. He tugged his coat tighter around himself to ward off the brisk Chicago wind and hurried to the curb to hail a cab. A taxi pulled over, and he climbed in, giving the cabbie an address downtown. He stared out the window, preoccupied with thoughts of the coming meeting with his agent. He was two months behind on his next book, and Charlie was calling him on the carpet about it.

It wasn't like he planned to be so far behind on his writing. His sister, Daisy, had been in a car accident, then she got married. He'd been busy. And distracted. Charlie knew all that, but this meeting was to remind James he had obligations to meet. Publishers to satisfy. It was only his past success that granted him the leeway he'd already received. But their patience was running thin.

The steely gray sky passed in a blur as the cab drove deeper into Chicago. The forecast called for snow. Again. It was only mid-November, but they'd already had several snowfalls. The curse of living next to Lake Michigan. James was ready for spring. Or to move to a warmer climate.

At least he didn't have to shovel. That was one perk of apartment living. Two of his brothers had houses in the suburbs. Sometimes—especially when his upstairs neighbor had a party—he wished he lived in a house, but then he remembered he'd have to mow and shovel snow and decided he was happy where he was.

A horn blared as the cab made an abrupt lane change and pulled up to the curb. James paid the driver and got out, jogging into the building. He took the elevator to the tenth floor.

"Hello, Mr. O'Malley."

One side of James's mouth tipped up as the receptionist greeted him. He sauntered forward to lean against her desk. "Hi, Jane."

The young woman blushed and giggled before schooling her features into a more professional mask. "I'll let Charlie know you're here."

He let his smile bloom and nodded. "Thank you."

Her smile peeked out again as she picked up the phone.

James wandered over to the waiting area and sat, resting an ankle atop his knee. He stared down the hall to his right, willing Charlie to appear. He just wanted to get this over with.

"So, how have you been?" Jane asked.

He glanced over to see her peering above her tall desk.

"Can't complain. Busy." As much as he flirted with her, he had no interest in getting involved with his agent's receptionist. She was pretty, but much too young for him. There was a time it wouldn't have mattered, but at thirty-six, he wasn't interested in fleeting trysts anymore.

"James."

At the sound of Charlie's voice, he looked to his right. His agent, Charlie Mills, stood in the mouth of the hallway. He stood smiling at her. "Hello. You look lovely as always, Charlie." And she did. His agent was a beautiful woman. The ivory pantsuit and blue peep-toe heels she wore only emphasized that.

She rolled her eyes. "Cut the crap." She gestured with her head down the hallway, her red ponytail bobbing. "Come on."

James blew out a breath and followed her down the hall into her office.

"Have a seat." She pointed to a chair across from her desk.

He sank into it, crossing his ankle over his knee again. She settled behind her desk, folding her hands over the blotter.

"So. You know why you're here." It wasn't a question.

"Yeah. And I don't know why you called me down here. I told you in my last email I was working on the book. You'll have the first five chapters soon."

"Soon was a week ago, James. It was due eight weeks before that."

"I know." He folded his hands in his lap and looked out the window. She didn't have the best view. Just more buildings.

Charlie sighed. "Look, I just need something, okay? How close are you?"

James scratched the back of his head, scrunching his face. Boy, he didn't want to answer that question.

"James."

The warning note in her voice had him blowing out a breath. He wondered if she got that tone from her ex-Marine husband or if it came naturally. "I have a chapter. And a rough outline."

Her eyebrows shot up. "That's it?"

He nodded. "Yeah. I know it's not a lot."

She scoffed. "You got that right. The whole book is due in three months. Can you make up the time?"

"Yes." And he could. If he could concentrate. After all the

crap that happened in the last few months, it had scrambled his ability to focus.

"Then do it. I don't care what you have to do, whether it's lock yourself in your apartment, take a trip somewhere—hell, you could take a trip to the moon for all I care, so long as you finish that book." She sat forward. "You're a moneymaker for your publishing house, so they're giving you some wiggle room. This meeting is just a reminder that if you don't submit a finished manuscript by the deadline in three months, you have to return your advance."

"I'm aware." It was spelled out in his contract.

"It also means you'll have a hard time finding another publishing deal."

His mouth flattened. She was just piling it on today. None of this was anything he didn't already know. It sucked to have it shoved in his face, though. "I know."

"Good. So, we have an understanding, yes? You're going to do whatever's necessary to write that book, right? Because I don't have to tell you, I don't appreciate having my chain jerked around and then not get paid."

He grinned. "So I can jerk your chain as long as you get your money?"

A smile quirked one corner of her mouth. "Shut up, jack-ass. Go write your book."

James laughed and stood. "Been great talking to you as always, Charlie." He extended a hand over her desk.

She rose and took it, her expression turning serious. "Whatever's going on in that pretty head of yours, fix it. Before it takes you down."

He inhaled, nodding. "I will." Releasing her hand, he turned and walked out of her office, his face morphing into a frown. The question was, how?

James's phone rang as he exited the building. Glancing at the screen, he raised a hand to hail a cab. His brother Ian's name appeared. He answered as a taxi pulled up, and he got in.

"Hey, what's up?"

"Nori called. Seems Lance filed for custody of Olive."

"What?" His cousin Sofie divorced her husband earlier in the year and put the bastard in jail for abuse. He wasn't even supposed to be out yet. "Isn't he still in jail?"

"Nope. Apparently, he was released about a month ago because of overcrowding."

James scoffed.

"Yeah. Anyway, Sofie and Olive left the Stone Creek and went down to Colorado with a friend of Asa's, Knox Duvall. Lance showed up in Pine Ridge, and Sofie was worried he would try to kidnap Olive. Then the custody papers showed up. Nori said Sofie and Knox are getting married to help fight it."

Married? James stared out the window for a moment in stunned silence. "Why would she need to get married to fight it? How does Lance carry more weight as an abusive ex-con than she does as a loving mother?"

"Because he got his job back and found himself a fiancée. Some finance manager for a bank who lives in their old building. He's trying to paint Sofie as unfit."

"No judge will believe that. Sofie's a great mom."

"I know that, but if Lance buys off the judge, it won't matter. Anyway, Silas hired her one of the best family lawyers he and Asa could find. That's not the entire reason I called, though."

"Oh?" James frowned.

"With Sofie gone and Nori and Silas going to Colorado for the wedding, Daisy could use some help. You're the only one of us with a flexible schedule. Do you think you could fly out there and help her out until Nori gets back after Thanksgiving?"

James closed his eyes and leaned his head against the seat for a second. "This is bad timing, Ian. I just got reamed out by my agent because I haven't submitted anything on my next book. The publishing house is threatening to revoke my advance if I don't deliver the manuscript on time."

Ian paused. "How long do you have?"

"Three months."

"Why are you worrying? You've written books in less than a month before."

"Yeah, but this one's different."

"How so?"

"Nothing's coming to me. It's a new series, so that means new characters, and I just can't get a handle on the guy." And it was driving him crazy. Every time he sat down to write, he never got more than a few paragraphs because he couldn't connect with his character.

"Maybe this is perfect timing, then. Could be you just need a change of scenery?"

James snorted. "I've had a change of scenery recently, remember? We were all out west for Daisy's wedding."

"Right, but we were there to party, not for you to work."

His frown returned. He had a point. Maybe staring at something other than his office walls would do him good. "Fine." He blew out a breath. "I'll fly out today."

About the Author

Ashley started writing in her teens and never stopped. Her first novel, Smoky Mountain Murder, came out in 2016, and she has since published two more series and has plans for more. When not writing, you can find her with her nose stuck in a book or watching some terrible disaster movie on SyFy. An avid baseball fan, she also enjoys crafting and cooking. She lives in Ohio with her husband, two kids, three cats, and one very wild shepherd mix.

Website: https://ashleyaquinn.com

[g] goodreads.com/ashleyaquinn

[a] amazon.com/Ashley-A-Quinn/e/B07HCT4QST